# BLACK LUST

The pirate's eyes smouldered as if a fever raged in him, while his full lips writhed in a smile that made her shudder. "Dunnot be afeared," he said slowly.

She attempted to stand, but his arms suddenly pinned her to the chair.

"Let me go! Let me go, you beast!"

"Beast, am I? Well, well, my lass, mebbe I'll give thee cause to call me that. Mebbe thee'll be less likely to call me that when I've done so. I've tamed hawks as proud as thee afore now, made them coo like turtle doves." And with a snarling laugh he tore the bodice of her dress.

She screamed, and knew a terror greater than any she'd ever known. For suddenly she realized that not only was her honor at stake—but the last chance at life for the man she loved. . . .

PEERLES........ .....RIGUE.
ROMANCE ....
RAFAEL SA....
HISTORI....
SOLD M....
THROUGHOUT THE ....

If you have enjoyed this novel, be sure to watch
for all the great Sabatini adventures:

*CAPTAIN BLOOD RETURNS*

*MISTRESS WILDING*

*THE SEA-HAWK*

*SCARAMOUCHE*

*THE FORTUNES OF CAPTAIN BLOOD*

*MASTER AT ARMS*

*forthcoming from Ballantine Books*

# The
# Black Swan

By
Rafael Sabatini

BALLANTINE BOOKS • NEW YORK

ISBN 0-345-24864-3-150

This edition published by arrangement with
Houghton Mifflin Company

Manufactured in the United States of America

First Ballantine Books Edition: March, 1976

# Contents

# Fortune and Major Sands

MAJOR SANDS, conscious of his high deserts, was disposed to receive with condescension the gifts which he perceived that Fortune offered him. She could not bribe him with them into a regard for her discernment. He had seen her shower favours upon the worthless and defraud the meritorious of their just reward. And she had kept him waiting. If at last she turned to him, he supposed that it was less from any gracious sense of justice in herself than because Major Sands had known how to constrain her.

This, from all the evidence I have sifted, I take to have been the complexion of his thoughts as he lounged beside the day-bed set for Miss Priscilla Harradine under the awning of brown sailcloth which had been improvised on the high poop of the Centaur.

The trim yellow ship lay at anchor in the spacious bay of Fort Royal, which she had made her first port of call after the short run from Barbados. They were taking fresh water aboard, and this was providing an occasion to induce them to take other things. In the forechains the Negro steward and the cook were receiving a bombardment of mangled English and smooth French from a cluster of periaguas, laden with fruit and vegetables, that bumped and scraped alongside, manned by whites, half-castes, Negroes and Caribs, all of them vociferous in their eagerness to sell.

At the head of the entrance ladder stood Captain Bransome in a stiff-skirted coat of dark blue with tarnished gold lace, refusing admission to the gabardined and persistent Jew in the cockboat at the foot of it, who was offering him bargains in cocoa, ginger, and spices.

Inshore, across the pellucid jade-green waters of the bay, gently ruffled by the north-easterly breeze that was sweetly tempering the torrid heat of the sun, rose the ramage of masts and spars of the shipping riding there at anchor. Beyond this the little town of Fort Royal showed sharply white against the emerald green undulating slopes of Martinique, slopes dominated in the north by the volcanic mass of Mont Pelé which thrust its rugged summit into the cobalt sky.

Captain Bransome, his glance alternating between the Jew who would not be dismissed, and a longboat that half a mile away was heading for the ship, removed his round black castor. Under this his head was swathed in a blue cotton handkerchief, as being cooler than a periwig. He stood mopping his brow whilst he waited. He was feeling the heat in the ponderous European finery which, out of regard for the dignity of his office of master, he donned whenever putting into port.

On the poop above, despite the breeze and the shadow of the awning, Major Sands, too, was feeling the heat, inclining as he did to a rather fleshly habit of body, and this despite a protracted sojourn in the Tropic of Cancer. He had come out five years ago whilst King Charles II was still alive. He had volunteered for service overseas in the conviction that in the New World he would find that fortune which eluded him in the Old. The necessity was imposed upon him by a dissolute father who had gamed and drunk the broad family estates in Wiltshire. Major Sands's inheritance, therefore, had been scanty. At least, it did not include —and for this he daily returned thanks to his Maker— the wasteful, improvident proclivities of his sire. The Major was no man for hazards. In contrast with his profligate father, he was of that cold and calculating temperament which, when allied with intelligence, will carry a man far. In Major Sands the intelligence was absent; but like most men in his case he was not aware of it. If he had not realized his hopes strictly in accordance with the expectations that had sent him overseas, he perceived that he was about to realize them very fully, nevertheless. And however unforeseen the circumstances to which the fact was due, this nowise

2

troubled his perception that the achievement proceeded from his own merit and address. Hence his disdainful attitude towards Fortune. The issue, after all, was a simple one. He had come out to the West Indies in quest of fortune. And in the West Indies he had found it. He had achieved what he came to achieve. Could cause and effect be linked more closely?

This fortune which he had won, or the winning of which awaited now his pleasure, reclined on a day-bed of cane and carved oak, and was extremely good to look upon. Slim and straight, clean-limbed and moderately tall, Priscilla Harradine displayed an outward grace of body that was but the reflection of an inner grace of mind. The young face under the shadow of the wide-brimmed hat was of a winning loveliness; it was of that delicate tint that went with the deep golden of her hair, and it offered little evidence of long years spent in the blistering climate of Antigua. If there was spirit in her resolute little chin and firmly modelled lips, there was only tenderness and candour in the eyes, wide-set and intelligent and of a colour that was something between the deep blue of the sky and the jade-green of the sea on which they gazed. She wore a high-waisted gown of ivory-coloured silk, and the escalloped edges of her bodice were finely laced with gold. Languidly she waved a fan, fashioned from the vivid green-and-scarlet of parrots' feathers, in the heart of which a little oval mirror had been set.

Her father, Sir John Harradine, had been actuated by motives similar to those of Major Sands in exiling himself from England to a remote colonial settlement. His fortunes, too, had been at a low ebb; and as much for the sake of his only and motherless child as for his own, he had accepted the position of Captain-General of the Leeward Islands, the offer of which a friend at court had procured for him. Great opportunities of fortune came the way of an alert colonial governor. Sir John had known how to seize them and squeeze them during the six years that his governorship had lasted, and when at last he died—prematurely cut off by a tropical fever—he was in a position to make amends to his daughter for the years of exile she had shared with him, by leaving her mistress of a very substantial fortune and of a very fair estate in his native Kent which a trustworthy agent in England had acquired for him.

It had been Sir John's wish that she should go home at once to this, and to his sister who would guide her. On his deathbed he protested that too much of her youth already had she wasted in the West Indies through his selfishness. For this he begged her pardon, and so died.

They had been constant companions and good friends, she and her father. She missed him sorely, and might have missed him more, might have been dejected by his death into a deeper sense of loneliness, but for the ready friendship, attention, and service of Major Sands.

Bartholomew Sands had acted as the Captain-General's second-in-command. He had lived at Government House with them so long that Miss Priscilla had come to look upon him as of the family, and was glad enough to lean upon him now. And the Major was even more glad to be leaned upon. His hopes of succeeding Sir John in the governorship of Antigua were slight. Not that in his view he lacked the ability. He knew that he had ability to spare. But court favour in these matters, he supposed, counted for more than talent or experience; and court favour no doubt would be filling the vacant post with some inept fribble from home.

The perception of this quickened his further perception that his first duty was to Miss Priscilla. He told her so, and overwhelmed the child by this display of what she accounted an altruistic nobility. For she was under the assumption that his natural place was in her father's vacant seat, an assumption which he was far from wishing to dispel. It might well be so, he opined; but it could matter little when weighed against her possible need of him. She would be going home to England now. The voyage was long, tedious, and fraught with many perils. To him it was as inconceivable as it was intolerable that she should take this voyage unaccompanied and unprotected. Even though he should jeopardize his chances of the succession of the governorship as a consequence of leaving the island

4

at such a time, yet his sense of duty to herself and his regard for her left him no choice. Also, he added, with impressive conviction, it was what her father would have wished.

Overbearing her gentle objections to this self-sacrifice, he had given himself leave of absence, and had appointed Captain Grey to the lieutenant-governorship until fresh orders should come from Whitehall.

And so he had shipped himself with her aboard the Centaur, and with her at first had been her black waiting-woman Isabella. Unfortunately, the Negress had suffered so terribly from seasickness that it was impossible to take her across the ocean, and they had been constrained to land her at Barbados, so that henceforth Miss Priscilla must wait upon herself.

Major Sands had chosen the Centaur for her fine roominess and seaworthy qualities despite the fact that before setting a course for home her master had business to transact farther south in Barbados. If anything, the Major actually welcomed this prolongation of the voyage, and consequently of this close and intimate association with Miss Priscilla. It was in his calculating nature to proceed slowly, to spoil nothing by precipitancy. He realized that his wooing of Sir John Harradine's heiress, which, indeed, had not begun until after Sir John's death had cast her, as it were, upon his hands, must be conducted yet some little way before he could account that he had won her. There were certain disadvantages to be overcome, certain possible prejudices to be broken down. After all, although undoubtedly a very personable man—a fact of which his mirror gave him the most confident assurances—there was an undeniable disparity of age between them. Miss Priscilla was not yet twenty-five, whilst Major Sands had already turned his back on forty, and was growing rather bald under his golden periwig. At first he had clearly perceived that she was but too conscious of his years. She had treated him with an almost filial deference, which had brought him some pain and more dismay. With the close association that had been theirs and the suggestive skill with which he had come to establish a sense of approximate coevality, this attitude

5

in her was being gradually dispelled. He looked now to the voyage to enable him to complete the work so well begun. He would be a dolt, indeed, if he could not contrive that this extremely desirable lady and her equally desirable fortune should be contracted to him before they cast anchor in Plymouth Roads. It was upon this that he had staked his slender chances of succession to the governorship of Antigua. But, as I have said, Major Sands was no gambler. And this was no gambler's throw. He knew himself, his person-ableness, his charms and his arts, well enough, to be confident of the issue. He had merely exchanged a possibility for a certainty; the certainty of that fortune which he had originally come overseas to seek, and which lay now all but within his grasp.

This was his settled conviction as he leaned forward in his chair, leaned nearer to tempt her with the Peru-vian sweetmeats in the silver box he proffered, pro-cured for her with that touching anticipation of her every possible wish which by now she must have come to remark in him.

She stirred against the cushion of purple velvet with its gold tassels, which his solicitous hands had fetched from the cabin and placed behind her. She shook her head in refusal, but smiled upon him with a gentleness that was almost tender.

'You are so watchful of my comfort, Major Sands, that it is almost ungracious to refuse anything you bring. But . . .' She waved her green-and-scarlet fan.

He feigned ill-humour, which may not have been entirely feigned. 'If I am to be Major Sands to you to the end of my days, faith, I'll bring you nothing more. I am called Bartholomew, ma'am. Bartholomew.'

'A fine name,' said she. 'But too fine and long for common everyday use, in such heat as this.'

His answer to that was almost eager. Disregarding her rallying note, he chose to take her literally. 'I have been called Bart upon occasion, by my friends. It's what my mother called me always. I make you free of it, Priscilla.'

'I am honoured, Bart,' she laughed, and so rejoiced him.

Four couplets sounded from the ship's belfry. It brought her to sit up as if it had been a signal.

'Eight bells, and we are still at anchor. Captain Bransome said we should be gone before now.' She rose. 'What keeps us here, I wonder.'

As if to seek an answer to her question, she moved from the shadow of the awning. Major Sands, who had risen with her, stepped beside her to the taffrail.

The cockboat with the baffled Jew was already on its way back to the shore. The periaguas were falling away, their occupants still vociferous, chopping wit now with some sailors who leaned upon the bulwarks. But the longboat, which Captain Bransome had been watching, was coming alongside at the foot of the entrance ladder. One of the naked brown Caribs by whom she was manned knelt in the prow to seize a bight of rope and steady her against the vessel's side.

From her stern-sheets rose the tall, slim, vigorous figure of a man in a suit of pale blue taffetas with silver lace. About the wide brim of his black hat curled a pale blue ostrich plume, and the hand he put forth to steady himself upon the ladder was gloved and emerged from a cloud of fine lace.

'Odds life!' quoth Major Sands, in amazement at this modishness off Martinique. 'And who may this be?'

His amazement increased to behold the practised agility with which this modish fellow came swiftly up that awkward ladder. He was followed, more clumsily, by a half-caste in a cotton shirt and breeches of hairy, untanned hide, who carried a cloak, a rapier, and a sling of purple leather, stiff with bullion, from the ends of which protruded the chased silver butts of a brace of pistols.

The newcomer reached the deck. A moment he paused, tall and commanding at the ladder's head; then he stepped down into the waist, and doffed his hat in courteous response to the Captain's similar salutation. He revealed a swarthy countenance below a glossy black periwig that was sedulously curled.

The Captain barked an order. Two of the hands sprang to the main hatch for a canvas sling, and went to lower it from the bulwarks.

By this the watchers on the poop saw first one chest and then another hauled up to the deck.

'He comes to stay, it seems,' said Major Sands.

'He has the air of a person of importance,' ventured Miss Priscilla.

The Major was perversely moved to contradict her. 'You judge by his foppish finery. But externals, my dear, can be deceptive. Look at his servant, if that rascal is his servant. He has the air of a buccaneer.'

'We are in the Indies, Bart,' she reminded him.

'Why, so we are. And somehow this gallant seems out of place in them. I wonder who he is.'

A shrill blast from the bo'sun's whistle was piping the hands to quarters, and the ship suddenly became alive with briskly moving men.

As the creak of windlass and the clatter of chain announced the weighing of the anchor, and the hands went swarming aloft to set the sails, the Major realized that their departure had been delayed because they had waited for this voyager to come aboard. For the second time he vaguely asked of the northeasterly breeze: 'I wonder who the devil he may be?'

His tone was hardly good-humored. It was faintly tinged by the resentment that their privacy as the sole passengers aboard the Centaur should be invaded. This resentment would have been less unreasonable could he have known that this voyager was sent by Fortune to teach Major Sands not to treat her favours lightly.

## 2

## Monsieur de Bernis

TO SAY that their curiosity on the subject of the new-comer was gratified in the course of the next hour, when they met him at dinner, would not be merely an overstatement, it would be in utter conflict with the fact. That meeting, which took place in the great cabin, where dinner was served, merely went to excite a deeper curiosity.

He was presented to his two fellow passengers by Captain Bransome as Monsieur Charles de Bernis, from which it transpired that he was French. But the fact was hardly to have been suspected from the smooth fluency of his English, which bore only the faintest trace of a Gallic accent. If his nationality betrayed itself at all, it was only in a certain freedom of gesture, and, to the prominent blue English eyes of Major Sands, in a slightly exaggerated air of courtliness. Major Sands, who had come prepared to dislike him, was glad to discover in the fellow's personality no cause to do otherwise. If there had been nothing else against the man, his foreign origin would have been more than enough; for Major Sands had a lofty disdain for all those who did not share his own good fortune of having been born a Briton.

Monsieur de Bernis was very tall, and if spare he yet conveyed a sense of toughness. The lean leg in its creaseless pale blue stocking looked as if made of whipcord. He was very swarthy, and bore, as Major Sands perceived at once, a curious likeness to his late Majesty King Charles II in his younger days; for the Frenchman could be scarcely more than thirty-five. He had the same hatchet face with its prominent cheekbones, the same jutting chin and nose, the same tiny black moustache above full lips about which hovered the same faintly sardonic expression that had marked the countenance of the Stuart sovereign. Under intensely black brows his eyes were dark and large, and although normally soft and velvety, they could, as he soon revealed, by a blazing directness of glance be extremely disconcerting.

If his fellow passengers were interested in him, it could hardly be said that he returned the compliment at first. The very quality of his courtesy towards them seemed in itself to raise a barrier beyond which he held aloof. His air was preoccupied, and such concern as his conversation manifested whilst they ate was directed to the matter of his destination.

9

In this he seemed to be resuming an earlier discussion between himself and the master of the Centaur.

'Even if you will not put in at Mariegalante, Captain, I cannot perceive that it could delay or inconvenience you to send me ashore in a boat.'

'That's because ye don't understand my reasons,' said Bransome. 'I've no mind to sail within ten miles o' Guadeloupe. If trouble comes my way, faith, I can deal with it. But I'm not seeking it. This is my last voyage, and I want it safe and peaceful. I've a wife and four children at home in Devon, and it's time I were seeing something of them. So I'm giving a wide berth to a pirate's nest like Guadeloupe. It's bad enough to be taking you to Sainte Croix.'

'Oh, that . . .' The Frenchman smiled and waved a long brown hand, tossing back the fine Mechlin from his wrist.

But Bransome frowned at the deprecatory gesture. 'Ye may smile, Mossoo. Ye may smile. But I know what I knows. Your French West India Company ain't above suspicion. All they asks is a bargain, and they don't care how they come by it. There's many a freight goes into Sainte Croix to be sold there for a tenth of its value. The French West India Company asks no questions, so long as it can deal on such terms as they. And it don't need to ask no questions. The truth's plain enough. It shrieks. And that's the fact. Maybe ye didn't know it.'

The Captain, a man in middle life, broad and powerful, ruddy of hair and complexion, lent emphasis to his statement and colour to the annoyance it stirred in him by bringing down on the table a massive freckled hand on which the red hairs gleamed like fire.

'Sainte Croix since I've undertaken to carry you there. And that's bad enough, as I say. But no Guadeloupe for me.'

Mistress Priscilla stirred in her seat. She leaned forward.

'Do you speak of pirates, Captain Bransome?'

'Aye!' said Bransome. 'And that's the fact.'

Conceiving her alarmed, the Major entered the discussion with the object of reassuring her.

'Faith, it's not a fact to be mentioned before a lady.

10

And anyway, it's a fact for the timorous only nowadays.'

'Oho!' Vehemently Captain Bransome blew out his cheeks.

'Buccaneers,' said Major Sands, 'are things of the past.'

The Captain's face was seen to turn a deeper red. His contradiction took the form of elaborate sarcasm. 'To be sure, it's as safe cruising in the Caribbean today as on any of the English lakes.'

After that he gave his attention to his dinner, whilst Major Sands addressed himself to Monsieur de Bernis.

'You go with us, then, no farther than Sainte Croix?' His manner was more pleasant than it had yet been, for his good-humour was being restored by the discovery that this intrusion was to be only a short one.

'No farther,' said Monsieur de Bernis.

The laconic answer did not encourage questions. Nevertheless Major Sands persisted.

'You will have interests in Sainte Croix?'

'No interests. No. I seek a ship, A ship to take me to France.' It was characteristic of him to speak in short, sharp sentences.

The Major was puzzled. 'But, surely, being aboard so fine a ship as this, you might travel comfortably to Plymouth, and there find a sloop to put you across the Channel.'

'True,' said Monsieur de Bernis. 'True! I had not thought of it.'

The Major was conscious of a sudden apprehension that he might have said too much. To his dismay he heard Miss Priscilla voicing the idea which he feared he might have given to the Frenchman.

'You will think of it now, monsieur?'

Monsieur de Bernis' dark eyes glowed as they rested upon her; but his smile was wistful.

'By my faith, mademoiselle, you must compel a man to do so.'

Major Sands sniffed audibly at what he accounted an expression of irrepressible impudent Gallic gallantry. Then, after a slight pause, Monsieur de Bernis added with a deepening of his wistful smile:

'But, alas! A friend awaits me in Sainte Croix. I am to cross with him to France,'

The Major interposed, a mild astonishment in his voice.

'I thought it was at Guadeloupe that you desired to be put ashore; and that your going to Sainte Croix was forced upon you by the Captain.'

If he thought to discompose Monsieur de Bernis by confronting him with this contradiction, he was soon disillusioned. The Frenchman turned to him slowly, still smiling, but the wistfulness had given place to a contemptuous amusement.

'But why unveil the innocent deception which courtesy to a lady thrust upon me? It is more shrewd than kind, Major Sands.'

Major Sands flushed. He writhed under the Frenchman's superior smile, and in his discomfort blundered grossly.

'What need for deceptions, sir?'

'Add, too: what need for courtesy? Each to his nature, sir. You convict me of a polite deceit, and discover yourself to be of a rude candour. Each of us in his different way is admirable.'

'That is something to which I can't agree at all. Stab me if I can.'

'Let mademoiselle pronounce between us, then,' the Frenchman smilingly invited.

But Miss Priscilla shook her golden head. 'That would be to pronounce against one of you. Too invidious a task.'

'Forgive me, then, for venturing to set it. We'll leave the matter undecided.' He turned to Captain Bransome, 'You said, I think, Captain, that you are calling at Dominica.' Thus he turned the conversation into different channels.

The Major was left with an uncomfortable sense of being diminished. It rankled in him, and found expression later when with Miss Priscilla he was once more upon the poop.

'I do not think the Frenchman was pleased at being put down,' said he.

At table the Major's scarcely veiled hostility to the stranger had offended her sense of fitness. In her eyes

12

he had compared badly with the suave and easy Frenchman. His present smugness revived her irritation.

'Was he put down?' said she. 'I did not observe it.'

'You did not . . .' The prominent pale eyes seemed to swell in his florid face. Then he laughed boisterously. 'You were day-dreaming, Priscilla, surely. You cannot have attended. I let him see plainly that I was not to be hoodwinked by his contradictions. I'm never slow to perceive deceit. It annoyed him to be so easily exposed.'

'He dissembled his annoyance very creditably.'

'Oh, aye! As a dissembler I give him full credit. But I could see that I had touched him. Stab me, I could. D'ye perceive the extent of his dissimulation? First it was only that he had not thought of crossing the ocean in the Centaur. Then it was that he has a friend awaiting him in Sainte Croix, and I, knowing all the while that Sainte Croix was forced upon him by the Captain who could not be persuaded to land him, as he wished, at Guadeloupe. I wonder what the fellow has to hide that he should be so desperately clumsy?'

'Whatever it is, it can be no affair of ours.'

'You make too sure, perhaps. After all, I am an officer of the Crown, and it's scarcely less than my duty to be aware of all that happens in these waters.'

'Why plague yourself? In a day or two he will have left us again.'

'To be sure. And I thank God for't.'

'I see little cause for thanksgiving. Monsieur de Bernis should prove a lively companion on a voyage.'

The Major's brows were raised. 'You conceive him lively?'

'Did not you? Was there no wit in his parries when you engaged him?'

'Wit! Lord! I thought him as clumsy a liar as I have met.'

A black hat embellished by a sweeping plume of blue appeared above the break of the quarter-deck. Monsieur de Bernis was ascending the companion. He came to join them on the poop.

The Major was disposed to regard his advent as an unbidden intrusion. But Miss Priscilla's eyes gleamed a

13

welcome to the courtly Frenchman; and when she moved aside invitingly to the head of the day-bed, so as to make room for him to sit beside her, Major Sands must mask his vexation as best he could in chill civilities.

Martinique by now was falling hazily astern, and the Centaur under a full spread of canvas was beating to westward with a larboard list that gently canted her yellow deck.

Monsieur de Bernis commended the north-easterly breeze in terms of one familiar with such matters. They were fortunate in it, he opined. At this season of the year, the prevailing wind was from the north. He expressed the further opinion that if it held they should be off Dominica before tomorrow's dawn.

The Major, not to be left behind by Monsieur de Bernis in the display of knowledge of Caribbean matters, announced himself astonished that Captain Bransome should be putting in at an island mainly peopled by Caribs, with only an indifferent French settlement at Roseau. The readiness of the Frenchman's answer took him by surprise.

'For freights in the ordinary way I should agree with you, Major. Roseau would not be worth a visit; but for a captain trading on his own account it can be very profitable. This, you may suppose to be the case of Captain Bransome.'

The accuracy of his surmise was revealed upon the morrow, when they lay at anchor before Roseau, on the western side of Dominica. Bransome, who traded in partnership with his owners, went ashore for a purchase of hides, for which he had left himself abundant room under hatches. He knew of some French traders here, from whom he could buy at half the price he would have to pay in Martinique or elsewhere; for the Caribs who slew and flayed the beasts were content with infinitely less than it cost to procure and maintain the Negro slaves who did the work in the more established settlements.

Since the loading of the hides was to delay them there for a day or two, Monsieur de Bernis proposed to his fellow passengers an excursion to the interior of the

14

island, a proposal so warmly approved by Miss Priscilla that it was instantly adopted.

They procured ponies ashore, and the three of them, attended only by Pierre, de Bernis' half-caste servant, rode out to view that marvel of Dominica, the boiling lake, and the fertile plains watered by the Layou.

The Major would have insisted upon an escort. But Monsieur de Bernis, again displaying his knowledge of these regions, assured them that they would find the Caribs of Dominica a gentle, friendly race, from whom no evil was to be apprehended.

'If it were otherwise,' he concluded, 'the whole ship's company would not suffice to protect us, and I should never have proposed the jaunt.'

Priscilla rode that day between her two cavaliers; but it was the ready-witted de Bernis who chiefly held her attention, until Major Sands began to wonder whether the fellow's remarkable resemblance to his late Majesty might not extend beyond his personal appearance. Monsieur de Bernis made it plain, the Major thought, that he was endowed with the same gifts of spontaneous gallantry; and the Major was vexed to perceive signs that he possessed something of King Charles's attraction for the opposite sex.

His alarm might have gone considerably deeper but for the soothing knowledge that in a day or two this long-legged, gipsy-faced interloper would drop out of their lives at Sainte Croix. What Miss Priscilla could discern in the man, that she should bestow so much of her attention upon him, the Major could not imagine. As compared with his own solid worth, the fellow was no better than a shallow fribble. It was inconceivable that Priscilla should be dazzled by his pinchbeck glitter. And yet, women, even the best of them, were often, he knew, led into error by a lack of discernment. Therefore it was matter for thankfulness that this adventurer's contact with their own lives was destined to be so transient. If it were protracted, the rascal might become aware of the great fortune Miss Priscilla had inherited, and undoubtedly he would find in this an incentive to exert all the arts of attraction which such a fellow might command.

That he was an adventurer Major Sands was persuaded. He flattered himself that he could read a man at a glance, and his every instinct warned him against this saturnine rascal. His persuasions were confirmed that very evening at Roseau.

On the beach there, when they had relinquished their ponies, they came upon a burly, elderly, rudely clad Frenchman, who reeked of rum and tobacco, one of the traders from whom Captain Bransome was purchasing his hides. The man halted before them as if thunder-struck, and stared in round-eyed wonder at Monsieur de Bernis for a long moment. Then a queer grin spread upon his weather-beaten face, he pulled a ragged hat from a grizzled, ill-kempt head, with a courtesy rendered ironical by exaggeration.

Major Sands knew no French. But the impudently familiar tone of the greeting was not to be mistaken.

'C'est bien toi, de Bernis? Pardieu! Je ne croyais pas te revoir.'

De Bernis checked to answer him, and his reply reflected the other's easy, half-mocking tone. 'Et toi, mon drôle? Ah, tu fais le marchand de peaux maintenant?'

Major Sands moved on with Miss Priscilla, leaving de Bernis in talk with his oddly met acquaintance. The Major was curiously amused.

'A queer encounter for our fine gentleman. Most queer. Like the quality of his friends. More than ever I wonder who the devil he may be.'

But Miss Priscilla was impatient of his wonder and his amusement. She found him petty. She knew the islands better, it seemed, than did he. She knew that colonial life could impose the oddest associations on a man, and that only the rash or the ignorant would draw conclusions from them.

She said something of the kind.

'Odds life, ma'am! D'ye defend him?'

'I've not perceived him to be attacked, unless you mean to attack him, Bart. After all, Monsieur de Bernis has never pretended that he comes to us from Versailles.'

'That will be because he doubts if it would carry conviction. Pish, child! The fellow's an adventurer.'

Her agreement shocked and dismayed him more than contradiction could have done.

'So I had supposed,' she smiled distractingly. 'I love adventurers and the adventurous.'

Only the fact that de Bernis came striding to overtake them saved her from a homily. But her answer, which the Major accounted flippant, rankled with him; and it may have been due to this that after supper that night, when they were all assembled in the great cabin, he alluded to the matter of that meeting. 'That was a queer chance, Monsieur de Bernis, your coming face to face with an acquaintance here on Dominica.'

'A queer chance, indeed,' the Frenchman agreed readily. 'That was an old brother-in-arms.'

The Major's sandy brows went up. 'Ye've been a soldier, sir?'

There was an odd light in the Frenchman's eyes as for a long moment they considered his questioner. He seemed faintly amused. 'Oh, after a fashion,' he said at last. Then he swung to Bransome, who sat at his ease now, in cotton shirt and calico drawers, the European finery discarded. 'It was Lafarche, Captain. He tells me that he is trading with you.' And he went on: 'We were on Santa Catalina together under the Sieur Simon, and amongst the very few who survived the Spanish raid there of Perez de Guzman. Lafarche and I and two others, who had hidden ourselves in a maize field, when all was lost, got away that night in an open boat, and contrived to reach the Main. I was wounded, and my left arm had been broken by a piece of langrel during the bombardment. But all evils do not come to hurt us, as the Italians say. It saved my life. For it was my uselessness drove me into hiding, where the other three afterwards joined me. They were the first wounds I took. I was under twenty at the time. Only my youth and my vigour saved my arm and my life in the trials and hardships that followed. So far as I know we were the only four who escaped alive of the hundred and twenty men who were on Santa Catalina with Simon. When Perez took the island, he ruthlessly avenged the defence it had made by putting to the sword every man who had remained alive. A vile massacre. A wanton cruelty.'

17

He fell pensive, and might have left the matter there but that Miss Priscilla broke the ensuing silence to press him for more details.

In yielding, he told her of the colony which Mansvelt had established on Santa Catalina, of how they had gone to work to cultivate the land, planting maize and plantains, sweet potatoes, cassava, and tobacco. Whilst she listened to him with parted lips and softened eyes, he drew a picture of the flourishing condition which had been reached by the plantations when Don Juan Perez de Guzman came over from Panama, with four ships and an overwhelming force, to wreak his mischief. He told of Simon's proud answer when summoned to surrender: that he held the settlement for the English Crown, and that sooner than yield it up, he and those with him would yield up their lives. He stirred their blood by the picture he drew of the gallant stand made by that little garrison against the overwhelming Spanish odds. And he moved them to compassion by the tale of the massacre that followed and the wanton destruction of the plantations so laboriously hoed.

When he reached the end, there was a smile at once grim and wistful on his lean, gipsy-tinted face. The deep lines in it, lines far deeper than were warranted by his years, became more marked.

'The Spaniards paid for it at Porto Bello and at Panama and elsewhere. My God, how they paid! But not all the Spanish blood that has since been shed could avenge the brutal, cowardly destruction of the English and the French who were in alliance at Santa Catalina.'

He had impressed himself upon them by that glimpse into his past and into the history of West Indian settlements. Even the Major, however he might struggle against it, found himself caught in the spell of this queer fellow's personality.

Later, when supper was done, and the table had been cleared, Monsieur de Bernis went to fetch a guitar from among the effects in his cabin. Seated on the stern-locker, with his back to the great window that stood open to the purple tropical night, he sang some little songs of his native Provence and one or two

18

queerly moving Spanish airs set in the minor key, of the kind that were freely composed in Malaga.

Rendered by his mellow baritone voice they had power to leave Miss Priscilla with stinging eyes and an ache at the heart; and even Major Sands was moved to admit that Monsieur de Bernis had a prodigious fine gift of song. But he took care to make the admission with patronage, as if to mark the gulf that lay between himself and his charge on the one hand and this stranger, met by chance, on the other. He accounted it a necessary precaution, because he could not be blind to the impression the fellow was making upon Miss Priscilla's inexperience. It was also, no doubt, because of this that on the morrow the Major permitted himself a sneer at Monsieur de Bernis' expense. It went near to making a breach between himself and the lady in his charge.

They were leaning at the time upon the carved rail of the quarter-deck to watch the loading, conducted under the jealous eyes of Captain Bransome, himself, who was not content to leave the matter to the quarter-master and the boatswain.

The coamings were off the main hatch, and by slings from the yardarm the bales of hides were being hoisted aboard from the rafts that brought them alongside. In the waist a dozen hairy seamen, naked above their belts, heaved and sweated in the merciless heat, whilst down in the stifling, reeking gloom of the hold others laboured at the stowage. The Captain, in cotton shirt and drawers, the blue kerchief swathing his cropped red head, his ruddy, freckled face agleam with sweat, moved hither and thither, directing the hoisting and stowing, and at times, from sheer exuberance of energy, lending a powerful hand at the ropes.

Into this sweltering bustle stepped Monsieur de Bernis from the gangway that led aft. As a concession to the heat he wore no coat. In the bulging white cambric shirt with its wealth of ruffles, clothing him above a pair of claret breeches, he looked cool and easy despite his heavy black periwig and broad black hat.

He greeted Bransome with familiar ease, and not only Bransome, but Sproat, the boatswain. From the bulwarks he stood surveying the rafts below with their

19

silent crews of naked Caribs and noisily directing French overseers. He called down to them—Major Sands assumed it to be some French ribaldry—and set them laughing and answering him with raucously merry freedom. He said something to the hands about the hatchway, and had them presently all agrin. Then, when the trader Lafarche came climbing to the deck, mopping himself, and demanding rum, there was de Bernis supporting the demand, and thrusting Bransome before him to the after gangway, whilst himself he followed, bringing Lafarche with him, an arm flung carelessly about the villainous old trader's shoulder.

'A raffish fellow, without dignity or sense of discipline,' was the Major's disgusted comment.

Miss Priscilla looked at him sideways, and a little frown puckered her brow at the root of her daintily chiselled nose.

'That is not how I judge him.'

'No?' He was surprised. He uncrossed his plump legs, took his elbows from the poop-rail, and stood up, a heavy figure rendered the more ponderous by an air of self-sufficiency.

'Yet seeing him there, so very much at ease with that riffraff, how else should he be read? I should be sorry to see myself in the like case. Stab me, I should.'

'You stand in no danger of it.'

'I thank you. No.'

'Because a man needs to be very sure of himself before he can condescend so far.' It was a little cruel. But his sneering tone of superiority had annoyed her curiously.

Astonishment froze him. 'I . . . I do not think I understand. Stab me if I do.'

She was as merciless in her explanation, unintimidated by his frosty tone.

'I see in Monsieur de Bernis a man placed by birth and experience above the petty need of standing upon his dignity.'

The Major collected the wits that had been scattered by angry amazement. After a gasping moment, he laughed. Derision he thought was the surest corrosive to apply to such heresies.

'Lord! Here's assumption! And birth, you say. Fan me, ye winds! What tokens of birth do you perceive in the tawdry fellow?'

'His name; his bearing; his . . .'

But the Major let her get no further. Again he laughed. 'His name? The "de," you mean. Faith, it's borne by many who have long since lost pretensions to gentility, and by many who never had a right to it. Do we even know that it is his name? As for his bearing, pray consider it. You saw him down there, making himself one with the hands, and the rest. Would a gentleman so comport himself?'

'We come back to the beginning,' said she coolly. 'I have given you reason why such as he may do it without loss. You do not answer me.'

He found her exasperating. But he did not tell her so. He curbed his rising heat. A lady so well endowed must be humoured by a prudent man who looks to make her his wife. And Major Sands was a very prudent man.

'But, dear Priscilla, it is because you will not be answered. You are a little obstinate, child.' He smiled to humour her. 'You should trust to my riper judgment of men. You should so, stab me.' And then he changed his tone. 'But why waste breath on a man who tomorrow or the next day will have gone, and whom we shall never see again?'

She sighed, and gently waved her fan. It may be that her next words were uttered merely to plague and punish him. 'I take no satisfaction in the thought. We meet so few whom we are concerned ever to meet again. To me Monsieur de Bernis is one of those few.'

'In that case,' said he, holding himself hard to keep his voice cool and level, 'I thank God the gentleman is so soon to go his ways. In these outlandish settlements you have had little chance, my dear, of learning—ah—discrimination in the choice of associates. A few months in England will give you a very different outlook.'

'Yes. That is probable,' said she, with a sweet submissiveness. 'Until now I have been compelled to accept the associations which circumstance has thrust upon me. In England it will be mine to choose.'

This was a little devastating in its ambiguity. If he was left in doubt of her real meaning, he was in no doubt that, before England was reached and the choice afforded her, he would have placed her beyond the need of exercising it in so far as a husband was concerned.

But she had not yet completed her task of chastening his superciliousness.

'As for Monsieur de Bernis, it yet might be possible to persuade him to make the voyage with us. Good company upon a voyage is not to be disdained. The time can be monstrous tedious.'

He stared at her, his florid face inflamed. She smiled up at him over the edge of her fan, very sweetly.

'Will you try to persuade him, Bart?'

'I? Persuade him?' He spoke in horror. 'Stab my vitals! Persuade him? I? You jest, of course.'

She laughed a trilling little enigmatic laugh, and was content to leave the matter there.

Later, whilst still they lingered on the quarter, they were sought by Monsieur de Bernis. He came laden with a basket woven of palmetto, containing fresh oranges and limes. He brought it as an offering to Miss Priscilla, announcing that he had sent Pierre, his half-caste servant, ashore to gather the fruit for her that morning. Graciously she accepted, thanking him. He waved the thanks aside.

'A very trifling gift.'

'In gifts, sir, it is the thought that counts.'

The Major was left considering that he must practise thoughtfulness in future. He remained silent and brooding, whilst Monsieur de Bernis hung there in talk with Miss Priscilla. The Frenchman was gay, witty, and amusing, and to the Major it seemed that Miss Priscilla was very easily moved to laughter. His stolidity leaving him little skill in the lighter social arts, he became increasingly uneasy. What if this French adventurer, growing too conscious of Miss Priscilla's attractions, were after all to decide to make the voyage to Europe on the Centaur? What if Miss Priscilla, whose laughter and general manner seemed in the Major's jaundiced eyes to be almost tinged with wantonness, should so far forget her dignity as, herself, to invite de Bernis to such a course?

Major Sands, inwardly cursing the delays resulting from these loadings of hides, was surly and uneasy all that day. His chance, however, and his revenge upon the man who had occasioned him these pangs was unexpectedly to be vouchsafed him that evening at supper.

3

## Bransome's Prayer

THE Centaur left Dominica a little before sunset, and with the wind on her starboard quarter set a westerly course for the Isle of Aves, so as to give a wide berth to Guadeloupe.

Having conned the ship, the Captain went below to supper, and came in high good-humour to the spacious cabin, flanked to port and starboard by the lesser cabins which his passengers were now occupying.

The great horn windows in the stern stood wide to the air and to the green receding mass of the island, which Captain Bransome announced without a sigh that he would never see again. His good-humour was rooted in the fact that his last call made and his cargo safely stowed, he was now definitely setting his face towards home and the serene ease in the bosom of a family that scarcely knew him. Nevertheless, he went in confidence that, like himself, this family looked forward joyously to his retirement from the sea and to assisting him in garnering the reward for all these years of labour bravely shouldered and for all the perils and hardships confronted without shrinking.

Contentment made him more than ordinarily loquacious, as he sat there in shirt and drawers, a burly,

23

jovial figure at the head of his own table, with Sam, the white-jacketed Negro steward, in attendance and Monsieur de Bernis' servant lending him assistance. A feast was spread that evening. There was fresh meat and turtle and vegetables taken aboard that day, and the roasted flesh of a great albacore that Monsieur de Bernis had caught in the course of the afternoon; and in honour of what to him was a great occasion, Captain Bransome regaled them with a sweet Peruvian wine which his own rude taste accounted very choice.

In this wine Monsieur de Bernis pledged his safe return and many happy years in the bosom of that family of which so far the Captain had seen so little.

'Seems queer,' the Captain said, 'that a man should scarcely know his own children. Unnatural. There's four fine lads well-nigh grown to manhood, and all but strangers to me that got 'em.' A pensive smile lighted the broad ruddy features of his good-humoured face. 'But the future is ours now, and it'll have to make amends to me for the past. Aye, and to that sweet patient woman o' mine who waits at Babbicombe. I'll be beside her now to show her that the years I've been away ha'n't been wasted. And this last voyage o' mine'll prove the most prosperous of all. There's a mort o' money in them hides when we comes to market them at home. Old Lafarche has served me well this trip.'

The mention of the old French trader shifted the current of his thoughts. He looked at Monsieur de Bernis, who sat alone on one side of the board, his back to the light, opposite the Major and the lady who were side by side on the master's right.

'Queer, your meeting the old buccaneer again like that, by chance, after all these years. And queer, too, that I should not have remembered who ye were, for all that your name was kind of familiar, until old Lafarche reminded me.'

'Yes,' de Bernis quietly agreed. 'Life is a matter of queer chances. It made me feel old to meet him and to see into what he has grown. That's the result of beginning life whilst most men are still at school.'

The Major had pricked up his ears. Here were interesting facts. Facts to be investigated.

24

'D'ye say that French trader was once a buccaneer?'

It was de Bernis who answered him. 'Faith, we were little better at Santa Catalina. And after that we sailed with Morgan.'

'With Morgan?' The Major could hardly believe his ears. 'D'ye mean Henry Morgan?'

'Sir Henry Morgan. Yes. He that is now Governor of Jamaica.'

'But . . .' The Major paused, frowning. 'D'ye say that you, too, sailed with him? With Morgan?'

Monsieur de Bernis did not seem to remark the incredulity in the other's voice. He answered simply and naturally.

'Why, yes. And I marched with him, too. I was at Porto Bello with him, and at Panama. At Panama I was in command of the French contingent of his forces. We took a proud vengeance then for the blood that was shed at Santa Catalina.'

Miss Priscilla looked brightly alert and eager. Without knowledge of West Indian affairs to perceive the implications that had shocked the Major, she was aware only that here was another story of brave doings, and hoped that Monsieur de Bernis would be induced to tell it. But the Major's face was blank and seemed to have lost some of its high colour. He reflected with satisfaction upon his own shrewdness which had discerned this man's true quality under his airs and graces, his swaggering gallantry and his troubadour arts. In dubbing him an adventurer he had erred on the side of charity.

There fell a long pause, during which Monsieur de Bernis helped himself to a slab of guava cheese and poured himself another cup of the Peruvian wine. He was setting down the squat bottle when at last the Major exploded.

'So that ye're just . . . just a damned pirate! A damned pirate! And, stab me, ye've the effrontery to confess it!'

Miss Priscilla and the Captain cried out upon him simultaneously in alarm.

'Bart!' ejaculated the lady.

'Major Sands, sir!' exclaimed the Captain.

Condemnation was in the voice of each. But Monsieur de Bernis showed no resentment. He smiled upon their dismay and waved a long fine hand to pacify them.

'A pirate?' Almost he seemed amused. 'Ah, no. A filibuster, please. A buccaneer.'

The Major curled his heavy lip. 'And the difference?'

'The difference? Oh, but all the difference in the world.'

Captain Bransome came to the rescue with the explanation which Monsieur de Bernis seemed to disdain to offer. The buccaneers had a sort of charter behind them. They had been encouraged by the Governments of both England and France, because they had kept in check the rapacity of Spain, confining their raids to Spanish ships and Spanish settlements.

Monsieur de Bernis was moved by this to take up the tale. 'And doing it as I'll swear none others could have done it. You would not sneer, Major Sands, had you crossed Darien with us.'

He was launched upon reminiscences. He began to tell them of that incredibly arduous journey made partly on foot and partly by water on the Chagres River. He described the hardships they had confronted and overcome: how for eight days they had gone without food, save an occasional evil-tasting musk-flavoured alligator's egg; how they had been constrained to eat strips of hide, consuming even their own belts to cheat their famished stomachs; and how it was in a spent condition that at last they had staggered into sight of Panama, which, forewarned, had mobilized to receive them, with guns and horses, outnumbering them in men by three to one.

'If the Spaniards had only driven in their cattle from the savannah where we lay the night before the battle, starvation must have made us an easy prey to them. I should not now be telling you of these things. But the cattle were there, the steers and horses, and we took and killed what we required, and ate the flesh almost raw. And so, by the grace of God, we found the strength to deliver the attack, and carry the town in the teeth of its defenders.'

26

'By the grace of God!' said the Major, scandalized. 'It is blasphemy, sir.'

De Bernis was singularly patient. 'Ye're intolerant, Major,' was all he said.

'Of thieving rogues? To be sure, I am. I call a thing by its proper name. Ye can throw no glamour over the sack of Panama, sir. With whatever arts you tell the tale of it, it remains a thieving raid, and the men who took part in it—Morgan and his cutthroats—were just bloodthirsty, thieving scoundrels.'

Before such direct offensiveness Captain Bransome became deeply alarmed. Whatever Monsieur de Bernis might be today, it was certain that, since once he had followed the trade of a buccaneer, there must be wild blood in him. If it were roused, there might be mischief done; and he wanted none of that aboard the Centaur. He was considering intervention, when the Frenchman, who, whatever he may have felt, still betrayed no outward sign of irritation, forestalled him.

'By my faith, Major, do you realize that what you say is almost treason? It is a reproach to your King, who does not share your so sensitive honesty. For if he regarded Henry Morgan as you describe him, he would never have raised him to the dignity of knighthood and made him Governor of Jamaica.'

'And that's the fact,' Captain Bransome supported him, hoping to curb the Major's rashness. 'And ye should also be told that Monsieur de Bernis here holds the appointment of Sir Henry Morgan's lieutenant, to help him keep order upon the seas.'

Contradiction came not from the Major, but from Monsieur de Bernis himself.

'Ah, but that is over now. I have resigned my post. Like yourself, Captain, I am going home to enjoy the rest I have earned.'

'No matter for that. The fact that ye held the post, held the King's commission in spite of Panama and Porto Bello and the rest, should be answer enough for Major Sands.'

But Major Sands was not to be put down. 'Ye know very well that was but setting a thief to catch a thief. You may sing the praises of your buccaneers never so eloquently, sir. But you know they had become such a

27

pest that to deliver the seas of them your friend Henry Morgan was bribed with a knighthood and a King's commission to turn upon his old associates.'

Monsieur de Bernis shrugged, and sank back into his chair, quietly sipping his wine. His manner, faintly contemptuous, showed that he withdrew from the discussion. Captain Bransome took it up in his place.

'However it may have been, we've Sir Henry Morgan to thank for it that we can sail in safety now. That at least will be something to his credit.'

The Major sneered. 'He's been constrained to it,' was his grudging admission. 'They've had him home once, and very nearly hanged him for the disloyal way in which he neglected the duty for which he was paid and commissioned. As if loyalty were to be looked for in such men. It was only that danger awakened him to the necessity to keep faith with those who had paid him in advance. I'll own that since then he seems to have gone more vigorously about the business of sweeping the seas clean. But that don't make me forget that it was he and his kind who fouled them.'

'Don't grudge him his due, Major,' Bransome pleaded. 'It's to be doubted if another could ha' done what he has done. It needed him with his own lads behind him to tackle the disorders afloat, and put an end to them.'

But the Major would not yield. In the heat of argument and exasperation he plunged recklessly into matters from which, yesterday, concern for Priscilla had made him steer them. 'Put an end to it? I seem to have heard of a buccaneering villain named Tom Leach who still goes roaring up and down the Caribbean, setting Morgan at defiance.'

Bransome's face darkened. 'Tom Leach, aye. Rot his soul! But Morgan'll get him. It's known from Campeche to Trinidad and from Trinidad to the Bahamas that Morgan is offering five hundred pounds for the head of the last of the buccaneers.'

Monsieur de Bernis stirred. He set down his wine-glass.

'That is not a buccaneer, Captain. It offends me to hear you say it. Tom Leach is just a nasty pirate.'

'And that's the fact,' Bransome approved him. 'As

28

wicked a cut-throat as was ever loose upon the seas. An inhuman beast, without honour and without mercy, making war upon all, and intent only upon robbery and plunder.'

And he fell to relating horrors of Leach's performance, until de Bernis raised a long graceful hand to check him.

'You nauseate Miss Priscilla.'

Made aware of her pallor, the Captain begged her pardon, and closed the subject with a prayer.

'God send that filthy villain may soon come to moorings in execution dock.'

Miss Priscilla intervened.

'You have talked enough of pirates,' she censured them, and rendered the Major at last aware of his enormity.

She leaned across to Monsieur de Bernis, smiling up at him, perhaps all the more sweetly because she desired to reward him for his admirable patience and self-restraint under provocation that had been gross. 'Monsieur de Bernis, will you not fetch your guitar, and sing to us again?'

The Frenchman rose to do her bidding, whilst Major Sands was left to marvel ill-humouredly that all that had been revealed touching this adventurer's abominable antecedents should have made so little impression upon the lady in his charge. Decidedly she was in urgent need of a season of the sedate dignity of English county life to bring the world into correct perspective to her eyes.

# 4

## The Pursuit

THE historical truth of the situation, as it concerned Sir Henry Morgan and the notorious Tom Leach, emerges so clearly from that conversation in the cabin of the Centaur that little remains to be added by a commentator.

Morgan had certainly been shaken up by the authorities at home for his lack of zeal in the prosecution of the task entrusted to him of exterminating the sea-brigands who infested the Caribbean. He had been admonished with more severity than justice; for, after all, in the short time that had elapsed since his own retirement from the Brotherhood of the Coast, he had wrought miracles in the discharge of the duty assumed. The very force of his example had in itself gone far. The very fact that he had ranged himself under the banners of law and order, with the consequent disbanding of the buccaneer fleet of which he had been the admiral, had compelled the men who had followed him to drift back gradually to the peaceful arts of logwood-cutting, planting, and boucanning proper. Many more had been induced to quit the seas by the general amnesty Morgan had been authorized to proclaim, backed by a grant of twenty-five acres of land to every filibuster who should choose to take advantage of it. Those who defiantly remained afloat he pursued so actively and relentlessly as to have deserved better of the Government than a reprimand and the threat of deposition and worse. Because in spite of his endeavours there were some sea-robbers who still eluded him, the authorities at home did not scruple to suggest that Morgan might be playing a double game and might be receiving tribute from those who still remained at large.

Sir Henry was not merely enraged by the insinuation; he was fearful of a solid indictment being built upon it which might end by depriving him of his head. It made the old pirate realize that in accepting a knighthood and the King's commission he had given stern hostages to Fortune. And whilst he may have cursed the one and the other, he addressed himself fearfully to the business of satisfying his terrible taskmasters. The business was rendered heavy by the lawless activities of his old associate Tom Leach, whom Major Sands had named. Tom Leach, as crafty a seaman as he was a brutal, remorseless scoundrel, had gathered about him a host of those buccaneers who were reluctant to forsake their old ways of life, and with these, in a powerful forty-gun ship, the Black Swan, he was in strength upon the Caribbean and wreaking fearful havoc. Being outlawed now, an Ishmael with every man's hand against him, he practised none of the old discrimination of the Brethren of the Coast, as the buccaneers had been called. He was just a brigand, making war upon every ship that sailed, and caring nothing what flag was flown by the vessels he captured, stripped, and sank.

For four anxious months, Morgan had been hunting him in vain, and so as to encourage others to hunt him, he had put the price of five hundred pounds upon the ruffian's head. Not only had Leach eluded him and grown ever more defiant in his depredations, but two months ago off Granada, when two ships of the Jamaica squadron had cornered him, he had delivered battle so successfully that he had sunk one of the Government frigates and disabled the other.

Well might Captain Bransome have uttered his prayer that this evil villain should soon come to moorings in execution dock. The following morning was to bring him the urgent dread that, if the prayer was to be answered at all, it was not likely to be answered in time to be of profit to the Centaur.

Going early on deck to take the air and summon his fellow passengers to breakfast, Monsieur de Bernis found the Captain on the poop, levelling a telescope at a ship some three or four miles away to eastward on their starboard quarter. Beside him stood Major Sands

31

in his burnt-red coat and Miss Priscilla very dainty in a gown of lettuce-green with ivory lace that revealed the lissom beauty of her milk-white neck.

The wind which had veered to the north had freshened a little since dawn, and swept the ship with a grateful coolness. With topsails furled, and a considerable list to larboard, the Centaur was rippling through the sea on a course almost due west. She was still some leagues south-east of Aves, and land was nowhere in sight.

The master lowered his telescope as de Bernis came up. Turning his head, and seeing the Frenchman, he first pointed with the glass, then proffered it.

'Tell me what you make of her, Mossoo.'

Monsieur de Bernis took the glass. He had not observed the grave look in Bransome's eyes, for he displayed no urgency in complying. He paused first to exchange a greeting with Miss Priscilla and the Major. But when at last he did bear the glass to his eye, he kept it there for an unconscionable time. When he lowered it, his countenance reflected the gravity worn by the Captain's. Even then he did not speak. He stepped deliberately to the side, and setting his elbows on the rail for steadiness, levelled the glass once more. This time his observations were even more protracted.

He scanned the tall black hull of that distant ship and the black beak-head carved in the shape of a swan with a gilded crest. He attempted to count the gun ports on her larboard flank as far as this was revealed by the course she was steering. With the same leisureliness he surveyed the mountain of canvas under which she moved, with every sail unfurled, and above which flew no flag.

So long was he in this inspection that at last the Captain's hard-held patience slipped from him.

'Well, sir? Well? What d'ye make of her?'

Monsieur de Bernis lowered the glass again, and faced his questioner. He was calm and smiling.

'A fine, powerful ship,' he said casually, and turned to the others. 'Breakfast waits in the cabin.'

The Major, whose appetite was never feeble, required no further invitation. He departed, taking Miss Priscilla with him.

As they disappeared into the gangway leading aft, the smile left the face of Monsieur de Bernis. Solemnly his long dark eyes met the Captain's uneasily questioning glance.

'I desired not to alarm the lady. It is as I think you already suspect. Tom Leach's ship. The Black Swan.'

'Ye're certain?'

'As certain as that she's steering to cross your course.'

The Captain swore in his red beard. 'And this on my last voyage!' he complained. 'Fate might ha' let me end my sailing days in peace. Ye think . . . D'ye think she means to attack me?'

Monsieur de Bernis shrugged. 'It is Tom Leach. And he steers to cross your course.'

The Captain fell to ranting and swearing as a man will who is spirited and yet conscious of impotence when beset. 'The black-hearted, blackguardly swine! What's your fine Sir Henry Morgan doing to leave him loose upon the seas? What for did the King knight him and make him Governor of Jamaica?'

'Sir Henry will get him in the end. Be sure of that.'

The Frenchman's calm in the face of this overwhelming peril served only to increase the Captain's fury. 'In the end! In the end! And how will that help me? What's to be done?'

'What can you do?'

'I must fight or run.'

'Which would you prefer?'

Bransome considered, merely to explode in exasperation. 'How can I fight? She carries twice my guns, and, if it comes to boarding, her men outnumber mine by ten to one or more.'

'You will run, then?'

'How can I run? She has twice my canvas.' Bransome was grim.

In the waist some of the hands newly descended from aloft were shading their eyes to survey the distant ship, but idly, without suspicion yet of her identity.

De Bernis returned to the study of her through the telescope. He spoke presently with the glass still to his eye. 'For all her canvas, her sailing's laboured,' he pronounced. 'She's been overlong at sea. Her bottom's foul. That's plain.' He lowered the glass again. 'In your place, Captain, I should come a point or two nearer to the wind. You'ld beat up against it a deal more nimbly than will she in her present stale condition.'

The advice seemed to exasperate Bransome. 'But whither will that lead me? The nearest landfall on that course is Porto Rico, and that over two hundred miles away.'

'What matter? If this breeze holds, she'll never gain on you to windward. She'll sail her worst close-hauled. You may even outsail her. But if you do no more than keep the present distance, you are safe.'

'That's if the breeze holds. And who's to warrant me the breeze'll hold? It's an unnatural wind for this time o' year.' He swore again in his frenzy of indecision. 'If I was to go about, and run for Dominica again? It's none so far, and safest, after all.'

'But it's down wind, and down wind, with all her canvas spread, she'll overhaul you quickly for all her foulness.'

Bransome, however, was rendered obstinate by panic, and another hope had come to vitiate his reasoning. 'Towards Dominica we're likeliest to meet other shipping.' Without waiting for the Frenchman's answer, he stepped to the poop-rail and bawled an order to the quartermaster at the whipstaff to put down the helm.

And now it was de Bernis who departed from his calm. He rapped out an oath in his vexation at this folly, and began an argument which Bransome cut short with the reminder that it was he who commanded aboard the Centaur. He would listen to advice; but he would take no orders.

With a lurching plunge the Centaur luffed alee, then came even on her keel and raced south before the wind.

The seamen in the waist, who had fallen agape at this abrupt manœuvre, were ordered aloft again to unfurl, not only the topsails which they had just come down from furling, but also the topgallants. Even as they sprang to the ratlines, in obedience, the great black ship, now left astern on the larboard quarter, was seen to alter her course and swing in pursuit, thus dispelling any possible doubt that might have lingered on the score of her intentions.

At once it became clear aboard the Centaur that they were running before an enemy. Unaccountably, as it seemed, realization spread through the ship. The hands came tumbling from the forecastle in alarm, and stood about the hatch-coaming in the waist, staring and muttering.

Bransome, now on the quarter-deck, whither de Bernis had followed him, remained a long while with the telescope to his eye. When at last he lowered it, he displayed a face of consternation, from which most of the habitual ruddy colour had departed.

'You was right,' he confessed. 'She's overhauling us fast. We'll do better, though, when the topsails are spread. But even so we'll never make Dominica before that hell-hound is on our rudder. What's to do, Mossoo? Shall I go about again?'

In the obvious urgency of his need, humbled by the realization that if he had taken de Bernis' advice in the first instance, he would now be in better case, he appealed again to that experienced fighting seaman.

Monsieur de Bernis took time to answer. He was plunged in thought, a heavy frown between narrowed eyes. Bransome assumed him to be making mental calculations, and the assumption seemed confirmed when the Frenchman spoke.

'It is too late,' he said at last. 'Consider the time you would lose, and the way, whilst she with the weather-gauge of you, would need to veer but a point or two so as to steer athwart your hawse. No, Captain. You are committed to your present course. It means now that you must not only run, but fight.'

'God of Heaven! In what case am I to fight? To fight such a ship as that?'

'I've seen victory snatched against longer odds.'

Bransome took heart from the other's grim calm. 'And, anyhow,' said he, 'with his back to the wall, a man has no choice but to fight, no matter the odds. Have ye anything in mind, Mossoo?'

35

Thus plainly invited, Monsieur de Bernis became brisk and authoritative.

'What hands do you muster?'

'Twenty-six, all told, including quartermaster and bo'sun. Leach'll have three hundred or more.'

'Therefore, he must be allowed no chance to board us. Give me charge of your guns, and I'll show you how a main-deck should be fought, so long as you provide me with the chance to fight it.'

The Captain's gloom was further lightened. 'I'm in luck, at least, in having you aboard, Monsieur de Bernis.'

'I hope it may prove as lucky for me in the end,' was the sardonic answer.

He summoned Pierre, the half-caste, from the bulkhead below against which he was leaning, awaiting his master's orders.

'Tiens, mon fils.' Monsieur de Bernis stripped off the sky-blue coat he was wearing, the fine cambric shirt with its delicate ruffles, his hat, his periwig, his shoes and stockings, delivering all to Pierre with orders to bestow them in his cabin. Then, naked above the waist, displaying a lean, muscular brown torso, and with a scarf tied about his cropped head, he was ready to take the command of the gun-deck which Bransome so very gladly made over to him.

By this time the crew was fully aware of what was coming. The steadiness of the men, displayed when Sproat, the bo'sun, piped them to their quarters, was at least encouraging.

Eight of them, with Purvey, the master-gunner, were told off to compose a gun-crew. Captain Bransome addressed them briefly. He informed them that Monsieur de Bernis would take command on the gun-deck and that it was upon the gun-deck that this fight would be fought, so that the safety of all was in their hands.

Monsieur de Bernis, now sharply authoritative, ordered them at once below to clear the gun-tackles, to load and run out the guns. Before following, he had a last word with the Captain. Standing by the ornately carved rail of the quarter-deck, at the head of the companion, he spoke incisively.

'You've placed the responsibility on us. I will do my part. You may depend on that. But it rests with you to give me the opportunity of doing it. Here timorousness, caution, will not serve. The odds are heavily against us in this gamble. That we must accept. We stake all—your ship, our lives—upon a lucky shot or two between wind and water. Handle your ship so as to give me every chance of it you can. You will have to take great risks. But take them boldly. Audacity, then, Captain! All the audacity you can command.'

Bransome nodded. His face was set, his air resolute. 'Aye, aye,' he answered.

Monsieur de Bernis' bold dark eyes pondered him a moment, and approved him. A glance aloft, where every stitch of canvas now wooed the breeze, a glance astern, over the larboard quarter where the pursuing ship came ploughing after them, and de Bernis went down the companion and crossed the waist, to lower himself through an open scuttle to the deck below.

He dropped from the brilliant blaze of a cloudless day into a gloom that was shot at regular intervals by narrow wedges of sunlight from the larboard gun-ports.

Under the direction of Purvey, the guns were being run out and made fast.

Stooping almost double in that confined space, with the reek of spun yarn in his nostrils, de Bernis busied himself in taking stock of the material with which he was to endeavour to command the fortunes of the day.

# 5

## Board and Board

IN THE great cabin, Miss Priscilla and Major Sands broke their fast, happily ignorant of what was coming. They marvelled a little at the absence of the Captain, and they marvelled a little more at the absence of their fellow passenger. But rendered sharp-set by the sea air, and having waited a reasonable time to satisfy the demands of courtesy, they yielded to Sam's soft invitation to table, and with the Negro to wait upon them fell to with an appetite.

They saw the soft-footed Pierre enter and pass into his master's cabin, bearing a bundle. To the question Miss Priscilla addressed to him, he answered after his usual laconic fashion that Monsieur de Bernis was on deck and would breakfast there. He collected from Sam some food and wine, and went off, to bear it to his master on the gun-deck.

They thought it odd, but lacked curiosity to investigate.

After breakfast, Miss Priscilla went to sit on the cushioned stern-locker under the open ports. Monsieur de Bernis' guitar still lay there, where last night he had left it. She took it up, and ran inexpert fingers carelessly across the strings, producing a jangle of sound. She swung sideways upon the locker, and turned her gaze seaward.

'A ship!' she cried, in pleased excitement, and by the cry brought Major Sands to stand beside her and to stare with her at the great black ship driving forward in their wake.

The Major commented upon the beauty of the vessel with the sun aslant across her yards, lending a cloud effect to the billowing canvas under which she moved; and for some time they remained there, watching her,

38

little suspecting the doom with which her black flanks were pregnant.

Neither of them observed the altered course of the Centaur, obvious though it was rendered by the position of the sun. Nor at first did they give heed to the sounds of unusual bustle that beat upon the deck overhead, the patter of feet, the dragging of tackles, or again to the noisier movements in the wardroom immediately underneath them, where the two brass culverins that acted as stern-chasers were being run out under the orders of Monsieur de Bernis.

Down there in the sweltering gloom, where men moved bowed like apes for lack of head room, the Frenchman had been briskly at work.

The ten guns with which he was to challenge the Black Swan's forty, waited, their leaden aprons removed, their touch-holes primed, all ready to be touched off.

De Bernis had laid them himself, approximately, so as to fire high and sweep the shrouds of the pursuer. The broad target of her sails offered him an infinitely better chance of crippling her than he could hope to achieve by a shot aimed at her hull of which so little would be presented to him. If he could thus injure her sailing power, it would afterwards be theirs to elect whether to be content to escape, or whether to stay to tackle her with the advantage of unimpaired mobility.

From the wardroom ports astern, crouching beside one of the brass stern-chasers which had moved his scorn, Monsieur de Bernis watched the pirate racing after them and rapidly lessening the gap between. Thus an hour passed, counting from the moment when the Centaur had gone about. The Black Swan was overhauling its prey even more swiftly than Monsieur de Bernis had reckoned possible. Very soon now she was less than half a mile astern, and Monsieur de Bernis judged that they were within range.

He sent the wardroom gunner forward, to warn Purvey to stand ready, and waited in growing impatience for Bransome to put up his helm. But moments passed, and still the Centaur held to her course, as if Bransome had no thought but to continue running.

Then from below the pirate's beak-head came a white bulge of smoke, followed half a heart-beat later by the boom of a gun. A shower of spray was flung up by a round shot, taking the water fifty yards astern of the Centaur.

To de Bernis this was like a call to action, and so he judged that it must be to Bransome. Quitting his observation post, he sped forward to the gun-deck, where the matches glowed in the gloom, as the gunners blew upon them. And there he waited for the Black Swan to come into view of the larboard gunports.

In the cabin above, that single shot had disturbed the complacency of the watchers on the stern-locker. They stared blankly at each other in their uneasy surprise, the soldier vehemently desiring his vitals to be stabbed. Then Miss Priscilla sprang to her feet, and together they went on deck to seek an explanation.

They were allowed, however, to go no farther than the waist, where they were met by the grim faces of the mustered seamen. They needed no other confirmation of their fears that here all was not well. They received it, nevertheless, in the order to return at once below, roared at them by the Captain from the quarter-deck.

The Major's face empurpled. He spoke between remonstrance and indignation. 'Captain! Captain!' And then he added the question: 'What is happening here?'

'Hell is happening!' he was fiercely informed. 'Take the lady out of it. Get below decks, where she'll be under cover.'

The Major threw a chest, and advanced a step on legs that were stiff with dignity. 'I demand to know . . .' he began. And there the thunder of another gun interrupted him. This time the spray from the shot rattled against the timbers of their larboard quarter.

'Will you stay until a falling spar or worse strikes you across your foolish head? D'ye need to be told that we're in action? Get the lady under cover, man.'

Priscilla tugged at the Major's red sleeve. She was very white, and undoubtedly afraid. Yet all that she said to him was: 'Come, Bart. We embarrass them. Take me back.'

Despite simmering resentment of the tone the Captain had taken with him, he obeyed her without further argument. The suddenness of this troubling of their serenity bewildered him. Also, although Major Sands was brave enough ashore, he experienced here a daunting clutch at his heart from his sense of helplessness on an element that was foreign to him and in a form of warfare of which he knew nothing. Nor did the presence of Miss Priscilla help to encourage him. The sense of responsibility for her safety increased his discomfort. Before he had reconducted her, a seaman standing by had muttered to him that they were being chased by that hell's bastard Tom Leach.

Back in the great cabin, staring once more from her stern-ports at the oncoming enemy, the Major dissembled his dismay with the laudable aim of reassuring Miss Priscilla. He strove to quiet her alarm with assurances in which he, himself, had no faith.

And at the same time, on the quarter-deck, de Bernis, who in furious impatience had come up from below, was demanding to know what Bransome might be waiting for, and peremptorily ordering him to reef his topsails and bring the Centaur up to the wind so that her guns might come into action.

'You're surely mad,' the Captain answered him. 'She'll be upon us before we can get under way again.'

'That's because ye've delayed overlong already. Ye've increased the risk. That's all. But we must take it. We stake all now upon my chance to cripple her sailing power. Come, man! There's no more time to lose. Never mind reefing. Put up your helm, and leave the rest to me.'

Between an instinctive reluctance to a manœuvre that was a pure gambler's throw and resentment aroused by the Frenchman's hectoring tone, Captain Bransome was perversely indignant.

'Get off my quarter-deck!' he roared. 'Do you command this ship, sir, or do I?'

De Bernis clutched the Captain's arm and pointed astern. 'Look, man! Look!'

The pirate was lowering and raising her fore topsail.

It was the signal to heave to. Instantly de Bernis' quick mind had seen what advantage might be taken of it.

'It's your chance, man! Heaven-sent! You've but to pretend to comply. She'll be off her guard.' He flung an arm upwards to point to the Union flag aloft. 'Strike your colours, and heave to across her bows. Then leave it to me to put a whole broadside athwart her hawse.'

The Captain, however, shared none of the Frenchman's eager hopes. He seemed only alarmed by a proposal so redolent of buccaneering treachery.

'By God's death!' he answered. 'She'll sink us in reply.'

'If I shear away her shrouds, she'll be in no case to bring her guns to bear.'

'And if ye don't?'

'Things will be not a whit worse than they already are.'

Under the Frenchman's dark, compelling eyes the Captain's opposition visibly weakened. He saw that this was their last desperate chance. That there was no longer any choice. As if reading his mind, de Bernis urged him once again.

'Heave to, Captain. Give the word.'

'Aye, aye. It's all that's left to do, I suppose.'

'To it, then!' De Bernis left him, leapt down to the waist, and vanished once more through the scuttle to the deck below.

Even as he disappeared, Tom Leach, grown impatient, sent a charge of langrel from his fore-chasers through the shrouds of the Centaur, so as to quicken her master's compliance with his signals. In a tangle of cordage, a couple of spars came crashing to the deck.

Below, de Bernis heard the thuds and conjectured what had happened. He was not at all dismayed. The event, he concluded, must put an end to any lingering hesitation of Captain Bransome's. He ordered his gunners to stand ready. Himself he snatched from one of them a linstock, and, crouching by the middle one of the five larboard guns, waited for the Centaur to go about.

Whilst he waited thus, he heard again the boom of

cannon, and felt the vessel shudder under the heavy impact of a hit astern. Then he was flung violently against a bulkhead as the Centaur wildly yawed.

He recovered his balance, and for a moment his hopes ran high. She was heaving to. He perceived that she was veering. He saw the face of the waters shifting below. But he waited in vain for a sight of the pursuing ship. Only an empty sea confronted him. And at last he reached the exasperating conclusion that, in heaving to, Bransome had put his helm to starboard. Cursing him for a lubberly fool, de Bernis sped aft to the wardroom to verify his suspicion. Here he found a dismayed explanation of what was happening. That hit, of which he had felt the impact, had, by a monstrous chance, smashed the head of the Centaur's rudder, throwing her steering-tackles out of action. As if it did not suffice a malignant Fate that with damaged shrouds she should rapidly be losing way, now, with the helm out of control, she was left to yaw this way and that, as the wind took her.

Through the stern-ports the Black Swan was now visible to de Bernis, bearing down upon them at an alarming rate, and this, although she was already shortening sail, preparatory to boarding.

Bransome had waited too long to make the only throw that it was theirs to make. When at last he was willing to obey Monsieur de Bernis' persuasions, he suffered the common fate of him who will not when he may. A lucky shot from one of the pirate's powerful fore-chasers had rendered him helpless.

The wardroom gunner, a fair-haired, vigorous lad, turned a scared face upon Monsieur de Bernis when he came up to view the damage.

'We're beat, sir. They have us surely now.'

For a moment de Bernis stooped there, considering the tall ship that was scarcely five hundred yards astern. His lean, lined, swarthy face was set; his dark eyes steady and impassive. He went down on one knee beside one of the brass culverins, and laid it again. He laid it carefully, calm and unhurried, realizing that this slenderest of chances was the last one of which the Centaur still disposed. At this short range it was possible that the little brass cannon, which earlier had aroused his scorn, might be effective.

Rising, he took the smouldering match from the gunner's hand, blew upon it, touched off the gun, and stepped nimbly aside to avoid the recoil. But even as the gun went off, the Centaur yielding to a puff of wind, yawed again, swinging her stern a point or two alee. The Centaur fired her first and last shot into the void.

De Bernis looked at the young gunner, squatting there on his naked heels, and laughed in grim bitterness.

'C'est fini, mon gars. All is over. Next we shall have the grappling-hooks aboard, and then . . .' He shrugged, and tossed the useless match through the port.

White-faced, the lad swore through his strong young teeth. He raved a little about Tom Leach, desiring a red-hot hell for him.

'It looks as if it would be our turn first,' sighed de Bernis. Then he, too, broke out passionately for a moment. 'Ah! Sang de Dieu! What was needed here was a fighting seaman on the poop; not a lubberly merchant master. I should have stayed with him, and made him handle her as she should have been handled. Then any fool might have served these guns. But what use to talk now?'

He stood squarely in the port, in the space which the gun's recoil had left, watching the pirate's advance. She had further shortened sail, and she was creeping forward slowly now, but none the less surely, upon a prey no longer able to escape her. She held her fire, and waited to board, so as to do no further damage.

From where he stood, de Bernis could see the men on her bowsprit busy with the gaskets of her spritsail, and two others standing in the fore-chains holding the grapnels ready.

The gunner heard him muttering between his teeth. Then he turned, suddenly brisk.

'Up above with you, my lad, and bid the others on the gun-deck up with you. There's no more to be done down here.'

As for Monsieur de Bernis, himself, he took a short

cut. He crawled out through the square port, steadying himself precariously against one of the stanchions of the shallow gallery over the counter.

Then, facing inwards, his bare feet upon the sill, he drew himself upright, and raised his right arm, so as to clutch one of the posts, which was within easy reach. Then, with the strength and agility of an ape, he swung clear and hoisted himself until he could bring his left hand to clutch the gallery rail. He heaved again nimbly, and his right hand followed. Another heave, and his elbow was on a level with the rail. He threw a leg over it, and so disappeared from the view of the amazed young gunner below.

To Miss Priscilla and the Major came then the most terrifying of all their experiences of that dreadful morning, when they beheld this half-naked figure clambering through the stern-windows of the coach.

The Major, who had meanwhile armed himself for eventualities, laid a hand to his sword, and would have drawn it had not the Frenchman's speech made it known to them that it was indeed he, taking this shortest way to reach his cabin. His aspect was terrifying, with face and hands and naked torso befouled by sweat and powder. His voice came harsh with scorn.

'The fight is fought. The lubberly Bransome was well advised to think of turning farmer. He should have thought of it before. Better for him, and better for those who sail with him. The fool never gave me a chance to use the guns. In God's name, why do such men go to sea? It's as if I took holy orders. Leach is saving gunpowder because he wants the ship. That's plain. He's going to board.'

From what he had told them, they were left to surmise the part which the momentarily forgotten Frenchman had played in the action.

Miss Priscilla, assuming that her only resource now lay in the lap of Heaven, fell on her knees to pray. The Major looked on, helplessly, foolishly fierce.

Monsieur de Bernis, however, displayed in this desperate pass neither fear nor helplessness.

'Ah, but courage, mademoiselle. Compose yourself. I am here. It may be that you are in no danger.

45

It may be. I can do things sometimes. You shall see. Have faith in me. A little faith.'

He flung away on that, into his own cabin, calling for Pierre, who was there, awaiting him.

Priscilla rose from her knees to question the Major.

In his heart Major Sands could not suppose that the Frenchman was anything but vaingloriously boastful. A theatrical fellow who would attitudinize in the very face of death. But he made gallant shift to stifle that conviction, so as to comfort her distress.

'I do not know what he can do. Stab me, I don't. But he seems confident. A resourceful fellow, I should judge. Remember, too, that he has been a buccaneer, and knows their ways. Dog don't eat dog, they say.'

Thus, vaguely, he mumbled on, though in his heart there was no hope. From what they had heard as lately as last night of the ways of Tom Leach, he could only assume that death would be his portion, and only pray that it might be a swift one. Fearful as the prospect might be, yet a deeper agony clawed him on behalf of Priscilla Harradine. Beholding her, so sweet and lovely in her distress, he feared for her the worse fate of being allowed to live, the prey of such a beast as Leach. It even crossed his agonized mind to kill her where she stood, considering this, in the pass to which things were come, the highest and noblest proof he could give of his love and reverence. But the thought took no root in his will. Inert he remained standing by the locker on which she sat, conscious for once of his own utter futility, and offering her cheerlessly vague words of comfort.

Thus, until the sunlight was eclipsed for them by the bulk of the great black ship. She came, her bulwarks lined with men, gliding up astern on their larboard quarter, and so cast her chilling, sinister shadow athwart the stern-ports where Miss Priscilla sat. Across the short gap of water came a trumpet call from the pirate's deck. They heard, too, the roll of drums, and presently there was a volley of musketry.

It brought Miss Priscilla quivering to her feet, and urged the Major to set a protecting arm about her slimness.

And then from his cabin Monsieur de Bernis re-emerged at last, followed by his servant. He came now, not merely cleansed of his grime, but restored to his normal courtly habit. He had resumed his curled black periwig, his fine ruffled shirt, and his doublet of violet taffetas with its deep cuffs reversed in black and the buttonholes richly laced with silver. In addition, he was booted, in fine black Cordovan leather, and he had armed himself, not only with a long rapier, but with a pair of pistols, slung before him, after the fashion of the buccaneers, in the ends of a stole, which, like his baldrick, was of purple leather stiff with silver bullion.

They stared at him in wonder. That he should have been at such pains with his toilet at such a time was surprising enough. But the ease of his bearing was more surprising still.

He smiled upon their wide-eyed wonder. He explained himself. 'Captain Leach is a great man. The last of the great buccaneers. He is to be received with ceremony.'

He was moving forward towards them when the deck under their feet shuddered to a thudding, crashing impact, followed by rending of timbers, the ringing clank of grapnels, the snapping of spars, and the long, harsh rattle of volley upon volley of musketry.

Flung forward, Monsieur de Bernis clutched the table to steady himself. The Major dropped to his knees, whilst Miss Priscilla, hurtling across the cabin, found refuge in the Frenchman's arms.

'Save me!' she gasped. 'Save me!'

Holding her, the man's tight lips under the little black moustache softened into a smile. One of his long shapely hands stroked the golden head that lay against his breast, and it may be that the firm, calm touch of him soothed her more than his actual words.

'I hope to do so. It may well be possible.'

Deeply resentful of a situation which gave the Frenchman license for the intimacy of his attitude, the Major, gathering himself up, glared at him.

'Why, what can you do?' he growled ungraciously.

'We are going to see. Perhaps much. Perhaps little. But to do much, it is necessary that you obey me.' His manner became stern. 'Contradict nothing that I say,

47

whatever it may be, and whatever you may think. Remember that, if you please, or you may destroy us all.'

Overhead a thunder of feet went rolling across the deck, to inform them that the pirates were aboard the Centaur. A babel of shouts and screams, mingled with a din of pistol shots and musketry fire, and, under all, the deeper diapason of the inarticulate muttering of men in conflict made up the hideous, terrifying sound of battle joined. Something dark and bulky flashed downwards past the stern-ports. They realized that it was the body of a man flung overboard from the poop. Another, and yet another, followed.

Miss Priscilla, in a fresh access of fear, clung yet more closely to Monsieur de Bernis.

'It will not last,' he said, his voice quiet. 'Leach has three hundred men at least; the Centaur little more than a score.'

His straining ears caught an approaching sound, and he added on a firmer note: 'You will obey me? Implicitly? Give me your word. It is important.'

'Yes, yes. Whatever you may say.'

'And you, Major Sands?'

Gloomily the Major gave the demanded promise. He had scarcely uttered it when along the gangway from the waist came the padding of a score of naked feet and a raucous mutter of voices quickly growing louder and nearer.

Overhead the sounds, if they had not diminished in volume, had changed in character, at least to the attentive, expert ears of Monsieur de Bernis. There were still the stamping and the shouting. But they were mixed now with sounds of horrible, obscene laughter, and a firing of muskets which de Bernis knew to be no more than the wanton sporting, the triumphant joy-fire of the buccaneers.

The brief fight was over. The invaders had swept like a tidal wave across the decks of the Centaur cutting down all resistance.

The padding feet and muttering voices in the gangway, drowning now more distant sounds, announced to him the approach of those who came below to appraise the value of their capture, and to deal with any who might still be found alive under decks.

The cabin door was flung violently inwards upon its hinges, to crash against a bulkhead. Through the dark gap swarmed a little mob of half-naked men, most of them with gaudily swathed heads, their sunburned, bearded faces alight with evil exultation. They came with weapons in their hands and foulness on their lips.

Beholding the four tenants of the cabin—for Pierre stood in the background, simulating impassivity, despite a greyness overspreading his deep tan—the ruffians checked a moment. Then one of them, at sight of the girl, loosed a hideous view-holloa, and on that they were surging forward again, when Monsieur de Bernis, calm to the point of seeming contemptuous, put himself in their way.

His hands were on the silver-mounted butts of the pistols in his stole; but the fact that he did not trouble to draw them lent him an added authority.

'Hold! I'll burn the brains of the first man who advances farther. I am de Bernis. Fetch your Captain Leach to me.'

<br>

## 6

### The Partnership

WHETHER because they knew the name of this man who once had sailed with Morgan, a name which he announced in a tone to imply its high significance, or whether because his very manner, so cool and assured, had an intimidating effect upon them, those evil ruffians stood arrested, at gaze, their leader balancing a blood-stained machete in his powerful hand. Thus, whilst a man might have counted ten. Then, as they were beginning to mutter lewdly decked demands that this man who stood so boldly before them should explain himself, a fellow of middle height, whose body and movements held something of the lithe strength of the panther, came thrusting through them to the front. It was Tom Leach.

He was breeched in red, and his blood-smeared shirt hung open from the neck to waist, the sleeves rolled high to display the powerful muscles of his long hairy arms. Black curls clustered about a low, animal brow; his nose, a thin, cruel beak, was set close between a pair of quick-moving eyes that were almost black. Instead of the cutlass or machete more generally favoured on boarding occasions by such men, Leach was armed with a rapier, a weapon with which to his abiding pride he was accounted of a deadly skill.

'What in hell's here?' he cried, as he advanced.

But when he stood clear and slightly ahead of that press of scoundrels, he checked as they had done before the elegant, commanding figure, so straight and tall that was confronting him. In his coppery face the little eyes flashed as if in surprise, and then narrowed like a cat's. He caught his breath for an ejaculation.

'May I be sunk into everlasting hell if it isna Topgallant Charley!' And he added a foul oath in token of his profound amazement.

Monsieur de Bernis took a step forward. He removed a hand from a pistol-butt, and proffered it.

'Well met, my friend. You were always to be found where you were wanted. But never more opportune than now. You come to save me trouble. You arrive just as I am on my way to seek you. On my way to Guadeloupe, for a ship and men to sail to find you. And behold, Tom! You have the complacency to drop from the skies to our deck. C'est charmant!'

With eyes still narrowed, his attitude slightly crouching, as if his muscles were gathered for a spring, the ruffian disregarded the proffered hand.

'Will ye cozen me, de Bernis? Thee was always a sly rogue, thee was. But not sly enough for Tom Leach.'

Born on the banks of the Lune, which he had quitted so as to follow a calling on the seas, which he had originally intended should be honest, his speech retained the broad burr of the north country, just as his nature retained its dour mistrustfulness. 'I last heard

50

tell o' ye wi' Morgan. Morgan's right-hand man ye was when ye quit th' Brotherhood o' th' Coast, along o' that treacherous turncoat.'

Monsieur de Bernis displayed the mild amusement he might bestow upon absurdity. 'Of course, I was given to choose,' he said with irony. 'A fine choice: between that and execution dock. As long as I was in Morgan's hands, I had to dance to the tune he piped. But you knew nothing of de Bernis if you supposed his heart was in the jig. I took my first chance to slip away and join you. And behold me.'

'To join me? To join me, d'ye say? I never knew as ye loved me.'

'We always love those we need. And, faith, I need you. And I don't come empty-handed. You're the only leader left with men enough and spirit enough for the enterprise I'm set on. I bring you fortune, Tom. Fortune such as ye may have met in dreams, but never waking. Something better than poor merchantmen like this, with paltry cargoes of hides and logwood, over which the French traders at Guadeloupe or Sainte Croix will impudently swindle you.'

Leach advanced a step, holding his rapier, like a whip, in his two hands at the end of his lowered arms. 'What's th' enterprise?'

'A plate fleet, Tom. No less. To sail in a month from now.'

There was the faintest kindling of interest tempering the mistrust in those watchful little eyes. 'Sailing whence?'

The Frenchman laughed, and shook his head. 'Nay, now. We'll leave that till later.'

Leach understood. But his lips tightened. 'I'll need to know more o' this or ever I says aught to it.'

'Of course you shall know more. Enough to make you sharp-set.'

The pirate's view of Miss Priscilla, partly screened hitherto by the bulk of Major Sands, happened to be left clear at this moment by a movement of the Major's. His eyes quickened evilly.

'Who be these? Who be th' doxy?' He would have advanced, but de Bernis stood resolutely in his way.

51

'My wife and her brother. I was taking them to Guadeloupe, to await there my return.'

The foolish Major cleared his throat to repudiate a relationship which offended him. But Priscilla, intuitively guessing the mad intention, warned him against it by a violent clutch upon his arm.

'Your wife?' The pirate's manner was a trifle daunted. His glance turned sour. 'I never heard tell you was married.'

'It happened lately. In Jamaica.' Airily de Bernis dismissed the matter. 'It's not important, Tom. We have this other business to settle now that we are met, so oddly opportune.'

Tom Leach considered him. 'It'll need a deal to make me believe you're honest, de Bernis. And if I find ye're not . . .'

De Bernis interrupted him. 'Suspicion makes you stupid, Tom. It was always the flaw in your nature. What manner of fool must I be not to be honest with you when I'm in your hands?'

Still considering him, Leach stroked his thin nose. 'Maybe. Maybe. But, by God, Charley, if thee looks to get spry wi' me, thee'll end by wishing thee'ld ne'er been born. D'ye call to mind Jack Clavering? He was just such another dawcock as thee, Charles, and thought he could make a fool o' Tom Leach. Ye may ha' heard tell how I plucked his feathers, until the poor bastard screamed to be let die. Thee's clever, Charley. Morgan always reckoned thee was clever. Artful as Old Nick hisself. But I's artful, too. Thee'd best remember it.'

'Ye're wasting breath,' said de Bernis contemptuously.

'Maybe. An' I've ways o' wasting other men's, too.'

Nevertheless, his resolve was taken, as he now showed. Abruptly he turned upon the ruffians waiting like hounds in leash behind him.

'Away wi' y' all. All but you, Wogan. And tell Mike to go through th' cargo so as he'll report to me when I come up.'

They went out noisily. Leach watched them depart, then he advanced to the table, pulled out a chair and

52

sat down, laying his slim sword on the board before him. 'Now, Charley. We'll hear more o' this plate fleet o' yours.' Yet as he spoke it was not at de Bernis that he looked, but at Miss Priscilla, over by the stern-locker with the Major; and his glance was neither nice nor reassuring.

Behind him stood Wogan, the buccaneer with the machete, who had led the invasion of the cabin: a tall, powerful, flat-featured scoundrel, black-bearded, with greasy black curls fringing the red scarf about his head and the bluest of eyes under thick black brows. He wore a gaping red shirt and loose breeches of rawhide, in the belt of which he carried a brace of pistols.

Monsieur de Bernis, entirely at his ease, moving with the authority of a man in his own house, went to open the door of one of the starboard cabins.

'Come, Priscilla,' he said quietly. 'And you, too, Bart.'

Instantly, and in relief, she moved to obey him.

Tom Leach stared annoyance and grumbled. 'What's this? Who says they shouldn't stay here?'

'By your leave, Captain,' was all that de Bernis answered him, with a chill dignity that seemed to exclude all argument. He held the door for his supposed wife and brother-in-law; and he closed it after they had passed out.

'Eh, by God!' said Leach, with an unpleasant little laugh. 'Seems you give yourself airs, like. Act as if thee was master here. Give orders, eh?'

'Only where my wife is concerned,' said the Frenchman quietly. He pulled a chair to the table, and paused by it to address his waiting servant. 'The rum, Pierre.'

The buccaneer's malevolent, suspicious eyes followed the loose-limbed half-caste as he moved to the carved buffet set against the forward bulkhead.

'Be yon another member o' thee family?' His sneering tone seemed to carry a menace.

De Bernis did not appear to observe it. 'He is my servant.' He sat down so as to face the buccaneer across the table. His air as he talked now was entirely genial, the air of a man chatting with friends and associates.

'We're in luck, Tom. That's plain. Otherwise you and I wouldn't be sitting here now in the cabin of the Centaur. If she had been handled by a man with fighting experience, if I, now, had been handling her today, ye'ld never have come board and board with her.'

'Would I not? Clever, isn't he, Wogan? Ye reckons ye can fight a ship better than me, eh? Thee's o'ermodest, Charley.'

De Bernis shook his head. 'I should never have stayed to fight. I'ld have shown you a dwindling counter, my lad. I'ld have beaten up wind; and foul and barnacled as you are, I'ld easily have outsailed you if it came to tacking. Ye've been overlong at sea, Tom. But it was always your way to take no risks except those you shouldn't take.'

Captain Leach opened wide now his wicked little eyes in genuine admiration.

'Thee's got good eyesight, by God, to ha' seen I'm barnacled.'

Pierre set before them a tray bearing a jack of rum, a jar of tobacco, pipes, a tinder-box, and three drinking-cans. Then he fell back to the buffet again, and remained there in attendance.

They poured for themselves in turn, and Wogan came to sit at the table's end, and filled himself a pipe of fine leaf. De Bernis did the same. But Tom Leach waved the jar disdainfully away when it was proffered to him.

'What's this business o' a plate fleet? Come, now. Let's have it.'

'Faith, it's soon told. Three Spanish ships due to sail for Cadiz in a month's time: a galleon of thirty guns as the treasure-ship, with two twenty-gun frigates to escort her. The treasure is as big as any that's ever been ventured in one bottom. Gold and silver worth over five hundred thousand pieces of eight, and bushels of pearls from the Rio de la Hacha, besides other baubles.'

Wogan stood arrested in the act of applying to his pipe the flame he had kindled. Both he and Leach stared with fallen jaws and faces almost awestricken at the mention of a treasure so fabulous. If this were true, there would be enough in their shares as captain and mate to make them rich for life. At the end of a gaping pause, Leach vented incredulity in oaths. Then flatly he added:

'I's not believing it. Sink me into hell if I can.'

'Nor I, neither, on my soul,' said Wogan.

Monsieur de Bernis smiled his quiet scorn of them. 'I said it was something ye may have met in dreams, but never waking. But it's true, for all that. Perhaps you'll understand, now, why I should have been on my way to Guadeloupe to find a ship in which to seek you, so that you might bear a hand in this; and also why I should account it a bounty of Providence that we're met as we are, with the second ship we'll need for the venture ready found for us, here, under our feet.'

It was a question-begging argument, in which two equally unbelievable statements were urged each in support of the other. Yet to the buccaneers, dazzled by the vastness of the prize and the cupidity it aroused in them, each of the Frenchman's incredible allegations served to lessen the incredibility of the other.

Tom Leach pulled his chair closer to the table, and set his bare elbows on it. 'Let us know more o' this. How did ye come to learn of it?'

'By one of those chances—of which our meeting is another—sent by the gods to those they favour.' And he told his tale: a smooth, well-knit, convincing story.

A month ago he had been cruising off the Caymans with Morgan. Morgan was looking for Tom Leach at the time, and de Bernis was in command of one of two frigates that accompanied Sir Henry's flagship. At daybreak one morning, after a stormy night, some five or six leagues south of the Grand Cayman, they came upon a sloop so battered by the gale that her timbers had parted and she was foundering. They were no more than in time to take off her crew. The men they rescued proved to be Spaniards. One of them was a gentleman of some consequence, a Spanish officer named Ojeda, who was in a frenzy to get to Hispaniola, whither the sloop had been steering when the gale caught her and blew her out of her course. This Spaniard's urgency was rendered the more desperate because he had been seriously injured the night before. A falling yardarm had pinned him to the deck. He swore that his back was broken. Anyway, he was certainly in great bodily pain and in almost equal pain of soul, for fear that he might not live to reach San Domingo and the Spanish Admiral there, for whom he had a message of the first importance.

'You'll be supposing,' said de Bernis, 'as I supposed, that the message must be fully as important as he announced it, to be giving so much preoccupation to a man in his desperate case. You'll understand that my curiosity was aroused. I offered to bear the message for him if he would entrust it to me, or convey it in a letter if he would write it. He repelled the offer with a terrified vehemence which only went to increase my curiosity. But the suggestion that he should write a letter remained working in his mind. Later in the day, persuaded that his end was near, he sent for me again, and begged me to fetch the master of the foundered sloop and to supply him with writing materials. I did this readily enough. I was not to guess that the cunning and scholarly don had hit upon a device that should render the letter meaningless to rude unlettered seamen, most of whom could not even read their own mother-tongue. He dictated it in Latin. I suppose that he must have spelled out each word to the master of the sloop, who must, himself, have remained in ignorance of what he wrote. It was crafty, and it must fully have succeeded but for that curiosity of mine.

'That evening the don quietly died. He fell into his last sleep with a mind completely at ease, since he was persuaded that his death would leave no duty unfulfilled. A very gallant gentleman.

'That night the master of the Spanish shop met with an accident that was never explained. He fell overboard. At least, so it was supposed next morning, when he could not be found. As no one but myself knew anything about the vital letter, his loss, whilst regretted, created no great excitement. But the letter was not lost. Fearing that some mischance might overtake him, I had taken the precaution of removing it from the lining of one of his sea-boots, where, for greater safety, he had stowed it.'

He was interrupted by the approving, crowing laughter of the two buccaneers. The delicate humour in which he had veiled an obvious deed of murder was of a kind they could savour fully. He smiled his acknowledgements of their appreciative understanding, and pursued his tale.

'It was then that I discovered the trick that the dead don had played us. I am not by any means an unlettered man, and once my knowledge of Latin was considerable. But at sea a man forgets these things. Besides, as I now know, the Latin used by the don was very pure and difficult—what scholars call classical. I could make nothing of it beyond some Roman numerals, which at first I supposed to be dates, and an odd word here and there. But back in Port Royal a week later, I sought a French priest of my acquaintance, and from him I had a translation of the document.'

He paused there and looked into those dark faces which his tale had rendered quick with eager interest. 'That should satisfy you,' he said, 'as to how the knowledge reached me. Once I possessed it, I saw that the time had come to quit Morgan and the service of the English Crown. But I should need assistance for what was to do, and at once I thought of you, and of how together we might reap this rich harvest. To old Morgan my tale was that I was hungering for France and home after all these years of wandering. And Morgan, suspecting nothing, let me go. I was sure that at Guadeloupe I should still find a few French adventurers willing to join me, and a ship that would serve to support you when I found you. And I also thought it likely that I should get a hint of your whereabouts. I knew, as Morgan knew, that you had been trading your prizes there of late.'

He ceased, and refreshed himself with a sip of rum.

Leach stirred on his seat, and took his elbows from the table. 'Aye, aye,' he growled, more in impatience than agreement. 'And th' information?'

'You have that already. A plate fleet, with the treasure I told you, sails for Cadiz in a month's time, when the trade winds will serve best. The letter giving the details, so as to impress the Spanish Admiral at San

Domingo with the need implicitly to obey the request, desired him to hold two ships of war in readiness, further to strengthen the escort for the ocean crossing to Spain. That is all.'

'All, man? All, d'ye say? But where'll this plate fleet sail from?'

Monsieur de Bernis, in the act of taking up the tinder-box, smiled as he answered: 'From somewhere between Campeche and Trinidad.'

The pirate's brow grew dark. 'Why not say between the North Pole and the South?' His tone was angry. 'D'ye mean ye don't know? If so be, what good's rest o' thee knowledge?'

Monsieur de Bernis' smile became more bland. 'To be sure I know. But that is my secret. That is what I bring to the association.'

He struck flint and steel, kindled a match and applied it to his pipe, ignoring the scowls of the buccaneers, who were stricken speechless. 'One thing more,' he added presently. 'From what I know of them, the three Spanish ships will scarcely carry more than a total of two hundred and fifty men. With two such ships as we now possess and the following you have, we should be more than a match for them.'

' 'Tisn't that as bothers me. What I want to know, and at once, is where this fleet is to be looked for: north, south, east, or west.'

The Frenchman shook his head. 'Ye don't need to know that, because I am here to lead you to the spot, as I will so soon as the articles are signed between us.'

'Thee's sure we'll be signing articles.'

'If I were not, I must be sure that you're a fool, Tom. D'ye dream ye'll ever have the chance again of such a fortune?'

'And d'ye dream I'll go hoodman-blind into a venture?'

'There's no hoodman-blind in this. You know all that's necessary. If you refuse, if you haven't the stomach for it, put me ashore at Guadeloupe. I don't doubt I'll . . .'

'Look'ee, Bernis, my stomach's high enough, as thee well knows. And ye should know, too, that I've ways to make men talk. Ye'll not be the first as I've woolded; not by a many. Or thee may have a match between toes if thee prefers it.'

De Bernis looked down his nose at him, and spoke with languid disdain.

'Why, you poor kestrel, if I were not a patient man, I'ld pistol you for that.'

'What d'ye say?' The pirate put a hand to the sword that lay on the table before him.

De Bernis paid no heed to the threatening movement. 'To suppose that I am of the stuff that is to be woolded into talking! If you want to lose your every chance of ever seeing a real of that treasure, talk to me again of woolding. I may be in need of you, but if the plate fleet tempts you at all, your need of me is far more urgent, and, perhaps, not only to lead you to it. I've told you I was on my way to Guadeloupe to find another ship for you. But since you've seized the Centaur, we have all we now require. That is, all but the man to command her. I am that man. You should know that I can fight a ship with anyone. So there it is. Will you take this chance of a fortune on which to quit? Or will you wait until the Jamaica squadron hunts you from the seas, or until Morgan sinks you, as he surely will if you wait long enough?' He paused, to add:

'Now, Captain, shall we talk of terms, like sensible men?'

Wogan at least was conquered. He moistened his lips with his tongue, and intervened. 'On me soul, Cap'n, Charley's none so unreasonable when all's said. Isn't he doing just what you'ld be after doing in his place?'

De Bernis sat back and pulled at his pipe, strengthened in the perception that the cupidity he had awakened would make the mate of the Black Swan an ally who would curb in his captain excesses which might result in the loss of this fabulous chance. Already the Irishman's expostulation was not without its effect upon Leach.

'What terms d'ye propose?' he asked in a surly voice.

'For myself a fifth share of the prize when we have it.'

'A fifth share!' Leach got to his feet in his indignation. He loosened a bombardment of blasphemy at the Frenchman, then swung to Wogan. 'Is this your reasonable man, Ned?'

'The treasure,' de Bernis blandly reminded him, 'is worth perhaps a million pieces of eight. And it's not the sort of mangy cargo ye have to trade in Guadeloupe for a tenth of its worth.'

They fell to wrangling after that like a couple of hucksters, and they might have come to quarrelling but that Wogan, with his mind on the main issue, was intent upon keeping the peace at all costs. At long last, it was Leach who yielded, and this largely in consequence of Wogan's pacificatory persuasions.

Pen, ink, and paper were fetched, and Pierre was sent on deck, to summon any three men as representatives of the crew, to come and settle with the leaders, and to sign on the men's behalf, the terms of the articles, to be drawn in accordance with buccaneering custom.

Leach and his fellows all departed together when it was done, leaving de Bernis alone in the cabin to stay or follow as he pleased.

The buccaneer captain went out in a villainous mood, with the sense of having been worsted in the deal, and recklessly he vented his humour upon Wogan whom he largely blamed.

'Och, now, Captain, darling,' the mate mollified him, 'would ye be growing hot about nothin' at all. If he'ld asked for a half share, I'ld have promised it, so I would. For what's a promise, now?'

Leach checked in the ship's waist, which was now a shambles slippery with blood. For the horrors spread there about the main hatch, he had no thought or care. He had long since grown callous to the sight of slaughtered men. His mind was entirely on what Wogan had just said.

He looked up questioningly into the tall Irishman's face. Wogan looked down at him and grinned. 'When we've gutted the plate fleet and the treasure's under hatches, sure it's another talk we'll be having with Master Charley. Maybe he'll be more reasonable then. And what odds if he's not? There's the doxy, too,

Captain. A trim little craft, so she is. I saw ye'd an eye for her, small blame to ye.'

The Captain's close-set little eyes flashed evilly.

'The French,' said Wogan, 'have a proverb that all things come to him who knows how to wait. It's knowing how to wait is the art of it, Captain.'

'Ah!' said Captain Leach. 'I think I'll know how to wait. Seems to me as if we'd captured more nor a cargo o' hides today.'

## 7

## *Topgallant*

MONSIEUR DE BERNIS removed the pistol-bearing stole from about his neck, lifted over his head the baldrick, to the carriages of which his long rapier was attached, and delivered one and the other to Pierre, with orders to bestow them in his cabin. They had been assumed chiefly for decorative purposes, and they had served their turn.

Next he went to open the door of the cabin into which he had ushered his fellow voyagers, and invited them to come forth again.

They came, Miss Priscilla pale and shaken, yet making a spirited attempt to conceal her feelings, the Major, also pallid, but truculent, and with no notion of dissembling.

'Perhaps you'll tell us, sir, precisely what you intend by us,' he demanded aggressively.

They might have observed had they looked more closely that de Bernis, himself, wore the strained, jaded air of a man who has passed through an ordeal. But not on that account did his patience desert him. He ignored the Major, however, and addressed himself entirely to the lady, who had come to lean against the table.

'Be assured, at least, that I intend the best that I can do.'

But Major Sands did not mean to be ignored. 'Why should you?' he demanded. 'Being what you are, why should you?'

De Bernis smiled wearily. 'I see that you've been eavesdropping. I can but assure you, and you, mademoiselle, that in spite of what I am, you shall be as safe as I can contrive to make you.'

Miss Priscilla looked at him with troubled eyes. 'Was it true, what you told that pirate? Are you, indeed, associating yourself with those . . . those men?'

Monsieur de Bernis took time to answer her. 'The question implies a doubt. You find it incredible. From you that is a compliment. I thank you for it. But I may not encourage it.'

'Then your service to Captain Bransome, your taking command on the gun-deck, was a pretence?'

'A reasonable inference.' He shrugged. 'It is useless to argue against facts. Remembering that, you will perhaps remember that it is also a fact that, for the time being at least, I have made you safe from Captain Leach and his crew. If the word of a buccaneer counts for anything with you, believe that it will be my aim to send you safely home to England. Unfortunately, this is not possible at once. Delays are unavoidable now. And there may be anxieties and discomforts. But I hope—and, indeed, I am confident—nothing worse. Meanwhile, I will beg you to keep the cabin, where I shall contrive that you are private.'

Upon that he left them to go on deck.

In the gloom of the gangway he only just saved himself from tripping over a body. It proved to be that of Sam the steward, who had been caught there and cut down by the buccaneers when they had been on their way to invade the cabin. Monsieur de Bernis verified that the Negro was dead, and passed on.

He came out into the horrible shambles of the waist, still strewn with the bodies of the fallen men who had composed the crew of the Centaur and of three or four buccaneers whom they had cut down before being, themselves, overwhelmed.

Captain Bransome lay, with a cloven skull, where he

had fallen at the foot of the companion, so that to go up to the quarter-deck de Bernis had to step over the body of that good-natured burly fellow, who last night had been rejoicing in the thought that this was his last voyage. His last voyage it had proved, indeed, and it had ended sooner far than he had been expecting.

If de Bernis thought of this and bestowed an inward sigh on that honest life, so ruthlessly and wantonly extinguished in the very moment of reaching for the reward of its industry and courage, his countenance remained nevertheless set and impassive, as he went up the companion, a brave, jaunty figure in his violet and silver.

From a knot of men gathered about the main hatch, from which the coaming had been removed, came a hailing cheer for him in a sudden cry of:

'Topgallant! Topgallant!'

It informed him that the news of his presence and identity and of the enterprise to which he was to lead them had already spread through the ranks of Tom Leach's followers.

The cry was taken up by others on the forecastle. It drowned the sounds of merriment that were emerging from the galley, to tell of ruffians finding entertainment there.

De Bernis paused, midway in his ascent of the companion, and half-turned to wave a hand in acknowledgement to his acclaimers. Then he went on, and stepped upon the quarter-deck, to meet the lowering glance of Leach. The Captain engaged there with Wogan and a score of hands, considering the tangle overhead which had resulted from the boarding, and dictating measures for disengaging the two vessels, which now, with yards almost bare, were drifting slowly before the breeze. Aboard both ships hands were already aloft, clearing the yards of the Black Swan's foremast from those of the Centaur's mizzen. In boarding, the buccaneers had grappled their fore-chains to the after-chains of the Centaur, so as to avoid coming alongside her gun-ports, lest, as a last act of despairing rage, the merchantman should have fired a broadside when in touch, even at the risk of herself

63

being sunk. A gangway still connected the forecastle of the Black Swan with the poop of the Centaur.

It was in the articles that Monsieur de Bernis had signed with Captain Leach that the Frenchman should take command of the captured vessel with a prize crew from the Black Swan. De Bernis had insisted upon this, claiming it as due to a leader of his distinction among buccaneers. Grudgingly Captain Leach had yielded the point. But now that de Bernis came on deck to exercise his command, he was to learn that the other had found a way to curtail it.

'Wogan stays aboard wi' you,' he was curtly informed. 'Ye'll need a lieutenant. And ye'll have Halliwell for your sailing-master.'

De Bernis was under no delusion as to his real intention. These men were placed here by the pirate's suspicious nature to keep him honest. He displayed, however, no sign of resentment.

'That suits me very well, provided it is understood they take their orders from me.' And he proceeded immediately to the assertion of his authority. 'We'll begin at once by getting the carpenters to work on the rudder-head, and swabbers to clean up the mess you've made on these decks. I like a tidy ship.'

Leach eyed him malevolently, with the suspicion of a sneer, but offered him no hindrance. Within ten minutes a score of hands were at the work. The grim evidences of the fight were heaved overboard, and with pails and swabs, a dozen bare-legged fellows were sluicing and swabbing the waist, the quarter-deck, and the poop, whilst from below came the sounds of the carpenters' hammers to announce the progress of repairs upon the rudder-head, so that the steering-tackles might be restored.

With the same brisk authority de Bernis took in hand the disentangling of the fouled rigging, himself ordering the raising and lowering of yards and spars so as to clear them, displaying in all that he did his practical seamanship, and ignoring Halliwell, the sailing-master, whom Leach had summoned.

An hour later, when the two ships were ready to part company, and none but the crew of a hundred men appointed to the Centaur remained aboard her,

Leach himself was disposed to return to his own vessel.

On the point of doing so, he must, of course, require at last of de Bernis to be informed of their destination.

'We steer a course due south-west, for the islands at the mouth of the Gulf of Maracaybo,' he was answered. 'If we should become separated, our rendezvous is off Cape de la Vela.'

'Is that our destination? Do we wait there for the plate fleet?' Keenness gleamed in the little dark eyes of the buccaneer as they watched de Bernis' countenance.

'Oh, no,' he was answered. 'That is merely the first stage of our voyage.'

'And from there?' Leach pressed him.

'That you shall learn when we get there.'

Leach's annoyance displayed itself. 'Look'ee, Bernis' . . . he was beginning with some vehemence. Then he checked, shrugged, turned on his heel, and so departed to his own ship, there to wait until the restoration of the Centaur's steering-tackles and repairs to her yards should enable them to proceed.

Meanwhile, the Black Swan was warped away by sweeps from the other vessel, and stood by, hove to.

Miss Priscilla and Major Sands were first made aware of this manœuvre by the sudden growth of daylight in the cabin following upon the withdrawal of the great screen formed by the hull of the Black Swan on their larboard quarter. It led to the breaking of the silence which had endured between them for some time. The Major, filled by what he conceived a just resentment of Miss Priscilla's obstinate reluctance fully to accept his definite conclusions concerning Monsieur de Bernis, had sat moodily sulking for the last half-hour.

Miss Priscilla, listless on the stern-locker, leaning sideways against a bulkhead, now called his attention to the other vessel's withdrawal.

He rose from his seat at the table, where he had been fortifying himself out of the rum left there by the buccaneers, and crossed in silence to her side.

'Heaven knows what it means for us,' she said.

His answer was first a dismal sigh, and then, since

65

what fills a man's mind excessively must be flowing over, he began again upon a theme which had already led them as near the edge of disagreement as was possible for two persons so closely allied by a common peril.

'It is incredible that you should for a moment have believed in this man, Priscilla. Incredible, stab me! Let it serve you as a warning against your own inexperience. Another time perhaps you will trust to my riper judgment.'

'There may not be another time,' she reminded him.

'Indeed, I fear that there may not be.'

'If there is, it will be thanks to Monsieur de Bernis.'

This was to reopen the discussion at its bitterest point. It looked as if it would lead again to sharp disagreement.

'To Monsieur de Bernis? To him! Thanks to him?' The Major turned away in his annoyance. He strode across the cabin and back again. He and Miss Priscilla were alone there, Pierre having withdrawn to the little pantry that had been the unfortunate Samuel's stronghold at the forward end of the cabin on the starboard side.

'You can still put trust in him? In this pirate rogue?'

'I can put trust in no one else. If he fails us . . .' She made a little gesture of helplessness to complete her meaning.

Major Sands would have given years of his life to have been able to reproach her with her lack of trust in himself. Since the circumstances denied him this consolation, he grew increasingly bitter.

'You can still say this after all that we have overheard? Knowing the devilry now afoot? Knowing that this rascal is making common cause with these other scoundrels? You can say this when he had the insolence to pass you off as his wife?'

'In what case should we be if he had not? That was something done to save me.'

'You are quite sure of that? 'Slife! Then ye're singularly trusting.'

66

Her pallor deepened before the implication of his sneer. But she flashed defiance of his mistrust. During the silence that had prevailed between them, she had been thinking deeply, reviewing the whole situation; and she had perceived at least one little feature that told strongly in de Bernis' favour. She mentioned it now.

'If his motives were as base as you imply, why did he trouble to spare you? Why did he pass you off as his brother-in-law?'

To the Major it was a startling question, to which at the moment he could discover no plausible answer. In that, however, he saw no reason why he should depart from his settled conviction, and admit an explanation favourable to de Bernis. 'Can I guess his base intentions?'

'Yet you are guessing them. Guessing them to be base. Why?' She smiled a little wanly. 'If he had let them cut your throat, you could not now be speaking evil of him.'

'Gadslife, madam!' He grew almost apoplectic. 'For obstinacy commend me to a woman. I hope the sequel may justify this stubborn, unreasonable belief in a blackguard. I hope it may. But, to be frank, I cannot hold the hope with confidence. Stab me if I can!'

'Now that is brave in you, Major Sands. Brave—is it not?—to have so little regard for the anxieties of a woman in my case.'

He was stung to penitence. 'Oh, forgive me, Priscilla. It is just my anxiety for you that goads me on. Blunderingly, perhaps. I would give my life for you, my dear . . .'

It was Monsieur de Bernis that interrupted him. 'Let us hope, my dear Major, that so much may not be required of you.'

Startled, Major Sands swung round, to see the Frenchman standing within the cabin doorway. He entered, and closed the door. He advanced towards them, his manner quietly assured. 'All is now arranged,' he informed them, in his pleasant, level voice. 'I am in command of this ship, and you will regard yourselves as my guests.'

'And Captain Bransome, sir?' she asked him, her

voice a little out of control, her eyes watching him the while.

His dark, saturnine face, however, was entirely unrevealing. It was as expressionless as his tone when he answered her after a perceptible pause.

'Captain Bransome did his duty by his ship. Had he behaved as bravely earlier, he might now be alive.'

'Dead! He is dead?' The horror of it drove her white to the very lips. It seemed so impossible that a man so vigorous and hearty, so full of life, going home in such fond expectancy of reunion with his wife and the family which scarcely knew him, should have been cut off so abruptly and cruelly.

De Bernis slightly inclined his head. 'He said last night that this was his last voyage. Oddly prophetic; yet falsely so. He is at peace. He looked to the future, he said, to make amends to him for the past. He is spared the discovery that the future can never do that.'

'My God!' cried the Major, 'this is horrible! And you can talk of it so? You might have saved that poor fellow . . .'

'Ah, that, no,' de Bernis interrupted. 'When I went on deck, it was already too late. Indeed, the fight was ended before Leach came down here.'

'And the others? The crew?'

In the same colourless voice de Bernis replied: 'It is not the practice of Captain Leach to take prisoners.'

Miss Priscilla uttered a groan, and sank her face into her hands. She was assailed by a feeling of nausea, of faintness. As from a distance she heard that level, pleasantly modulated voice speaking in its stiff, faultless English faintly softened by a Gallic accent.

'Let my sense of hospitality reassure you both. Here you are in no danger, beyond that of a little delay and inconvenience. Now that all is arranged, I can repeat the assurance with confidence.'

Hotly contemptuous came the answer from Major Sands: 'What is it worth, sir, this assurance from you who usurp the place of that murdered man?'

Monsieur de Bernis preserved an unruffled urbanity. 'Whatever it may be worth, it is all that I have to offer. You would be wise to rest content with it.'

He turned aside, to summon Pierre and give him

68

orders to lay dinner for five persons. He explained this, addressing himself to Miss Priscilla. 'My lieutenant and my sailing-master will take their meals with us. I would have spared you this but that it would scarcely be prudent. Beyond that, however, you need fear no invasion of your privacy, and, except during meals, this cabin will be exclusively your own.'

Her clear blue eyes considered him steadily and searchingly, from out of her pallid face. But his aloof and rather chilling impassivity baffled scrutiny. She inclined her head.

'We are in your power, sir. It only remains for us to thank you for any consideration you may show us.'

A little frown puckered his dark brow. 'In my power? Oh, that! Say, rather, under my protection.'

'Is there a difference?'

'When we are all in the power of circumstances, Priscilla.'

She imagined the beginnings of a disclosure in this, and would have pursued it, but the Major must at that moment come blundering in, indignantly.

'You make very free with Miss Harradine's name, sir.'

'Of necessity. Like the rest. Is she not my wife? And are you not my brother-in-law, my dear Bartholomew?'

The Major quivered, and glared at him. Perceiving the one and the other, Monsieur de Bernis stiffened as if he had been struck. He spoke now with an incisive edge to his tone. 'You embarrass me damnably. Another in my place might end it quickly. Pray remember that, Bartholomew. And be good enough, both of you, to address me as Charles, unless you want to endanger your necks with my own. The intimacy may be distasteful to you, Bartholomew. But less distasteful, I hope, than to find yourself swinging from a yardarm. That is not at all amusing.'

On that he went out again, leaving the Major in a fever of indignation.

'By God! That cut-throat had the audacity to threaten me, I think.' From that reckless beginning he would have continued recklessly to pour out his wrath had Priscilla not collected wit and strength to check him,

69

her eyes on the lean, soft-footed half-caste, who was busy with the table.

'After all, Bart,' she reminded him, 'Monsieur de Bernis did not invite Captain Leach to come aboard the Centaur.'

'But he welcomed him! He associates himself with this bloodthirsty scoundrel! He has confessed that it was his intention to join that murderer, and that the ruffian's assault of us was timely. What better is he?'

'I wonder,' said Miss Priscilla.

Amazement brimmed his pale eyes. 'You wonder? After what you've just heard? When you know him to be in command here in the place of that poor murdered Bransome?'

'Oh, but that proves nothing—as against all the rest.'

'Nothing? It proves that he's a damned pirate, a cut-throat villain . . .'

She was on her feet to check him; for Pierre, who had momentarily passed into the pantry, was coming forth again. 'And you prove that you're a fool,' was her interruption. 'And unless you can succeed in concealing it, you'll come by a fool's end before long, and you may drag others with you.'

He could only gasp and stare, shocked, scandalized beyond all expression that a child, so meek and gentle as he had always supposed Priscilla, should bring herself to address him—a man of his parts, an officer of his consequence—in such outrageous terms. It passed all understanding. He could but suppose that the events of that terrible morning must have unbalanced her reason. When he had recovered breath, he began remonstrances, which she cut short with the same incredible new-found manner. In a moment of Pierre's absence, she stepped close up to him, caught his arm in a tight grip, and muttered swiftly: 'Will you rant so before that man of his? Have you no sense of discretion?'

If she thus made him aware that she was justified of her apprehensions, nothing in his view could justify the terms she chose in which to convey her warning to him. He was profoundly annoyed, his sense of fitness outraged. He said so, pompously. And having said so lapsed again into a sullen silence in which she judged it best to leave him, since in that mood at least he could do no damage.

Thus until Monsieur de Bernis returned, accompanied now by the tall Irishman Wogan, and an extremely corpulent but nevertheless powerful-looking man, of middle height with enormous shoulders, an enormous dewlap, and features that were by contrast ridiculously small. He presented him as Halliwell, the sailing-master.

They got to table, and Pierre, ever swift and silent in his movements, a very shadow of a man, came forth to wait upon them.

De Bernis took the chair in which the ill-starred Bransome had sat, so care-free and good-humoured, as lately as last night. He placed Miss Priscilla and the Major on his right, with their backs to the light, Wogan on his immediate left, and the elephantine sailing-master beyond him.

It was a gloomy meal. At first the pirates were disposed to be hilarious. But something compelling in de Bernis' cold manner and the silent aloofness of the supposed Madame de Bernis and her supposed brother gradually damped their humour. Wogan's dark, flat-featured face became mask-like in sullen resentment. The sailing-master, however, a man of voracious appetite, considering nothing at table of an importance to compare with the victuals, discovered here all the entertainment he could desire in the fresh meat and vegetables in which the Centaur was well-found. Noisy and repulsive in his feeding, he paid little heed to anything else.

The Major curbed himself with difficulty from reproving the fellow's abominable table-manners. As for Miss Priscilla, overcome by the horrors of the day upon which these table companions placed a culminating horror, secretly racked by fears, and entirely miserable, yet bravely dissembling it, she made a pretence of eating that could have deceived no one who had been concerned to observe it.

## 8

# In Command

MONSIEUR DE BERNIS paced the high poop of the Centaur in the starlit, moonless, tropical night. His tall figure could be seen by those in the waist below, sharply silhouetted in black against the golden glow of the great poop-lamp as in his pacings he crossed and recrossed the ambit of its light.

The wind had dropped at sunset to the merest breeze, but without changing its quarter, and with her sails spread to receive it, the Centaur, her steering-tackles restored and spars repaired, led the way on that south-westerly course which Monsieur de Bernis had laid. An eighth of a mile or so astern three tall poop-lamps showed where Tom Leach followed in the Centaur's phosphorescent wake.

As a result of the softened wind, the night was hot, and most of the buccaneers who now made up her crew were above-decks. They swarmed in the waist and under the booms amidships on which the boats were stowed. There slush-lamps glowed like gigantic fireflies. About these they were gathered in groups, at seven-and-eleven, and intermittently the rattle of dice in the pannikins that did duty as dice-boxes would merge into the noise of their chatter and laughter with an occasional explosive oath or the loud calling of a main. On the forecastle someone scraped a fiddle, providing a discordant accompaniment to a bawdy song which, although by no means new to the audience, had not yet lost its power of provoking coarse hilarity.

Monsieur de Bernis heard little and heeded less of all this. His mind was preoccupied, turning inwards, away from his senses, to resolve a problem with which he was confronted.

Towards midnight he came down the companion,

and took his way towards the gangway leading to the cabin. Near the entrance to this, Wogan and Halliwell leaned against a bulkhead at the break of the poop in muttered talk. They fell silent at his approach, and gave him good-night as he passed them.

The entrance to the gangway was a black cavern. The slush-lamp swinging there to light it had been extinguished, and as de Bernis stepped into the gloom he was aware—for his perceptions were now restored to their normal keenness—that something moved there very softly. He checked, to be instantly reassured by a voice, breathing a word with ghostly softness.

'Monsieur!'

He went on, following the invisible and inaudible Pierre who had stood sentinel, and who, he surmised, would have been responsible for the fact that the lamp there was extinguished.

In the light of the cabin, after the door had been closed, the young half-caste's keen-eyed face with its prominent cheek-bones looked grave. He spoke swiftly, in French, his voice soft and liquid. He had been on his way to the deck to take the air, when, as he reached the entrance of the gangway, he had heard the voices of Halliwell and Wogan; and Wogan had mentioned the name of de Bernis in a tone that in itself had been informing to Pierre. He had gone quietly back, and had extinguished the light, so that he should not be seen. Then he had crept up to the entrance, and had stood there listening to the conversation of those two. It had disclosed to him the treachery in the minds of those whom Monsieur de Bernis had now joined, and Captain Leach was in it. The intention was to let him guide them to the plate fleet, and then pay him his share of the plunder in cold steel. Wogan had disclosed this to allay Halliwell's grumbling at the fifth share which under the articles de Bernis claimed for himself. Halliwell had accounted the claim preposterous and was blaming Leach for having agreed to such terms. Wogan had laughed at him for being such a fool as to believe that the terms would be kept. De Bernis should take what they chose to give him. If that didn't satisfy him—and there was no cause to be over-generous—

73

they'ld slit his throat for him, and so make an end of an impudent swaggering dawcock.

Halliwell, however, was not so easily to be reassured. De Bernis had always been known for a tricky, slippery devil, who had a way of defeating brute force by artifice. He called to mind more than one trick that de Bernis had played on the Spaniards at Panama, and but for which Morgan might never have had the town. He called to mind that it was de Bernis' wit had found a way to deal with the herd of wild bulls which the Spaniards had goaded into charging the buccaneers on the savannah. Halliwell had been there. He talked of what he had seen; and he knew the opinion in which de Bernis was held. It was not merely for his pimpish foppishness that they called him the Topgallant. In a tight place de Bernis knew how to supply just the little more that made all the difference to their sailing powers. Did Wogan and Leach suppose that de Bernis would not be fully aware of the possibility of just what they proposed?

'Sure now he may be aware of it. But it's the risk he has to take. How could he be helping himself?'

'I don't know,' said Halliwell. 'If I did, I should be as spry as de Bernis himself. Ye'll not persuade me he don't know what he's doing, and just what we might do.'

'Why shouldn't he be trusting us to keep faith?' Wogan had countered confidently. 'He's a buccaneer of the old sort. They respected articles. And we'll do nothing to alarm him. Until we have the plate fleet gutted, we'll just be humouring him and suffering all his impudence. But if there's too much of it, sure we'll be keeping the score, so we will. And it's the fine reckoning we'll be presenting at the end.'

And then Monsieur de Bernis had come down the companion, and the talk had ceased.

The Frenchman heard his servant out. He stood by the table, chin in hand, his face thoughtful, but neither surprised nor alarmed.

'Bien, mon fils,' he said, when Pierre had ended. And he added, after a moment: 'It is just what I supposed would happen.'

His calm seemed to fill his servant with alarm. 'But the danger, monsieur?'

'Ah, yes. The danger.' Monsieur de Bernis smiled upon the other's gravity. 'It is there. At the end of the voyage. Until then, we have something in hand. Until the plate fleet is gutted, as they say, they will humour me and suffer all the impudence I may show them. I may show them a good deal of it.' He laid a hand on the slim lad's shoulder. 'Thanks, Pierre, for your diligence. But no more of it. You take risks; and it is not necessary. Preserve yourself against my real need of you. And now, to bed with you. It has been a heavy day for us all.'

In the interests of his fellow voyagers, or, perhaps, purely from a chivalrous interest in Miss Priscilla, Monsieur de Bernis displayed next morning some of the impudence which Wogan and Halliwell condemned in him. Coming early on deck, and finding the two together there, he addressed to them as a command what might better have been preferred as a request.

'Madame de Bernis is in delicate health. Sometimes she sleeps late. I desire that the cabin be left to her in the morning, so that she may not be disturbed. You understand?'

Wogan's face darkened as he looked at the Frenchman standing before him so straight and aloof and with such airs of master. 'Sure now, I don't understand at all,' said he. 'What of breakfast? We must eat, I suppose, by your gracious leave.'

'You'll break your fast in the wardroom, or where else you choose. But not in the cabin.'

He did not wait for an answer, but passed on to make a round of inspection of the ship.

When he was out of earshot, Wogan breathed gustily in his indignation. 'Airs and graces, by God! It's not fine enough we are, you and me, Ned, for madam. The delicate piece! Well, well! Maybe there'll be another opinion before all's done. The delicate piece may have to learn to be less delicate, so she may. Meanwhile, what shall we be doing?'

'Same as you said last night,' grumbled the corpulent ship-master. 'Humour him. Pay out rope. So long as we break our fast, what odds where we breaks it? To tell you my mind, I found it none so joyful at table with them yesterday. Madam with as many simpers as a court-slut from Whitehall, and her brother mute but for grunts, and this Bernis with his fine, pimpish manners. Bah! I wonder the food didn't turn sour on my stomach.' He spat ostentatiously. 'Give me the wardroom by all means, says I. I likes to be at my ease at table.'

Wogan slapped him on the shoulder. 'And it's entirely right ye are, Ned. And, faith, we'll let him know it.'

So, presently, when de Bernis was returning, he found an Irishman awaiting him arrayed in sarcasm.

' 'Twas a fine notion yours, Charley, of the wardroom for Ned and me. We're much obliged. So well do we like it that we'll not be troubling your lively madam and her hilarious brother with any more of our company at all. Ye understand?'

'Perfectly. You have my leave to keep to the wardroom.' And he passed on, up the companion, to the quarter-deck.

The shipmaster and the lieutenant remained staring at each other a little dumbfounded.

'He gives us leave!' said Wogan at last. 'Did ye hear that now? He gives us leave. Glory be! I wonder if he has his match afloat for impudence.'

Meanwhile, now on the poop, leaning on the taffrail, and observing the Black Swan where she followed in their wake, her yards squared to the breeze, Monsieur de Bernis was thoughtfully frowning. It would be a half-hour or so later when he roused himself from his deep abstraction. As he took his elbows from the rail and suddenly drew himself erect, the deep lines of thought were smoothed out of his face. Into their place crept the creases of a speculative smile.

He turned, and came briskly down to the quarter-deck, where Halliwell was at the moment conning the ship and instructing the quartermaster at the whipstaff below.

He surprised him by commanding him to heave to and to signal to the Black Swan to heave to also. Further, he desired a boat to be manned and launched to take him aboard Tom Leach's ship. He had a word to say to her captain.

He was obeyed, of course, and a half-hour later he was climbing up the side of the Black Swan, on which the paint was blistering and cracked, to be received by Leach with a volley of blasphemous questions touching the purpose of this morning call and the time it wasted.

'As for time, we have time to spare. And even if we had not, it would still be my way to go surely rather than swiftly.'

He stood at the head of the entrance-ladder, tall, commanding, and oddly elegant for a buccaneer. Others of his kind had attempted modishness in their exteriors, but none had ever achieved it so completely as de Bernis. He had an instinctive sense of the value of dress and appointments, and of the authority and the aloofness necessary to authority which these can lend a man. It was just such a sense as this which had led Sir Henry Morgan to aim at splendour of apparel, but, lacking the inbred refinements of de Bernis' mind and the restraints which it imposes, he had never achieved more than a gaudy ostentation.

By contrast with the Frenchman, Leach in his gaping shirt and red breeches, wearing his own black hair in short clustering greasy curls, looked a coarse ruffian capable of commanding only by aggressiveness and noisy, blustering self-assertion.

'It would be your way, would it? Thee's come to give orders, then?'

'I've come to discuss with you our precise destination,' was the answer in that cold, level voice, a voice which seemed constantly to announce that, whatever emotions might be excited in its owner, fear would never be one of them.

The hands crowding the waist looked on with interest, and even with a certain admiration for de Bernis, an admiration by no means due only to his fine exterior and impressive manner, but nourished by all those legends which had come to be woven about his name as a result of his activities when he had sailed and marched with Morgan.

His answer meanwhile had curbed the aggressiveness of Leach. If there was one piece of information the pirate craved at that moment, it was just this

77

which de Bernis announced that he came to give him. Once in possession of that, he would soon know how to change the Frenchman's tone.

'Come below,' he said shortly, and led the way.

As they went, he beckoned first to one and then to another of the buccaneers to follow, and when they came to the spacious but unclean and untidy cabin, Bernis made the acquaintance of the mate and the sailing-master of the Black Swan. Both were short, sturdy scoundrels. Ellis, the mate, elected to take the place previously held there by Wogan, was a red flame of a man, with fiery hair and beard and red rims to a pair of pale cruel eyes that seemed to have no eyelashes. Bundry, the sailing-master, was dark with a pock-marked face that was of the colour of clay. He wore clothes of a decent, sober cut, and affected a certain fastidiousness of person and quiet dignity of manner.

They sat down, and an elderly Negro, clad only in a pair of cotton drawers and with the mark of the branding-iron on his shoulder, brought a punch of rum and limes and sugar, and then withdrew at a growl from Leach.

'Now, Charley,' the Captain invited his visitor, 'we's waiting.'

Monsieur de Bernis sat forward, leaned his elbows on the stained table, which was of solid, heavy oak, and faced Leach squarely. His opening was unexpected.

'I've been observing your sailing,' he said. 'Not that it was necessary, or that it told me much more than I had discerned yesterday. I've already said, as you may remember, that you've been overlong at sea.'

'And that's a fact,' Bundry cut in. 'Ye don't need to be a seaman to perceive it.'

'Ye'll talk when I bid you,' Leach growled at him, as if annoyed by this early agreement with anything that de Bernis might say. 'What next?'

Monsieur de Bernis paused a moment before continuing. Bundry's confirmation of his opening statement was as encouraging to him as it was unexpected, and as it had been irritating to the Captain. He was strengthened by the quick perception that he had here

78

an ally in what he came to do, and that, therefore, his task was suddenly rendered lighter than he could have hoped.

'I told you yesterday that so foul is your bottom that if I had been in command of the Centaur you'ld never have boarded her. In fact, Tom, you'ld still be chasing me if by now I hadn't sunk you, although you've forty fine guns and the Centaur only half that number of poor pieces.'

After a moment's surprise, Tom Leach received the statement with a loud, jeering laugh. Ellis grinned broadly. But Bundry's countenance, which the scarring of the smallpox had rendered naturally expressionless, remained grave, as de Bernis observed.

'Ye was ever a ruffling, fleering coxcomb, Charley, puffed up wi' your own conceit. But this beats anything I've ever heard even from you. There's a great fighting seaman, to be sure. The devil of a topgallant, high above all other canvas. Maybe thee'll tell us how thee'ld ha' done this miracle.'

'Your sailing-master isn't laughing,' said de Bernis.

'Eh?' Leach scowled inquiry at the solemn Bundry.

'That's because he guesses what's in my mind,' de Bernis continued. 'He's not without intelligence. He knows that if the Centaur with her well-greased keel had beaten up against the wind, she would probably have outsailed you.'

'Outsailing me is one thing, sinking me another. You spoke o' sinking me.'

'A ship that can be outsailed may be sunk if the other is skilfully and resolutely handled. In a sea-fight mobility is all. To swing into position swiftly, to loose a broadside, and to be off again, with masts in line, showing the narrowest mark to your opponent, that is the whole art of sea-fighting. And this the Centaur could have done, and would have done, had I been in her master's place. I'ld have turned and twisted about you like a panther about an elephant, taking my chance to strike before ever your barnacled keel would answer the helm to ward the blow.'

Leach shrugged contemptuously. 'Maybe ye would,

79

and maybe ye wouldn't. But whether ye would or whether ye wouldn't, what's this to do with our destination?'

'Aye,' said the fiery-faced Ellis. 'Let's hear something besides boasting from you.'

'You'll hear something very uncivil from me, unless your practice civility yourself,' he was coldly answered.

Leach smote the table with his fist. 'Hell!' he roared. 'Is it just to be talk and talk until we fall to quarrelling, or are we to come to business? I ask thee again, Charley, what's all this to do wi' our destination?'

'Everything. What I've been saying is meant to show you that you are in no case to go into serious action; and ye're not to make the mistake of under-rating the ships or the men of the plate fleet. They will be stout, well-found, well-manned frigates. The two ships we possess will readily account for them if properly handled. But you must first put yourself in case to handle them properly. The stake we play for is too heavy to admit of risks.'

'Ye said they would have no more nor two hundred and fifty men atween 'em.'

'But they've seventy guns to our sixty, and better guns than ours, and they are three keels to two; clean, nimble keels. Will you go shackled into the fight?'

Some of the aggressiveness departed out of Leach. But not all of it. He still sought to swagger. 'Od rot you! Why make difficulties?'

'I don't make them. They exist. I desire them removed.'

'Removed?'

'Removed. Ye must careen the Black Swan before we come to this engagement.'

'Careen!' Leach was aghast. 'Careen?' he repeated, his brow black with disagreement.

'Ye've no choice unless you want to court disaster.'

Bundry nodded, and his lips parted, obviously, it seemed, to express agreement. But Leach did not give him time.

'Sink me, man! Does thee think I needs to be taught my trade?'

'If ye refuse to careen, you'll prove that you do.'

'That's what thee says. But what thee says isn't gospel. With the Black Swan as she is, I'ld be quite ready to face your three Spaniards; aye, and account for them. Don't let me hear any more about careening. If ye weren't a fool, ye'ld realize that there's no time for it.'

'Time and to spare. We've a full month before the plate fleet sails. And that's more than you need to scour and grease your keel.'

To prove him wrong again, as de Bernis had done, was merely to drive Leach to entrench himself in obstinacy, which is ever the last refuge of a stupid man. 'Whether we've time or not, I'm not minded to do it. I'm not afeared enough of any Spaniard afloat. So leave that out. Let's come to business now. There's been enough idle talk. What's our destination?'

For a long moment de Bernis calmly considered him across the table. Then he tossed off the punch in his pannikin, pushed back his chair, and rose.

'Since ye're determined, that's the end of the matter. To engage the plate fleet with a ship in the foul state of the Black Swan is, as I said before, to court disaster. And that is something I never court. As for your destination, you may make it what you please.'

The three of them stared up at him in stupefaction, incredulously, reluctant to believe what he seemed to convey.

'What d'ye mean?' cried Ellis at last.

'That if Captain Leach chooses to sail his ships and his men to destruction, I'll be no party to it. You can seek other enterprises: merchantmen like the Centaur, with cargoes of logwood and hides, cocoa and spices. I'll be wishing you good-day.'

'Sit down!' Leach bawled at him. The Captain had come to his feet in his anger.

But Monsieur de Bernis remained standing. 'Do you wish to reconsider?'

'It's thee as had better consider. Thee'd better consider how we stand. Ye're aboard my ship, and, by God, I'll have no mutineers. Ye're here for a purpose, and that purpose ye'll fulfil.'

81

'In my own way. On my own terms,' said de Bernis, still imperturbable.

'In my way, dost hear? In my way. I am master here.'

'Ah? And if I refuse?'

'Ye'll maybe end on the yardarm. Maybe worse.'

'So!' said de Bernis. He raised his brows. He looked down his nose at Leach, considering him as he might have considered some curious and not too pleasant specimen. 'Do you know, Captain, that I have a suspicion that this crew of yours takes an interest in me, particularly since they've learnt I am to bring them to Spanish gold? They'll require to know why you are hanging me, Tom. What shall you tell them? That it is because I refuse to let you lead them to destruction? That it is because I insist that you shall take measures to make victory assured? Is that what you will tell them?'

He watched the dark, evil face before him; saw the expression change; saw a lessening of the colour glowing through his tan. He looked at the other two. In the face of Ellis he saw a reflection of the Captain's discomfiture. Bundry's looked almost distressed, and it was Bundry who spoke.

'When all's said, Captain, Bernis isn't altogether wrong.'

'I care nothing . . .' Leach was beginning, rallying his obstinacy, when Ellis interrupted him.

'We have to care, Captain. Damme! We have to. And that's the fact. Hell and the devil! Where's the sense o' quarrelling when our interests are all the same. Bernis wants to do his best for us all as well as for himself. What if his courage be less than your own, Tom?'

'Caution isn't altogether a fault,' came from Bundry. 'As a seaman I know him to be right about the state of the ship and the rest. If we was pressed for time, we might take a chance. But since we've time in hand, a' God's name let us spend it in making her properly seaworthy.'

Thus Leach found himself abandoned by his own officers, and by this defection realized that at present it was de Bernis who held the trumps. By the secret in his

82

possession of the whereabouts of that plate fleet, he could constrain them to his ways and they could use no constraint with him.

He controlled himself. He stamped down his anger, flung over it a pretence almost of bonhomie.

'Aye, ye're right. Where's the sense o' quarrelling? I can admit a fault. It's the way ye goes about things, Charley. Thee's all quills like a hedgehog. A' God's name, sit down, and fill your can, and let's agree things friendly.' He pushed the jack of rum across, with a propitiatory grin. Then he sat down again.

Monsieur de Bernis allowed himself to be propitiated. He permitted no faintest expression of triumph to escape him. He inclined his head a little, in acknowledgement, resumed his seat, and poured as he was invited.

'You agree, then, to career? That is settled?'

'Why, since not only you but Bundry here also thinks it's necessary, I suppose we must. Though frankly I'm not o' your ways o' thinking. But there. . . . It's agreed, yes.'

'In that case,' said de Bernis, 'the destination I came to discuss with you, our immediate destination, should be the Albuquerque Keys. There's an island there—Maldita—uninhabited, and well known to me of old, with a cove in which you can hide a dozen ships, and a long shelving beach that was made for careening. There's not a better place in all the Caribbean. You can lie snug there, and unsuspected, and it's convenient for another reason. . . .' He paused, raising an impressive forefinger. 'It lies within an easy two days' sail of the spot at which I mean to intercept the Spanish plate fleet.'

## 9

## Interlude

IT WAS on a Tuesday of the first week in June that
the Centaur was captured by Tom Leach. As a result
of Monsieur de Bernis' interview with him early on the
following morning, the two ships were brought a point
or two nearer to the northerly wind which continued to
prevail, and steered a course W.S.W. Consequently
their progress became more leisurely. Nevertheless, by
sunset on Thursday the watchman in the cross-trees
sighted land. It was Cape de la Vela, a mere haze in
the distance, abeam to larboard. Daybreak on Sunday
showed them ahead the low-lying group of the Albuquerques, which was their immediate destination.

The five days of that voyage had passed so quietly
and uneventfully aboard the Centaur that it almost
began to seem to Priscilla Harradine and Major Sands
as if there were, indeed, as Monsieur de Bernis had
assured them, no grounds for anxiety beyond those
begotten of this vexatious postponement of their return
to England.

Monsieur de Bernis, coming back from that success-
ful trial of strength with Captain Leach, derived from
it an added confidence. Although little or nothing of this
was to be discerned on that surface of his being, which
he had schooled himself to preserve unruffled whatever
wind might blow, yet it existed in the depths of him,
and lent an added if indefinable force to his authority.

From this, however, he knew how and when to
unbend.

Among buccaneers, whether ashore or afloat, there
was little discipline or regard for authority save only
when in action. At all other times the latest recruit
shipped considered himself the equal of his officers.

This, indeed, was the theory of their relations. But in practice some of the authority acquired by a captain in the course of engagements and in matters concerned with the handling and organization of a ship still clung to him at other times, and to preserve it for its own sake they would hold themselves as far aloof as they might without coming under suspicion of assumptions of personal superiority.

In this respect de Bernis presented a curious mixture. Stern, reserved, and cold of manner in all that concerned, however remotely, his command aboard the Centaur, as if he had been an officer of the Crown instead of a buccaneer leader, yet at other times he could so far unbend as completely to cast off the mantle of his rank and fraternize with the men. He would jest and laugh with them, drink with them, and even dice with them, and at seven-and-eleven he revealed himself formidable by the speed which practice had given him in the reckoning-up of chances. Once Wogan beheld him seated on a coil of rope on the forecastle with a crowd of buccaneers about him, listening in rapt silence, broken now and then by bursts of laughter, to his lively account of the taking of the Spanish Fort of San Lorenzo on the Chagres River. On another occasion—that was towards the end of the first dog-watch on the evening on which they had sighted Cape de la Vela—he fetched his guitar, and perched himself on the hatch-coaming, under the new moon, with those wild ruffians swarming about him to listen to the gay, tuneful little Spanish songs with which he enraptured them.

And yet, so delicately did he walk that tight-rope between familiarity and authority that none presumed upon his easy graciousness. Whilst the men came swiftly to an increased admiration, yet they did not entirely lose their awe of him, or a particle of the sense of his superiority inspired by his record, and supported by his bearing, his dress and appointments, and his precise, cultured speech.

Priscilla Harradine had been shrewdly right when she had told Major Sands that she perceived in Monsieur de Bernis a man placed by experience and natural endowments above the petty need of standing upon his dignity.

Wogan looked on in wonder and mistrust, vainly seeking to probe the secret of the magic in which de Bernis appeared to deal. The Irishman knew how to be one with the men at need—he could be as foul and lewd as the vilest of them—and he knew, at need, how to drive them. But he did not know by what arts a man could successfully do both at the same time. He consulted Halliwell upon this mystery. The shipmaster was prompt and contemptuous with an explanation.

'French tricks,' was his terse summary, which shed no light whatever upon Wogan's resentful darkness.

Major Sands was another interested and scornful observer.

Monsieur de Bernis had afforded him facilities for observation. On his return from that visit, on Wednesday morning, to the Black Swan, he had informed Miss Priscilla of the arrangements he had made with his lieutenant and his shipmaster. In future they would take their meals in the wardroom, so that her privacy in the cabin would not again be invaded.

'I would relieve you of my own company at the same time,' he added gravely. 'But the relationship in which it is prudent that we should appear to stand demands that I continue to intrude upon you.'

She protested with some vehemence against the underlying assumption.

'Can you suppose, sir, that I should be so ungracious as to desire it?'

'It would not be unreasonable when all is considered. After all, I am no better than these men.'

The steady glance of her blue-green eyes seemed to repudiate the statement with indignation. 'I should be sorry, indeed, to be of that opinion, sir.'

'Yet Major Sands, there, will tell you that it is the only opinion possible.'

The Major, in the background, cleared his throat. But he said nothing. It was certainly not in his mind to contradict the Frenchman. Nor could he think that Priscilla need have been so excessively courteous as to have troubled to do so. He was a little shocked, therefore, to hear her not merely persisting, but actually answering for him.

'Major Sands, like myself, has only gratitude for the consideration you have shown us. For all that you have done. He does not deceive himself as to what must have happened to us but for you. I beg you to believe it, sir.'

He smiled as he inclined his periwigged head. 'I do believe it. Major Sands leaves one in no doubt of his warm sincerity.' The Major's colour deepened under the buffet of that irony. But, without looking at him, Monsieur went on. 'I came to tell you also that there is no reason why you should keep to the cabin. You may without apprehension take the air on deck when you please. None will venture to molest you; though if any should I'll make an example of him that will not encourage others. I have had your awning set for you again on the poop.'

She thanked him, and he went out.

'I wonder,' said Major Sands, 'what the sarcastic hound expects of me.'

Miss Priscilla looked at him without approval. 'A little graciousness, perhaps,' she ventured.

'Graciousness? I am to be gracious to him?' He curbed resentment to become pedantic. 'Shall we preserve, even amid these troubles, our sense of proportion, Priscilla? Shall we consider precisely where this man stands and what he has done?'

'By all means. Let us consider, for instance, that he has preserved our lives. Is that nothing? Does it deserve no thanks?'

He spread his hands. 'That is to consider one side only of the question.'

'Is that not enough for us? With that side to consider, would a generous mind consider any other?'

The asperity of her tone pulled him up sharply. This, he perceived, would not do at all. Trouble and difficulty enough arose out of the events. He must certainly not allow them to jeopardize those dearest hopes of his, which had been blossoming with promise of so rich a fruition. He must remember that women were curious creatures, addicted to eccentricities of vision, allowing emotional influences to deflect the light of reason. There was no prevailing with them by hard common-sense alone. It provoked their hostility. He saw signs of this in Priscilla, and unless he changed his course to humour her, unless he addressed himself to her emotions, rather than to her intelligence, which he perceived to lie dormant, the argosy of his hopes might founder under him in these very difficult waters.

He assumed an air of gentle, patient melancholy.

'Dear Priscilla, do you realize, I wonder, the wrong you do me?' He sighed. 'You find me wanting in generosity. You are right. And yet how far from right. You are only halfway down my feelings. There are depths you have not suspected. Not suspected, stab me! You imagine, perhaps, that concern for myself is to be found down there; that this makes me impatient— ungracious, as you say. My dear! For myself I care nothing. For myself I could be gracious enough to this man. I should consider only that he has preserved my life. But my thought is all for you. All for you, stab me! If I am impatient, ungracious, it is because of my concern for you; for the distress, the anxieties, the fears that are afflicting you. How can I be patient in the face of this? Damme, Priscilla! How can I?'

Her indignation melted before this display of noble concern which held no thought of self. The fundamental sweetness of her nature welled up to make her ashamed.

'I am sorry, Bart. I am very stupid sometimes. Forgive me, dear.' She held out a hand to him in appeal.

He came nearer, gently smiling, and took it between both his own. He was suddenly inspired by the note of tenderness which penitence had brought into her voice. Dimly he recalled a line heard in a play, a line written by some poet or other, one of those absurd ranters who expressed themselves in stilted, pompous phrases, in which sometimes, Major Sands confessed to himself, one found a grain of sense amid a deal of nonsense. He marvelled at the queer opportuneness with which the line came now to the surface of his memory, not perceiving that it was his own commonplace thought which borrowed for itself the majestic robe of that expression: 'There is a tide in the affairs of man which taken at the flood leads on to fortune.'

88

Here now was the tide running strongly in his favour. Let him take it at the flood.

'My dear! What man in my place, loving you as I do, could have any other thought?'

'Dear Bart, I understand. I should have understood before.' She looked up with soft entreaty in her candid eyes.

He stroked the hand he held. Gently by that hand he began to draw her nearer. She suffered him to have his way.

'Do you suppose that it is easy for me to have patience, with such circumstances surrounding the woman I love?'

His tone had sunk to a fond, crooning murmur. Suddenly she seemed to freeze where she stood, almost in his arms. Her breath quickened, the colour ebbed from her face, and the candid eyes, that a moment ago had been so tender, held only alarm.

'What are you saying, Bart?' Her right hand was withdrawn from between his fondling palms; her left pushed him gently away. 'Are you . . .' she choked a little. 'Are you making love to me?'

In profound dismay he spread his hands. 'My dear!' he cried, protesting vaguely.

'Oh! How could you? How could you at such a time?'

What he understood from this came mercifully to temper his dismay. It was the time that was ill-chosen. He had been deceived, then. The tide, after all, was not yet at the flood. Her mind, distraught by peril, could hold the thought of nothing else. He had blundered by precipitancy. He had startled her. It only remained to beat a retreat in good order, and await a more propitious season for his next advance.

'At such a time!' he echoed. 'But—stab me!—it is just that. It is the time . . . the dreadful events . . . these terrible circumstances that quicken my tenderness, my urgent wish to have you know that you have beside you a man ready, as I have said before, to give his life for you. If I did not owe this to my affection for you, damme, there was my friendship for your father, my sense of duty to his memory. What is there here to dismay you?'

89

The trouble in her mind—reflected in her eyes—was hardly lessened; but it had changed its course. Her glance faltered. Confused, she turned away, and moved to the stern-ports through which the sunlight was now flooding.

With anxious eyes he followed the slim figure, admiring the graceful lines of it, the quiet elegance of her movements, and so waited. She spoke presently, when she had mastered herself.

'Forgive me, Bart. To be sure, I am a little fool. Don't let me appear also an ungrateful one. I owe you so much. I must have died, I think, but for the knowledge that you were standing by me in this awful time. You have made me realize it. It should not have been necessary.'

'It is not necessary now,' said he, very noble. 'Sink me if it is.' And then, being a fool, he must go on to spoil it. 'But I rejoice to hear, at least, that you are no longer in the persuasion that you owe everything to this French rogue.'

Now that is just what, in her generous anxiety to make amends for the injustice of her assumption, she had been in danger of forgetting. His words, acting as a sharp reminder, tempered her penitence. But she did not pursue the matter, intent at the moment upon making her peace with him.

She turned, and smiled a little shyly in the consciousness of the enormity of her late assumptions. 'Shall we take the air on deck, Bart?'

They went, and beyond the leering eyes of Wogan and Halliwell, on the quarter-deck, following her passage thence to the poop, none seemed to notice them.

Monsieur de Bernis was in the captain's cabin, which he had now made his own, astern, on the summit of the poop. He sat with open doors on account of the heat. Seeing their approach, he rose, and came forth, bringing cushions for her day-bed which she found set for her under the awning of sailcloth as it had been before the invasion of the Centaur by her present crew.

When this was done, he lingered on in amiable talk with them, like a courteous host. He mentioned their altered course, expressed a hope that the breeze might hold, spoke of their destination and the purpose for which they sought the Albuquerque Keys, and in answer to Miss Priscilla's questions regretted that circumstances would delay them there for the best part of a month.

The Major, morose, sat on the tail of the day-bed, of which Miss Priscilla occupied the head, making no contribution to the talk. The notion of spending a month at the Albuquerques filled him with disgust and indignation, and it was only by the exercise of all his powers of repression that he avoided saying so. The cool tone in which de Bernis made the announcement appeared to him as a climax of impudence. And it added fuel to his indignation to observe that Miss Priscilla did not appear to share his feelings. She seemed to accept the situation with a resignation that went very near complacency. His disgust reached its apex at a question which he heard her ask in a tone of quiet wonder.

'Monsieur de Bernis, how did you become a buccaneer?'

Monsieur de Bernis seemed startled by this question, coming so abruptly. He smiled a little as he looked down at her.

'You ask almost as if the fact were difficult to understand. It is a compliment, I suppose. But can you really be interested to know?'

'Should I ask such a question if I were not? The interest must be strong that drives me to an impertinence.'

'Not an impertinence,' he protested quietly. 'Most pertinent since your present situation depends so much upon the fact.' He paused a moment, and the long narrow face was overcast with thought, the dark eyes grew almost wistful. 'After all, there is so little that you do not know already. Did I not tell you that the Sieur Simon, he whom the Spaniards killed on Santa Catalina, was my uncle? I had come out with him to the New World, in quest of the liberty of action denied me at home in the Old. But there was no thought of lawlessness in my mind. We are Huguenots, we Bernis, from the Toulousain, and for a Huguenot in France there was only toleration. Today, since the King has revoked the Edict of Nantes, there is not even that. But already when I was a boy there were few opportunities for a Huguenot to find advancement in any career that was open to a gentleman.

'I was the youngest of seven sons, and a career was necessary to me. And so I took the chance my uncle offered me of seeking it in the New World. When he was killed at Santa Catalina, I was alone out here, without possessions and without friends, saving those poor fellows who had escaped with me. With them I went to join Morgan. Nothing else offered. Besides, the massacre on Santa Catalina had bred in me such a hatred of Spaniards that I was glad enough to march in any company that was hostile to Spain.

'With Morgan my rise was rapid. Birth, if it does nothing else for a man, will at least equip him for leadership. Opportunity served me, and I knew how to seize it. I showed Morgan that I knew how to make men follow me. My nationality, too, once I had displayed the gift of leadership, made me valuable to Morgan with whom there was always a considerable French contingent. I became his lieutenant, in command of his French following. With him, too, I learned to fight a ship, and I doubt if there was ever a higher school than his for that.

'When England's affairs ceased to justify her encouragement of the buccaneers, and Morgan decided to accept the governorship of Jamaica, I went with him, and took service with him under the English Crown. After all, there was no man living to whom I owed greater loyalty; and probably no man living whom Morgan trusted as fully as he trusted me.' He smiled down upon her as he ceased. 'That is all,' he said.

'So that,' she commented thoughtfully, 'your career is hardly to be spoken of as lawless, seeing that you ceased to be a buccaneer once buccaneers were declared without the law.'

But this was too much for Major Sands. 'If that was true once,' was his frosty interjection, 'it is unfortunately true no longer.'

Monsieur de Bernis laughed, as he turned to depart. 'But why unfortunately, Major? You, at least, should regard it as extremely fortunate.'

92

The Major had no answer for that. His look was foolish, and he reserved his comments upon what the Frenchman had told them until Monsieur de Bernis had gone down to the quarter-deck, where Halliwell stood taking the height of the sun.

'Morgan's trust in him hasn't prevented him from betraying it so as to return to piracy,' the Major condemned him.

But Miss Priscilla, wistfully pensive, either did not hear or did not heed him, for she made no answer. And the Major, remembering in time how the topic of Monsieur de Bernis invariably now led to the frontiers of acrimony, did not pursue the subject.

But he returned to it more than once before they reached the Albuquerques. His scorn of de Bernis was stimulated by that man's free-and-easy association with the ruffians who made up the crew, a matter to which he missed no opportunity of drawing Miss Priscilla's attention, so as to justify himself in her eyes for the feelings she was disposed to condemn in him.

That night when on the forecastle, under the new moon, de Bernis was singing to his audience of pirates, the Major and the lady were enjoying the cool on the poop. Across the length of the ship floated that mellow, moving baritone voice.

'It passes belief,' said the Major, in tones of disgust, 'that a man should make so free with a gang of cutthroats. Stab me, it does!'

He never knew whether Priscilla's words were intended for an answer.

'How beautifully he sings.'

## 10

## *Careened*

AT LAST, on the Sunday, they threaded the channel
that ran among the islands of the Albuquerque group,
and dropped anchor in ten fathoms, in the wide basin
of the lagoon on the eastern side of Maldita, the
northernmost of the keys. It was this, which, at the
instances of de Bernis, had been selected for the
careening of the Black Swan.

The cove was as secret and sheltered a place as he
had represented it, and in every particular Leach was
compelled to admit that it could not be better suited to
the purpose for which they came.

The lagoon was a pear-shaped basin, narrowing at
the neck, between a reef that fringed the southern half
of its sweep and a considerable scrub-crowned bluff
that screened it from the north. Sea-birds nested on the
heights of this bluff and it offered a fine emplacement
for guns to defend the entrance. Leach, however, without experience of fortifications and of fighting on land,
gave no thought of these possibilities, and de Bernis did
not appear to be disposed to school him in them.

The half-moon of beach, running from bluff to reef,
shelved so gradually that the anchorage was four or
five cables' length from high-water mark. This beach
was divided near the bluff by a fresh-water stream of
considerable proportions for so small an island. At the
summit of this beach, which was wide and very silvery
and along which turtles scuttled clumsily when the
clatter of the anchor chains came to disturb them, rose
a green wall of palm and pimento, and the air was
heavily fragrant with the scent of spices, which the hot
sun was drawing from the trees. The island, less than a
mile in width and little more than two miles long, was
densely wooded from end to end.

The two ships having come to anchor side by side, Leach lost no time. The boats were lowered from both of them, and men went ashore to fell timber for the building of stout rafts required for the work of lightening the Black Swan. This lightening occupied a full three days, in which time she was completely dismantled of all save her masts. Not only her forty ponderous guns, but everything else moveable, or that could be rendered moveable, went over the side, to be floated ashore on the rafts. Finally, eased of her ballast, she was ready to careen.

The work was merrily and briskly conducted by those lawless men. They brought to it a schoolboy zest. Seeing them wading to their armpits to receive and draw ashore the heavily laden rafts, maintaining the while a running fire of jest and laughter, like honest, care-free labourers, it was difficult to believe them men of blood and violence, predatory and ruthless, holding life as cheap as honour.

When at last the Black Swan was ready for beaching, the two hundred and fifty men who now composed her crew set about preparing themselves quarters ashore. There was more felling of trees to provide poles for the vast sailcloth pavilions which they erected along the summit of the beach in the neighbourhood of the fresh water. For their captain and his officers they built with incredible rapidity a roomy log hut thatched with palmetto; and they fitted it with hammocks and furnished it with tables and chairs that had been taken from the ship. And whilst the main body, industrious as a colony of ants, were about these operations, others were at work at the boucan fires which they had lighted and over which they were curing the turtles which they had caught.

At last, as the short Caribbean tide began to flow on the morning of the third day, which was Wednesday, the Black Swan slipped her anchor cables, which were picked up by the waiting boats, and the business of warping her ashore was taken in hand.

Almost naked, and sweating in the blistering sun, they toiled at the capstan in gangs, chanting as they slowly circled it and wound about it the straining, creaking hawsers which had been lashed to trees at the head of the beach. The very easy gradient and the fine soft sand assisting them, they made good progress at first. Then, as the water grew shallower, followed a spell of slow Herculean toil until they could bring rollers into action, and so render it comparatively easy again.

Most of the day was spent before at last the great black ship was careened, high and dry, one side of her heavily barnacled and weeded lower hull exposed, as she lay over on the other.

After this the buccaneers rested and feasted, and a couple of days of comparative idleness followed whilst they waited for the hot sun to do its work of drying the fouled keel, so as to make it easy to burn away the foulness.

Monsieur de Bernis meanwhile took his ease aboard the Centaur, where she rode at anchor in the limpid blue-green waters of the lagoon; and with him remained the members of his supposed family undisturbed until Wogan and Halliwell inspired Leach to disturb them.

The hundred men of the Centaur's prize crew went daily ashore to bear their part in the work, and returned nightly to their hammocks and sleeping-mats aboard. And there in the cool of the lovely tropical nights, after the heat and labours of the day, de Bernis would be moving freely amongst them, like a gay troubadour, to charm them with tale and song, thus deepening at once the contempt of Major Sands and the mistrust of Halliwell and Wogan.

Major Sands, ever intent to justify to Priscilla that scorn of his for the Frenchman which he knew offended her, took him to task for it on the day after the careening was complete.

It was just after eight bells, and the three of them were at dinner in the great cabin with Pierre to wait upon them, and to regale them with the fresh turtle and yams which one of the hands had brought aboard last night as a present for de Bernis. Save for the half-dozen buccaneers composing a watch, such as Leach insisted should be kept, the men were all ashore at the time, and all was quiet on the ship. It was nearing high water, and through the open stern-ports they had a view of the palm-fringed beach, three hundred yards away, deserted now, for the men were at meat in the shade of their pavilions.

Monsieur de Bernis listened patiently to the stuttered sentences in which the Major expressed his wonder that the Frenchman could find satisfaction in intimate association with the vile ruffians whom Leach had put aboard the Centaur.

'Satisfaction?' was the word that de Bernis took up, echoing it interrogatively. The narrow, saturnine face looked more saturnine than ever. 'Which of us does only that in which he takes satisfaction? He is fortunate, indeed, who can find real satisfaction in anything that he does. It has not often happened to me, Major. If it has often happened to you, your lot is enviable.'

'You mean, sir?'

'Why, that most of the things we do in this life, we do from sheer necessity: to ease pain, remove discomfort, preserve our lives, or earn a livelihood. These are the chief activities that engage most men. Do you not agree?'

'Stab me! You may be right. That may be the general rule of life. I hadn't thought of it. But here, now, what necessity do you obey when you go amongst these fellows?'

'But isn't it plain? I am sure that Miss Priscilla understands me.'

Calmly she met the gaze of his dark eyes. 'I think I do. You obey the necessity of disposing them favourably towards you.'

'And not merely towards me, but towards us all. Must I tell you that this Leach is a treacherous, headstrong, violent beast? Although I have associated myself with him, and although I believe that I hold him fast in the bonds of cupidity, yet I cannot be sure that perversity, stupidity, or the sheer evil that is in the fellow may not drive him to burst his bonds. Do not, therefore, turn the eye of scorn upon me because I am concerned to forge myself a buckler against the day of need. That buckler lies in winning the regard, even the affection, of these men.'

The Major made a wry face of disgust. 'Affection!'

he deprecated. 'Lord! There are some things that can be too dearly bought.'

'You may be right. For myself, I am slow to reach conclusions in these matters. But there is a detail to which you may not have given attention. If there should be an end of me, Major, there will certainly be an end of you and of Miss Priscilla. You will include no illusion on that score among the many illusions from which I have observed you to suffer.' He smiled upon the sudden utter blankness of the Major's countenance. 'Be sparing, therefore, in your contempt of the means by which I ensure your preservation with my own from any of the accidents to which such a nature as Captain Leach's might expose it.'

With that, and without awaiting any answer from Major Sands, he adroitly turned the conversation into other channels, addressing himself to Miss Priscilla whose eyes gleamed curiously as they now met his own. Almost, he could have supposed, she took satisfaction in the unanswerable rebuke which he had administered to the pompous soldier.

At about the same time and upon the very same topic, Wogan and Halliwell were entertaining Leach, who sat at dinner with them and with the fiery-faced Ellis and the quiet-mannered, pock-marked Bundry, in the log cabin that had been built for them.

Leach was not impressed at first. 'What's the odds?' he growled. 'Let him do as he likes until he brings us to the Spaniards. Then it'll be my turn, as he'll find out.'

To Ellis and Bundry there was news in this dark hint; for unlike Wogan and Halliwell they were not yet in the Captain's confidence as to how he intended to square matters with de Bernis for his intransigence over the articles. There was a queer kindling in the furnace of Ellis's countenance. But Bundry's eyelids drooped slowly like the membrane of a bird, and his face, with its clay-coloured pallor upon which the ardour of the sun could make no impression, grew more like a mask than ever.

The corpulent Halliwell leaned forward across the table. He spoke quietly. 'Can ye suppose, Cap'n, that possibility don't occur to him?'

'What if it do? He's here, isn't he? We've got him, haven't we? How's he to get away from us?'

Halliwell's little eyes were screwed up and almost disappeared into his bulging cheeks. 'Came and put himself into your hands, very trusting like, didn't he?' quoth his sly voice.

'Couldn't help his self as things fell out.' Leach was still contemptuous.

'Just so,' said Halliwell. 'Just so. 'Twas in his mind, as he told ye, to ha' gone to Guadeloupe for a ship and men wi' which to join us. But things fell out so as he didn't need to. It don't follow that he welcomes it. If he'd ha' joined us wi' a ship o' his own arming, and men o' his own recruiting, he'ld not be as helpless as he is now, would he? And ye're not supposing that Mossoo de Bernis of all men alive isn't awake to that and to what may happen to him.'

'Suppose he is. What, then? How in hell can he mend it?'

Impatiently Wogan flung into the discussion, so as to shed more light on the Captain's dullness.

'Och, now, don't ye see that's just what he may be trying to do?'

Leach sat up as if he had been stung. Wogan elaborated.

'There he is aboard yon ship wi' a hundred stout lads, and us careened here, high and dry, and as helpless as if our hands was tied behind our backs. What for is he at such pains to be making friends with them? Putting a spell on them with tales of his brave doings as a rover, and howling Spanish ditties to them in the moonlight, like a love-sick tom-cat? Will ye trust him with them? Or them with him, if it comes to that? There's Ned and me might wake up to find we've had our throats cut in our sleep, and him sailing away with the ship and the lads to try their luck by theirselves against the Spaniards and keep the treasure to theirselves. And you, Tom, careened. Careened here, with devil a ship in which to follow him and devil a notion which way to follow if ye had a ship.'

'By God!' roared Leach, and came to his feet on the oath. It was as if a pit had suddenly yawned at his feet. What manner of trusting fool had he been not to have seen this danger for himself?

He was flinging out of the cabin in a passion of suddenly aroused suspicions when the corpse-like Bundry seemed to come to life.

'Whither away, Captain?'

The cold, harsh voice checked the other's haste. Bundry was probably the only man amongst them all with power to do that. There was something oddly compelling about this cold, emotionless, calculating shipmaster.

'I am going to put it beyond Charley's power to play any of his tricks on us.'

Bundry was on his feet now. 'But ye'll remember that we depend upon him to bring us to the Spaniards?'

'I's not like to forget aught that matters.'

Content, Bundry let him go, and almost at once they heard him bawling for hands to man one of the boats and take him out to the Centaur. Before stepping into her, however, he summoned Wogan from the hut, and gave him brisk orders, which made him suddenly busy ashore.

And so it fell out that, as dinner was coming to an end in the great cabin of the Centaur, the door opened and Captain Leach walked in upon them unannounced.

He appeared less formidable than on the only other occasion when Miss Priscilla had seen him. Then he had been bare-legged and bare-armed, his shirt had hung open and was splashed with blood, and his hawk-like face had looked inexpressibly evil in the blood-lust it reflected. Today, at least his dress was reasonably decent. He wore no doublet, but his shirt was clean, and he was neatly shod in grey leather, with stockings also of grey.

He stood a moment within the doorway of the cabin observing them. His dark glance lingered on the neat virginal figure of Priscilla, and passed on only to be constantly returning to her, until she grew conscious of it and uncomfortable under its bold scrutiny which held for her something which if indefinable was nevertheless horrible and chilling. This, however, did not happen all at once.

Monsieur de Bernis, with an inaudible intake of breath, rose from his chair. If he had the scent of danger breast-high, nevertheless—indeed, perhaps, because of it—his manner was of a perfect and urbane serenity.

'Ah, Captain! You honour us unexpectedly.' He drew out a vacant chair and proffered it, smiling.

Captain Leach came forward. 'No need to sit. What I's come to say 's soon said.' He nodded to Major Sands, who accounting it prudent to copy de Bernis' example had also risen; and he bowed to Miss Priscilla. Repressing a shiver at the glance that accompanied the bow, she acknowledged it by a slight inclination of her head.

Monsieur de Bernis looked on with half-closed, languid eyes.

The Captain turned to him. 'I've given orders to have quarters got ready ashore for the crew o' th' Centaur. They're to stop ashore until the Black Swan is ready for sea.' His keen little eyes were intent for the slightest flicker on the face of de Bernis. 'Ye understand?' he snapped.

'The order, yes. But not the reason. The men were very comfortable here, and it was convenient.'

'Mebbe. But it's not as I wish it.' Slyly he added, 'I likes my own men under my own hand, Charley.'

'But of course,' said de Bernis,

This apparent indifference disappointed Leach. But it merely deepened his mistrust. He remembered having heard it said of Morgan's French lieutenant that he was never more alert than when he was looking languid and he could swear there was a languor now in the Frenchman's air.

There was a pause. The buccaneer's eyes slid once more to Miss Priscilla. He bowed a little again, with affectations of gallantry as he addressed her.

'I trust, ma'am, my next order will not displease or inconvenience you. I've good reason for 't.' Slowly, as if reluctant to depart from the contemplation of her, his eyes returned to de Bernis. 'I've also ordered them to build a hut for you ashore.'

But now, at last, de Bernis really displayed a flash of vexation. 'Is so much necessary? We are very comfortable here.' Contemptuously, as if to show Leach that he perfectly read his motives, he added, 'We can hardly run away with the ship.'

Leach stroked his chin and smiled. 'There's three of ye aboard: you and him and your servant yonder. I've knowed three men to sail a boat as big as this afore now.'

De Bernis raised his brows. 'By God, Leach, you want to laugh, I think.'

'Mebbe,' said Leech. 'But I mind me as, after all, 'twas by chance I came on ye. And if thee was to take it into thee head to be off, I'm in no case to go after thee. So thee'll come ashore this evening, and ashore thee'll stay.' He turned again to Priscilla. 'Ye'll forgive me, ma'am, for this, I hope. I'll see ye're made comfortable. Ye may bring what furniture ye please so as to make sure o' that. Ashore I'll be seeing something of ye, I hope.'

When at last he had gone, the Major and Priscilla beheld for the first time a departure in de Bernis from an imperturbability which they had been supposing irrefragable.

He stood with his chin buried in the lace at his throat, his countenance pale and disordered by anger, his hands clenched so that the knuckles showed white. Thus in silence which they did not venture to break. Then with a softly rapped oath, he turned on his heel and strode the length of the cabin to the stern-ports He stood there looking out over the water to the beach where all was now activity. Then again he turned and came slowly back. At last he threw up his head with a shrug and a laugh, like a man who has found what he was seeking.

'I don't understand at all,' said the Major at last. 'Stab my vitals, if I do.'

De Bernis flung him a glance like a blow in its undisguised contempt.

'What is there to puzzle you? The dog feared that I should corrupt the crew he had put aboard here. He perceived the possibility which you had not the wit to

102

perceive, else you would have spared me your discourtesies awhile ago.'

For once in his profound amazement the Major forgot to be resentful of an offensive tone. 'As God's my life!' he ejaculated. 'D'ye mean it was in your mind?'

De Bernis answered him in a tone made hard by impatience.

'It's not my mind I am disclosing to you. But Tom Leach's. And it's not a nice mind. Not at all a nice mind.'


## 11

'Ashore


MONSIEUR DE BERNIS surprised Captain Leach by following him almost immediately ashore. To the buccaneer's questions he rendered a ready account of his purpose.

'Since your timorous suspicions constrain Madame de Bernis to leave her quarters aboard, I will at least see that those prepared for her ashore are suitable. She is in delicate health.'

'I marvel, then, ye should ha' brought her roving wi' ye.'

De Bernis answered him impatiently. 'God mend your wit! I told you it was my intention to leave her in Guadeloupe, in her brother's care. Could I have left her in Jamaica, when I don't intend to return there?'

Leach perceived the reasonableness of this, and became amiable. Let de Bernis make what arrangements he accounted fit.

The Frenchman went amongst the men, and issued his orders. They were to build a log hut at the southern extremity of the beach, where the reef began, placing it just within the shelter of the trees. In its neighborhood they were to place a tent for Madame's brother and another for de Bernis' servant, Pierre. At that distance from the buccaneer encampment, with practically the whole length of that long beach between, Madame should be reasonably safe from disturbance.

Going to work with that speed which their numbers and experience made possible, all was ready before sunset. The timber, felled on the very edge of the jungle, made there an embayed clearing among the trees in which, by de Bernis' instructions, the hut was built. Thus it was screened from view except directly in front. The two small sailcloth tents were placed one on each horn of this little bay.

Some furniture brought from the ship: a table, four chairs, the day-bed from the poop, a tarred sheet to spread upon the ground, a couple of rugs wherewith partly to cover this, a slush lamp to hang from the rafters that carried the palmetto thatch, and some other odds and ends by means of which the cabin's single room was rendered reasonably inhabitable.

Miss Priscilla, despite her anxieties, displayed pleased surprise when she stood there that evening, and expressed her gratitude to Monsieur de Bernis for the pains he had taken to ensure her comfort. The quarters provided for her were so much better than anything that she had expected.

Nor was de Bernis, it appeared, the only one solicitous for her. Soon after her arrival, Tom Leach came to assure himself that all that was possible had been done for her comfort. He had assumed an ingratiating manner; he was all apologies for any inconvenience she might suffer in this change of quarters, and all solicitude to reduce this as far as might be possible. He ordered various odds and ends to be brought from among the landed furniture of the Black Swan, and desired her to use all frankness in telling him of anything further that might be done for her well-being. He lingered on in amiable, jocular talk awhile with her and with de Bernis and the Major who were in attendance, and finally went off with smirking expressions of goodwill.

De Bernis, who had remained impassive, looked at the Major whose bearing throughout had suggested that Tom Leach emitted an offensive smell.

'Timeo Danaos et dona ferentes,' he murmured.

'Ye know I don't speak French,' said the Major irritably, and he wondered why Miss Priscilla laughed.

He wondered that she could laugh at all, whatever the occasion, considering their circumstances. Himself he could perceive in them only grounds for despair. This despair was rendered the more acute by that morning's revelation that de Bernis, upon whom alone he could base such slender hopes as might be entertained of an ultimate deliverance, was by no means on the perfectly harmonious terms with that other scoundrel Leach which seemed necessary if this hope was not to be entirely illusory.

But there were worse vexations in store for Major Sands. When they came to retire that night, after the supper cooked by Pierre and served to them in the hut, the Major standing with Monsieur de Bernis in the open under the stars before the tent which had been provided for him, was suddenly moved to ask him what provision he had made for sleeping-quarters for himself. There was a moment's pause before the Frenchman answered him.

'It follows naturally, sir, that I share those prepared for my wife.'

The Major made a gurgling noise in his throat, as he swung to confront the Frenchman squarely.

'What security do you imagine the lady would enjoy if it were shown that she is not my wife? You have eyes, I suppose; and you saw the way Tom Leach looked at her when he came smirking round her here this evening with his loathsome affability.'

The Major tugged at his neckcloth. He felt as if he were choking.

'God's death!' he got out at last, in a voice thick with passion. 'And what, pray, is there to choose between Tom Leach and you?'

Monsieur de Bernis sucked in his breath quite audibly. His face showed white in the gloom. 'Runs your mind so?' he said at last. 'But what a poor, lame mind it is with which to run at conclusions! I wonder whither it will bear you in the end.' He uttered a short laugh. 'If I were what you are supposing, if my aims were such as you flatter me by deeming them, your

105

carcase, my dear Bartholomew, would by now be feeding the crayfish in that lagoon. Let the thought give you assurance of my honesty. Good-night!'

He was turning away when the Major caught him by the sleeve.

'I beg your pardon, de Bernis. Stab me! I should have seen that without being told.' Convinced by the other's clear argument, it was out of the depth of his relief that contrition rose. 'I've done you a monstrous wrong, damme! I admit it frankly.'

'Pshaw!' said de Bernis, and he moved off.

Miss Priscilla's hut had not been supplied with a door, this being deemed unnecessary. In its place, and to act as a curtain, Pierre had hung across the entrance a heavy rug which entirely screened the interior. From between the logs composing the walls the light was still gleaming when presently de Bernis approached it, having left his doublet with Pierre and carrying now a cloak and a pillow which his servant had given him.

He went down on one knee before the entrance, to dig a hole in the fine sand.

'Who is there?' came Priscilla's voice from beyond the curtaining rug.

'It is I,' De Bernis answered. "You have no cause for alarm. I shall be on guard. Sleep in peace.'

There was no answer from within.

De Bernis completed his digging. Then, wrapping himself in the cloak, he lay down fitting his hip into the hole, and disposing himself to slumber.

In the distance, at the other end of the beach, the fires over which the buccaneers had done their cooking were dying down. The noise of their voices had ceased, and all was quiet in their encampment. The moon, almost a half-disc by now, came up and the lagoon became a quivering sheet of quicksilver. The silken rustle of the incoming tide as its wavelets broke upon the fine sand was presently the only sound upon the stillness of the night.

But all were not asleep. A corner of the curtain masking the entrance of the hut, in which the light had been extinguished, was slowly, noiselessly, raised, and the faint moonlight beat down upon the white face of Priscilla.

Cautiously she looked out, and almost at once her eyes fell upon the long dark form of Monsieur de Bernis, stretched there at her very feet, with the deep, regular breathing of sleep.

Not at once was her head withdrawn. For some moments it remained visible as she pondered this sleeper, who made of his body a barrier for her protection. Then, very quietly the curtain fell again, and within the hut Priscilla sought her couch, and delivered herself up to slumber in the peaceful conviction that she was well guarded.

She was guarded more completely even than she knew. For in his tent a dozen yards away, Major Sands, disdaining to use the hammock provided for him, lay prone upon the sand, his head in shadow, but near the entrance of the tent, whence, himself sleepless, he could watch the sleeping custodian of the lady whom he had chosen for his wife. From which it would seem that the conviction which momentarily had moved the Major into penitence had been thrust out by the doubts that will beset a man in his circumstances.

Next day the Major paid the price of that unnecessary pernoctation. The morning found him blear-eyed, morose, and sullen. In the afternoon, he slept, partly because he could no longer combat drowsiness, partly because he realized the necessity of fortifying himself against another night of vigilance.

But after a second night of it, with a still drowsier day to follow, and an aching head which the heat, suddenly grown intense, rendered almost intolerable, the Major realized that this state of things could not continue. Whatever the Frenchman might be, the honesty of his intentions towards Miss Priscilla might now be considered tested. Besides, when all was said, the Major was within easy call, less than a dozen yards away, and he could trust himself not to sleep through an outcry.

And now followed arduous days for the buccaneers, hard-driven by Leach to the work awaiting them upon the hull of the careened ship. But drive them as he might, the heat retarded the operations, and despite the many hands at his command, only a comparative few could be employed at once in the task of burning off the barnacles and weeds. From sunrise until a little before noon, the men worked willingly enough. But when they had dined, they insisted upon sleeping, and let Leach storm and rant as he chose, they would not raise a finger during those torrid afternoons in which the sun beat down so pitilessly, and never a breath of wind came to temper the appalling heat.

In this they received a measure of encouragement from the attitude adopted by de Bernis. He was going freely amongst them here ashore, as he had done aboard the Centaur. He would saunter over to the encampment during the afternoon idleness, to laugh and joke with them, to regale them with stories of past deeds upon the Main in which he had borne a part, and, more often now, to fire their fancy on the score of the Spanish gold to which he was to lead them.

It was well for him, perhaps, that Major Sands did not hear him then, or he would have borne reports to Priscilla which must have destroyed her growing trust and confidence in de Bernis.

He painted word pictures for the men calculated to fire the gross appetites which he knew to be theirs, appetites which soon now they would have the means to glut. He thrilled them with the anticipation of the coarse delights which so much wealth would buy. They listened avidly in lawless, lewd anticipations he excited, and laughed with the unholy glee of the monstrous wicked, lawless children that they were at heart. It might be cruel to toil in this furnace, but soon there would be a golden unguent for their blistered backs. And, after all, they could take things easily. There was plenty of time before them. The plate fleet would not be putting to sea for another three weeks or so, and here at the Albuquerques they were within little more than a day's sailing of the spot where it was to be intercepted.

In this manner de Bernis intoxicated them with the prospect of the wealth that would be coming to each of them, and kept it clearly before the eyes of their minds that it was he, and nobody but he, would lead them to it.

Tom Leach, coming to learn that it was largely as a

result of the statements made by de Bernis that he found the men mutinously opposed to work during the heat of the day, came raging to him on the subject.

The Frenchman was not perturbed; he was airily platitudinous with proverbs about going surely by going slowly. He exasperated Leach by the opinion that there was plenty of time before them.

'Plenty o' time, ye daft loon? Time for what?'

'Before the plate fleet sails.'

'Damn the plate fleet!' swore Leach. 'Be that th' only fleet afloat? What of others as goes up and down the seas?'

'I see. You're afraid of being found here? Pshaw! You want to laugh, my friend. Be at ease. No ship is likely to come prowling into this cove.'

'Mebbe not. But if any did? What then, eh? Does thee think as I's comfortable here wi' ship high and dry, all helpless like? Plenty o' time, says you! Hell, man! I want to be on my keel again without no loss o' time. So I'll trouble thee not to go putting thee daft notions into folks' heads.'

De Bernis gave the required promise so as to pacify him. He gave it the more readily because the mischief was already done. Dilatoriness in that tropic heat accorded too well with the men's natural inclinations not to be indulged now that they had de Bernis' authoritative assertion that there was no need for any sweltering urgency.

Apart from that minor explosion from Leach, the first ten days on Maldita passed peacefully enough. By the end of that time, the burning and scraping on the hull was ended, and the carpenters could now get to work at caulking the seams, skilled labour this, which left the main body of the hands idle until they should presently come to the tarring and finally the greasing of the keel.

It was a time that naturally hung heavily upon the hands of Major Sands and Miss Priscilla, and more heavily perhaps on the soldier's than on the lady's. The Major, feeling the heat acutely as a result of his fleshly habit of body, waited in a condition of more or less complete inertness for the passage of time to bring him deliverance. The result of this was that his temper, naturally inclining to irascibility and querulousness, did not improve or dispose him to optimism concerning the future. Miss Priscilla, however, contrived to find for herself some occupation. She busied herself with Pierre in the preparation and cooking of food. She went out onto the reef with him, when he went fishing, and herself joined and found entertainment in the sport. Or she would go for excursions with him into the woods, in quest of yams and plantains, and once she crossed the island with him to its western side by a path which the half-caste had found over a long bald strip of ground reached within four or five hundred yards of the beach; a strip which thenceforward clove the dense jungle like an avenue, where only a thin layer of soil covered the rock, and, ascending towards the island's middle, sloped thence to the western shore, giving a backbone to Maldita.

Nor did she always take an escort on her excursions. In the early days on the island, she had wandered away by herself, climbing the reef and following the beach beyond it. Along this she had come upon a barrier of rock that rose like a wall some eight or nine feet high to bar her progress. Yet not to be so easily defeated, she had climbed the shallow bluff which rose here above the beach. From the summit, crowned with palms, with arnotto roses and scarlet hibiscus clustering about the boles, she had looked down into a little rock-bound cove and a limpid, sheltered pool within the embrace of it.

She must have come at least a mile from the encampment. She was quite alone; none ever came this way; and there was no remotest danger of surprise. So she yielded to the cool invitation of that pool, descended from the bluff, shed her light clothing on the sand where an overhanging rock made a sheltering canopy, and dived into the crystalline depths.

She came forth not only refreshed and invigorated, but enheartened by the discovery she had made. Under the friendly rock where her clothing lay, a rock which whilst giving shade was itself still hot from the passage of the sun, she let her body dry in the warm air, then resumed her garments, and made her way back to the encampment. Daily thereafter in the middle of the

110

morning she would disappear unostentatiously and alone. Making sure each time that she was not followed, she went to visit the bathing-pool of her discovery.

The disgruntled Major observing her comings and goings, or listening to her light chatter with Pierre when she was at work with him, or with de Bernis when he came to take his meals in the hut, marvelled that she could endure this state of things with so little apparent heaviness of heart. At moments he would ask himself whether such equanimity in adversity were not the result of an utter insensibility, an utter failure to apprehend the dangers by which she was surrounded and by which the Major was oppressed on her behalf. She could even laugh and at moments approach the borders of pertness with Tom Leach on those occasions, and they were none so rare, when he walked the length of the beach to pay them a visit.

If Monsieur de Bernis was not always there on these occasions, he had an uncanny trick of appearing suddenly amongst them, which the Major thought was just as well, for it saved him from the necessity of joining the conversation with that hawk-faced blackguard. He would sit sullenly by when Leach was with them, and if the pirate addressed him, as he occasionally did, the Major would answer gruffly in monosyllables, outraged in the soul of him that prudence should place him under the necessity of being even civil to such a scoundrel.

It was perhaps fortunate for him that Leach repaid contempt with contempt, regarding the Major as a negligible flabbiness without justification to existence save in the fact that he was brother to the delectable Madame de Bernis; though how this should happen, Leach could not begin to imagine. There was, he perceived, little resemblance to be traced between them. He startled them one day by saying so, adding, however, with heavy jocularity, that this was something for which the lady should daily give thanks to her Maker.

He made no attempt to dissemble his admiration for her, even when de Bernis was at hand. Nor did he confine himself to clumsy compliments. His attentions would take the shape now of a few bottles of Peruvian

111

wine, now of a box of guava cheese, or of almonds preserved in sugar, or some other delicacy from the landed stores of the Black Swan.

To Major Sands these attentions were infuriating, but not so infuriating as the apparent complacency with which Priscilla received them; for he lacked the wit to perceive the prudence which dictated her attitude towards the pirate. As for Monsieur de Bernis, he would lounge there at his ease, in the main indifferent and languid, but ever and anon pointedly asserting his position as a husband, and sometimes interposing it suddenly as a barrier when Leach's attentions approached the borders of excessiveness.

And Leach, thus checked, would turn upon him with the beginnings of a snarl, like that of a dog which sees a bone being snatched away from it. But under the languid, narrowed eyes of the long, saturnine Frenchman, the snarl would become a smile, half-mocking, half-cringing.

## 12

## The Guardian

THE infatuation of Tom Leach for the supposed Madame de Bernis—to employ a euphemistic indication of the emotions astir in his wild breast—became apparent to his officers. It was being treated by them with indifference, as merely a subject for lewd jests, until the shrewd-sighted Bundry pointed out the disadvantages that might result from it.

Alarmed by his cold reasoning, they improvised a council of war in the matter one day after dinner when the four of them were assembled with Leach in their hut.

Bundry was their spokesman, chosen because as fearless as he was passionless, he was the only one amongst them who dared to beard on so delicate a matter the violent Captain. The scarring by small-pox of his clay-coloured face had reduced it to a mask-like expressionlessness, which in itself made men apprehensive of him, for save in the twist of his lips or the gleam of his eyes, and this only when he so chose, he gave no indication of what might be passing in his mind. He had a clammy, chill, almost reptilian air, seeming utterly emotionless and as impervious to physical as to spiritual heat. In speech he was deliberate and precise, and he dressed his powerful stocky figure with a sober neatness, retained from the days when he had been a captain of merchantmen.

In that cold, deliberate voice of his and with that cold, deliberate manner he plainly and succinctly laid before the Captain their disapproval of the course his conduct appeared to be steering.

Leach flung into a hideous passion, roaring and snarling and threatening to rip the bowels out of any man who stood between him and his desires whatever they might be.

Wogan, Halliwell, and Ellis sat cowed under his ranting violence, beginning to regret that they should have brought up the subject.

But Bundry fixed him coldly with an eye as expressionless as a snake's, in the depths of which there dwelt perhaps some of that mesmeric power attributed to the colubrine gaze.

'Breathe your lungs, Captain. Breathe 'em freely. It may let out some o' the heat in ye. When ye're cooler, maybe ye'll listen to reason.'

'Reason? Damn reason!'

'That's what ye're doing,' said Bundry.

'Doing what?'

'Damning reason. And reason, I've noticed, ends by damning him that damns it. That's what'll happen to you, Captain, unless ye shorten sail.'

To Leach this sounded like a threat. If it did not diminish his wrath, at least, it abated his noise. He sat down again, and considered the pallid, almost sinister face before him with a malevolent glance.

'I's able enough to mind my own affairs, and I's not letting anyone else mind them for me. Understand that?'

'If it was a matter of your own affairs only,' said the phlegmatic Bundry, 'we'ld let you run aground, and be damned to you, Tom. But it happens also to be the affair of all of us. We're all in this bottom together, and we're not going to let any folly o' yours sink the ship before we've cast anchor in the golden harbour o' that Spanish treasure.'

'So it's by your leaves I move now, is it? It's what you'll let me do I must be minding, eh? By God, I wonder I don't pistol thee where thee sits, just to show who's master here.' He ran his wicked eyes over the others. 'And ye're all o' the same mind, I see,' he jeered at them.

It was Halliwell who nerved himself to answer. He slewed his corpulence forward on his chair, and leaned a massive arm on the table.

'Ye got to listen to reason, Cap'n. D'ye suppose Topgallant Charley don't notice what we're all noticing? And d'ye suppose he's the man to play tricks with? As dangerous a fellow under his pimpish clothes and cuckoldy fine manners as ever sailed the seas, and as ye should know, Tom.'

'Ah, bah! He's smooth enough wi' me. He dursn't be aught else.'

'Och, now, don't be deceiving yourself, Captain, darling,' flung in Wogan. 'Smooth he is, to be sure. But it's the smoothness of steel, not of velvet.'

'Why, ye poor gabies, he has a windpipe, I suppose.'

'What, then?' snapped Bundry, his voice harsh and dry.

'It'll slit as easily as another's. And that's what'll happen to it if Charley gets spry wi' me.'

'That,' said Bundry, 'is just what mustn't happen to it. He comes to us with the chance and secret of a fortune, and that's not to be put in jeopardy by any love-sick humours o' yours, Tom. Ye'd best remember it, and leave that woman of his alone.'

'And that's the fact,' said the fiery-faced Ellis. 'Until the treasure's under our hatches, ye'll have to curb your humours, Captain.'

'After that,' said Wogan to conciliate him, 'sure there's no one'll keep the doxy from you if you want her. It's only a little patience we're after asking of ye, Captain.'

Wogan laughed on that, and Ellis and Halliwell laughed with him, loud and heartily, thus breaking the restraint that had been growing there, and drawing, at last, an answering wicked smile from Leach.

But Bundry did not laugh. He was as rarely moved to laughter as to the display of any other emotion. His countenance remained a mask, his eyes—eyes that looked unnaturally black against the grey pallor of his seared face—riveting the Captain with that snake-like gaze, a queer, cold, compelling menace. This he maintained until with a jeer, representing it as a concession to their weak stomachs, Leach growled a contemptuous acquiescence in the circumspect course they thrust upon him.

The better to keep to his undertaking, the Captain did not that afternoon pay his usual visit to de Bernis' hut. When the next day came and went without his having crossed the brook which supplied a natural boundary to the buccaneer encampment, Priscilla ventured a comment upon it. She hoped that she might congratulate herself upon the Captain's abandonment of a habit which was as unpleasant as any experience that had yet been hers.

They had supped, and they were sitting in the little green bay before the hut, glad to breathe the cooling air of sunset. Neither of the men offered any comment upon Miss Priscilla's thanksgiving. A little spell of silence followed. But it appeared from the question presently asked by the Major that her words had touched off a train of thought in his mind. He turned to de Bernis, who sat on the lady's other side. The tone of this sorely tried man was querulous:

'Will you tell me, sir—it has long been in my mind to ask you—what you intend by us when you sail away on your thieving cruise against this Spanish fleet?'

Miss Priscilla frowned slightly in displeasure at the Major's tone and at the ruffling terms in which he chose to express himself.

As for Monsieur de Bernis, he seemed for once utterly taken aback by the soldier's question. It was a long moment before he commanded himself and smiled

115

his queer, slow smile. Then he spoke, but to evade, rather than to answer.

'Ah, Major! Are you very brave, I wonder; or just very stupid?'

'Sink me, sir!' spluttered the Major. 'I'll trouble you to explain yourself.'

'I mean, that sometimes you baffle me by the fanfaronade behind your foolish words.'

It took the Major a moment to recover his breath. 'Sir,' he said, 'I'll not take that from any man.'

'Indeed? You possess, then, the sole right to be provocative? A dangerous privilege. Especially here.' He rose to his feet, but lazily, half-stretching himself. 'I have already pointed out to you, my dear Bartholomew, that your preservation is the strongest proof you could possess of my good faith. But you should not abuse it.'

'Abuse it, sir?' The Major got up fuming, shaking off the restraining hand that the lady placed upon his arm. 'I asked you a plain question, and one to which both Miss Priscilla and I have the right, or so it seems to me, to an answer.'

'You asked it,' de Bernis answered him composedly, 'in uncivil and aggressive terms.'

'I call things by their proper names. By their proper names, blister me!'

De Bernis looked him over. 'Well, well! Be thankful that I don't return the compliment.'

He bowed in leave-taking to Miss Priscilla, put on his plumed hat, and sauntered off in the direction of the buccaneer encampment.

By the time the Major had recovered, de Bernis was twenty yards away. Even then he might have gone after him but for Miss Priscilla's almost stern command to him to sit down. He obeyed her mechanically, exploding as he did so.

'It's not be borne. Stab me! I'll not endure his insolence.'

'Why do you provoke it?' Miss Priscilla's cool voice asked him. 'Why not practise courtesy with him? Or don't you think that we owe him enough to warrant it?'

Her sarcasm added fuel to his anger. 'You defend

116

the knave! It is all that was wanting. You defend him, and against me. Me! In God's name, ma'am, what is he to you, this swaggering pirate hound?'

But Miss Priscilla remained as cool as if she had taken de Bernis for her model in deportment.

'That is not at all the question. The question is what he may be to you if you spare no pains to offend him. He has already made clear to you what should have been plain: that if he were indeed what you insist upon supposing him, he would already have disposed of your inconvenient and ungracious person.'

'Fan me, ye winds!' cried Major Sands, and stamped off before he should utter in the presence of a lady that which a gentleman might afterwards regret.

He found her utterly exasperating. The question that he had asked de Bernis was one that concerned her very closely. Life and death and even more might be involved in it; and yet, as if she did not understand the gravity of the case, she was attaching importance only to his manner, as if that were of any consequence where the matter was so perilous.

But in this the Major did her a serious injustice. She had certainly attached importance to his manner, and she censured it, because she realized the futility of alienating, perhaps exasperating, Monsieur de Bernis, upon whose good-will they depended so entirely, a good-will in which her belief was something more than instinctive. At the same time she had perceived not only the importance of the question asked by Major Sands, but also Monsieur de Bernis' evasion of it; and she was left wondering whether the evasion were simply the result of an irritation caused by the tactless tone the Major adopted, or whether there might be a deeper reason for it. Anxieties which had grown dormant lately, in this peaceful interlude, reawakened in her. She sought to allay them.

That night whilst de Bernis was sleeping at his post before the curtain of her hut, a hand descended gently upon his shoulder. Light as the touch was, he awakened so instantly that it was plain some part of his senses remained on guard even whilst he slept. In the instantaneous act of sitting up, he flung wide the cloak in which he was wrapped, and the moonlight gleamed

117

lividly upon a naked blade. He slept with his drawn sword beside him.

He found Miss Priscilla leaning over him, vaguely visible, a finger to her lips. He looked round swiftly in quest of what might have alarmed her. But all was still; the soft thud and rustle of the tide upon the beach and the resonant snores from the Major's tent were the only sounds upon the stillness of the night.

'What is it?' he softly asked, one leg already drawn under him to bring him to his feet.

A sibilant 'Hush!' reassured him. His muscles, gathered for the spring, relaxed. 'I want to talk to you, Monsieur de Bernis.'

'At your service,' said he.

He changed his position, so as to come to sit with his back to the hut, and she sat down beside him. It was a moment or two before she found opening words.

'Bart asked you a question today. You did not answer it. The terms he chose may be to blame. Naturally they offended you.'

'Ah, no,' he answered softly, subduing his voice to the pitch of her own. 'If a man is an oaf he offends himself, not me.'

She began to explain the Major, to make excuses for him, to account for his peremptoriness on the ground partly of the ways of life he had trodden, partly of the anxieties which were racking him on her behalf.

'This is not necessary, Miss Priscilla,' he presently interrupted her. 'I am not seriously perturbed; in fact, I am not perturbed at all. "Prevail by patience," is the motto of my house, and I have taken it for the guiding maxim of my life. I am not a man of senseless rages and swift fury, I do assure you.'

'There is not the need to assure me,' said she. 'I had observed it.'

She observed also now the oddness of this situation in which she found herself, and the oddness of hearing a man who had lived by lawlessness and who even now was a self-confessed pirate planning a raid upon a Spanish fleet, speaking demurely of his house and its lofty motto. The oddness lay in that whilst glaringly incongruous it seemed to hold no incongruity.

She did not, however, dwell upon the thought. She

had sought him here for a definite purpose, and this purpose she now pursued.

'You did not answer Bart's question,' she said again. 'It concerned, you'll remember, your intentions for us when you depart with these men upon this raid. Will you give me the answer now?'

That answer came after a thoughtful pause.

'I wait upon events.'

'Yet you must have some plan in mind, some project,' she pressed him. And after another pause in which he did not reply, she added softly: 'Hitherto I have completely trusted you. It is in this that I have found such peace as is possible in these conditions.'

'And now you trust me no longer.'

'Oh, not that. I should be in despair if that were so. But you'll understand my anxieties even if I have spared you the display of them.'

'You have been very brave in that. Oh, but singularly brave.' There was admiration approaching reverence in his tone. 'Your courage has helped me more than you suppose. Continue by it to help me, you will be helping me to help you.'

'Yet you will tell me nothing of your intentions? The knowledge would be a strength to me.'

'I have said that I wait upon events. But this I'll add: I firmly and honestly believe that you have no cause for any apprehension. It is my belief that I shall bring you safely through. I swear to do so if I live.'

'If you live!'

In the gloom he heard the catch in her breath, the sudden tremulousness of her tone. He made haste to reassure her. 'I should not have added that. It is idle to introduce a fresh doubt of your fate among all the anxieties troubling you.' And with a firm confidence he added: 'I shall live. Don't doubt it.'

'A fresh doubt of my fate!' she echoed. A half-laugh escaped her. 'How meanly you think of me!'

'Meanly?' he cried, his accent a protest. He did not understand. Nor did she enlighten him, although her next question was concerned with his preservation.

'Can you trust these men to keep faith with you? When the Spanish fleet is taken?'

He laughed softly. 'I am sure that I cannot. Once

119

there was honour among buccaneers. But today . . . And this beast Leach! He knows as much of honour as of mercy or of decency. Oh, no. They have no intention to keep faith with me.'

Alarm and bewilderment robbed her of breath. 'But then? If that is so, what hope have you?'

'The hope of prevailing by my wits. A very confident hope. Opportunity will present itself. It always does; but we do not always recognize it unless we are watching for it. And I am watching. Dismiss your alarms, madam. Only an extraordinary malignity of Fortune could thwart me. And Fortune surely could never be malign to you.'

'You will tell me nothing more?'

'At present there is nothing more to tell. But again I bid you to have faith in me, and to be confident that I shall bring you through unharmed.'

She was silent awhile. Then she sighed. 'Very well,' she breathed. 'Good-night, Monsieur de Bernis.'

Long after she had gone, he still sat there, thoughtful, where she had left him. His mind was busy with a problem, seeking the explanation of her outcry: 'How meanly you think of me!' Unless she meant that he thought meanly of her in thinking that her concern for his life was grounded solely in concern for her own, what else could she mean? And how could she possibly mean that?

13

*Lacrimae Rerum*

ON THE following morning, whilst Major Sands was sulking, like Achilles, in his tent, a shadow fell across the entrance, and Monsieur de Bernis stood before him in black silhouette against the sunlight. He carried his sheathed rapier tucked under his arm.

'I have observed, Major, that you grow too fat,' was the greeting with which he startled the soldier. 'You need to sweat a little, and to stretch your limbs. It will mend your humours. Take up your sword, and come with me.'

The Major, remembering the sharp words that had passed between them yesterday, conceived in this a derisory invitation to an adjustment of their differences. He got to his feet, with quickened breath and deepening colour.

'Blister me, sir! D'ye seek to put a quarrel on me? Have ye thought what will happen if I kill you?'

'I never build conjectures on the impossible.'

'By God, sir, your insolence is not to be borne! Not to be borne!' He snatched up sword and sword-belt. 'Have with you, then, whatever the consequences.'

Monsieur de Bernis sighed. 'Always will you be misunderstanding me. I propose exercise, and you talk of killing.'

'Whatever you propose, I am your man, stab me.'

They went out together, the Major breathing gustily, de Bernis calm and apparently amused.

Their departure was unwitnessed by Miss Priscilla, and so that it should go unperceived by others, de Bernis penetrated the woods for some little distance; then, under cover of the trees, led the way along a line parallel with the shore.

They went in silence until the Major, suspecting that they were being followed, halted to look behind him.

'It is only Pierre,' said de Bernis, without looking round. 'He comes to see that we are not interrupted.'

The Major plunged on, mystified, indignant, yet with no thought of avoiding an encounter upon which the other appeared determined, whatever might be the consequences. He panted up the rising ground that ran inwards from the bluff, and was bathed in perspiration by the time de Bernis had brought him out onto the little beach beyond it, and screened by it from the encampment of the buccaneers. On the summit of the bluff the Major saw now the figure of Pierre, and understood that he was posted there on guard.

Monsieur de Bernis removed his baldrick and drew his sword. The Major copied him in silence. Then from

121

his pocket the Frenchman took a piece of wood that was shaped like a tiny pear, with a slot opened at its apex. Into this slot, under the Major's bulging, uncomprehending eyes, he fitted the point of his sword, then tapped down the little wooden pear securely with a stone which he picked up from the beach.

'What the devil's this?' quoth the Major.

Monsieur de Bernis brought forth a second wooden object like the first and proffered it.

'Did you suppose I brought you on a blood-letting? Our situation will hardly admit of it, whatever may be your feelings. I told you you need to breathe your lungs, and stretch your limbs, and sweat a little.'

But now the Major, who was already sweating freely and at every pore and who conceived himself mocked, flung into a real passion.

'What the devil do you mean, sir? D'ye rally me? D'ye practise jests upon me?'

'Oh, but a little calm,' the other begged. 'The need for blood-letting may yet be thrust upon us. We rust for lack of practice. I do, if you do not, Major. That is all.' And more insistently he proffered the wooden pear again.

Between doubt and understanding the Major slowly took the object.

'I see,' he said, which was an obvious overstatement. 'It is for practice that you bring me here?' And he grumbled: 'You should have made it plainer.'

'Could I suppose that it was not plain?' De Bernis was beginning to remove his doublet.

The Major was glad enough to copy him in this. Then, as the thought of what they came to do grew upon him, a certain grim satisfaction grew with it. He had notions of himself as a swordsman. In younger days, at home, he had been the deadliest blade of his regiment. He would show this Frenchman something that would let him see that Major Sands was not a man with whom it was prudent to take liberties.

At last, stripped to the waist, they faced each other and came on guard.

The Major intent upon a brave display, attacked at once and fiercely. But whether he thrust or lunged, he remained always outside the guard of an opponent, who never once broke ground, however pressed. Notwithstanding this, the Frenchman remained so strictly upon the defensive as to leave the Major under the delusion that the ardour of his attack was so constraining his opponent. Thus until he found himself sharply admonished.

'More speed, Major. More speed, I beg. Press harder. You are giving me nothing to do.'

Goaded by what seemed a taunt, Major Sands momentarily increased the ferocity of his onslaught. But it spent itself idly against that guard, which, so swift, seemed yet so effortless.

Winded by his supreme exertion, the Major fell back to breathe, and lowered his point. The sweat ran from his cropped head—for they had removed their periwigs together with their upper garments. He dashed it from his brow with the back of his hand, and glared at the tall, lithe Frenchman, who remained so cool and whose breathing scarcely appeared to have quickened. Of what was the man made, that neither heat nor movement could leave an impression upon him?

He smiled into the Major's flushed, choleric face. 'You realize how urgent was your need to exercise yourself. I was right, you see. You are in even worse case than I. Lack of practice has made you slow.'

Sullenly the Major admitted it. And he knew it to be true. But he also began to suspect that at his speediest and best he would never have got past that guard, and the suspicion left his spirit wounded and resentful.

Presently when he regained his breath they resumed. But now de Bernis' tactics were quite different. Again the Major opened by attacking. But this time, in meeting a low thrust with a counter-parry which restored the blades to the line of the original engagement, the Frenchman straightened his arm in a riposte that made the Major jump backwards so as to avoid the point.

Monsieur de Bernis laughed. 'Too much effort,' he criticized. 'Play closer, Major. Keep the elbow nearer to your flank.' He went in to engage him, deflected a thrust intended to stop him, extended himself in a lunge, and hit the Major full upon the stomach.

They fell on guard again, and again, with the same ease de Bernis touched him. After that a series of swift disengages reduced the Major to utter impotency, at the culmination of which de Bernis inside his guard touched him upon his defenceless breast with the utmost deliberation.

'Assez,' he said, straightening himself. His own breath was coming more quickly now. 'For today, it is enough. I am less rusty than I feared. But not as keen as I should be; as I may need to be. Tomorrow we will try again, as much for your sake as for mine, Major. In your present condition I should tremble for you if you were opposed to a swordsman of any force at all.'

The Major was trembling for himself; trembling with suppressed anger. He had the sense to perceive that the expression of it must merely render him ridiculous. He sat down upon the beach to let his overheated body cool before resuming his clothes, whilst de Bernis, divesting himself of what garments he still retained, plunged into the sea to refresh himself.

They came back towards noon for dinner, with little said between them, the Major's indignation still simmering. It was not merely that he was under the humiliation of having been made to realize that the swordsmanship he had imagined so expert was rendered puerile by contrast with that of his opponent, but that he nourished a strong suspicion that Monsieur de Bernis had deliberately invited him to that passage at arms so as to intimidate him with an exposition of what must happen to him if he should permit acrimony seriously to embroil them.

By this conviction and the resentment springing from it, Major Sands added to the contempt in which he already held de Bernis for a thieving, cut-throat pirate, a further measure of contempt for being a posturing mountebank.

Fortunately, however, the indignation, which only their circumstances compelled him to repress, was diminished, together with that first impression of the Frenchman's motives, when on each of the next three mornings he was invited and went to repeat that practice in swordsmanship. Gradually he was brought to change his view and to believe that, after all, de Bernis had no object to serve beyond perfecting himself by practice against emergencies and inducing the Major to

124

do the same. In this growing conviction he became more tolerant of the Frenchman's hints and criticisms, and even began to seek to profit by them. But underneath it all a certain resentment still remained at the manner which de Bernis had adopted at the outset, and this prevented any softening of the Major's deep-rooted dislike for him.

Oddly enough, the growing friendliness between de Bernis and Miss Priscilla contributed little or nothing to these feelings. The easy and, in the Major's view, impudent familiarity of the Frenchman's bearing towards her, and her own apparent lack of resentment of this, was an irritation to him, it is true. But this merely because he perceived it to spring from a less perfect dignity on the part of Priscilla than he desired in the lady who was destined one day to become his wife. Jealousy never even tinged his emotions. It was too inconceivable that Miss Priscilla should ever lose sight of the social abyss that separated her from such a man as de Bernis.

He did not know—for he slept soundly now—that ever since that first occasion when anxiety had urged her, it had become her nightly habit, when all was still, to slip out of the tent, and to sit and talk there with the guardian of her threshold. Possibly it would not deeply have exercised him if he had known of it, provided that he had known at the same time of what they talked. For certainly these interviews were innocent of obvious tenderness. Commonly they were concerned with the events of the day. Nor were these always as trivial as might be supposed. One day, for instance—it was a Saturday, their fourteenth day upon Maldita—a riot had broken out among the buccaneers, which at one moment had threatened to split them into two opposing factions. One of the men had stabbed another, as a result of a quarrel over dice. Sides had been taken, and anger spreading like wildfire amongst those lawless men, a battle had begun to rage upon the beach.

Leach and his officers had flung themselves into the mêlée, and with voice and fists had sought to quell the riot. If they had not completely succeeded in restoring peace, at least they had secured an armistice, during

125

which Leach might hear the facts and pronounce upon them. But Leach had refused to do anything of the kind, refused to listen to the pleas either of those who demanded the life of the murderer, whose name was Shore, or of those who asserted that the murdered man was to blame for having accused Shore of cheating and smothered him in intolerable insult.

'It's no time to fall a-quarrelling among ourselves,' he told them. 'Keep your tempers and your knives for the Spaniards. No more o' this now.'

But they surged angrily clamant about him. As their captain it was his place to pass judgment. Unless he did so they would, themselves, do justice.

Leach's reluctance sprang from his perception that, however he delivered himself, he would have to face the hostility of the party opposed to his decision.

'There's a man dead,' he growled at them. 'Rot you in hell! Isn't that enough?'

Monsieur de Bernis, surging amongst them, no man knew whence, was speaking, and they fell silent to hear what he might have to say, the regard which he had known how to inspire in them asserting itself.

'There's a simple way of resolving the dispute, Tom,' said he.

'Ah! And what may that be?' Leach displayed no satisfaction at this uninvited intervention.

'The only fit judges are those who were witnesses to the quarrel.'

A roar approved him. When it had ceased, he continued:

'They are here, a full score of them. The dispute concerns none else. Let them decide whether Shore is to be hanged or not. Let it be decided on a show of hands, with the undertaking from the rest that they'll abide by the decision.'

It was a way out that commended itself to Leach, for it delivered him from the undesired responsibility. To his question based on de Bernis' suggestion, they readily gave their assent to abide by the decision of the majority, and by this they abode with that queer loyalty to a contract which the buccaneers could observe. The show of hands went against Shore. He was taken and hanged forthwith, and peace was at once restored in the encampment.

It was the mystery of this which Monsieur de Bernis expounded that night to Miss Priscilla, who could not understand the submissiveness of those who had so violently taken up the cudgels on the murderer's behalf.

'It was not his life that had concerned them,' he explained. 'Life is cheap enough amongst them at all times. It was the principle involved that mattered and over which they were quarrelling. The vote offered an equitable solution, and they had bound themselves to accept it.'

This led to questions from her and a lengthy dissertation from him upon the bonds and engagements recognized and respected by even the most lawless among buccaneers. Thus, since he was led into delving into past experiences of his own, she drew him into reminiscences which afforded her further glimpses of what his life had been. For always was it of himself that she contrived to make him talk.

One night—the seventeenth spent upon Maldita as he afterwards remembered, the date being fixed in his memory by that which happened on the morrow—she directly questioned him upon his future. Was it his intention indefinitely to prolong this dangerous roving life?

'Ah, that, no. Already you may account it closed. This business upon which I am now embarked will certainly see the end. I am troubled with nostalgy. It has been growing of late. It is quite true that I told Morgan my only desire is to quit the Caribbean and return home. At need I'll even change my religion, like Henry IV, so that I may tread the blessed soil of France again, see the vines and olives growing upon the hillside and hear the sweet accent of the Toulousain.'

He spoke in a softened, wistful voice, ended on a sigh, and fell silent, musing.

'I understand,' she said gently. 'But to change your religion? The call of country must be strong.'

He considered that, and suddenly laughed, but muting his mirth so as not to disturb the Major who slept in his tent a dozen yards away.

'It is as if a naked man were to speak of changing his coat. What hypocrites most of us are where faith is concerned. With the life that lies behind me I can still dwell on mine, and speak of changing it, as if some sacrifice were entailed.'

It was the first time that she had heard from him even an implied disparagement of his past. Hitherto he had spoken of it almost with complacency, as if piracy were a normal career, as if he saw in it nothing at which to take shame.

'You are still young enough,' she said, answering that thought of hers rather than his last words, 'to build anew.'

'But what shall I build me out of the materials I take with me from the Old World? Every man, remember, builds his future from the materials supplied him by his past.'

'Not entirely, surely. There are the materials he finds in his path as he advances. These may suffice him. You will make a family for yourself . . .'

He interrupted her at the very beginning of her picture of that future.

'A family? I?'

'But why not, then?'

'Do you conclude that all that may once have been decent and sound in me has been utterly stifled by the wild life I have lived?'

'I know the contrary.'

'How do you know it?'

'I have the evidence of my senses. I know you. I have come to know you a little, I think, in these few weeks. But what has that to do with my question?'

'This. What sort of a mother am I to find for my children?'

'I don't understand. That surely is matter for your own decision.'

'It is not. It has been decided for me. My past decides it. Unless I am to woo in disguise, pretending myself something that I am not. I have killed. I have plundered. I have done dreadful things, unutterable things. I have even amassed some wealth. I own lands,

128

in Jamaica and elsewhere, with plantations and the like. My proper mate among women would be some unfortunate soulless drab who would be indifferent to the source of the money that will support us. I am not so lost—lost though I may be—as to give such a mother to my children. Nor yet am I so lost as to presume to woo any woman of another kind. It is the only honesty remaining me; the last frail link with honour. If that were to snap, then should I be damned, indeed. No, no, sweet lady, whatever I may find to build in the Old World if I reach it, certainly it will not be a family.'

He had spoken with a deep, moving bitterness, different far from his habitual manner which alternated between hardness and flippancy, and commonly presented a blend of the two. A silence followed, and endured for some time. It endured until something light and moist dropped upon his left hand where it rested on his knee.

Startled he turned to her, sitting so close to him and leaning a little forward and sideways.

'Priscilla!' he breathed, tremulously, touched in his turn to discover that he should so profoundly have moved her pity.

She rose swiftly, hastily, as if in confusion. 'Goodnight!' she murmured in a small, quick voice. The heavy curtain rustled, and he was alone.

But with his head turned to the entrance, he called softly after her.

'I thank you for that tear dropped on the grave of a lost soul.'

Then he bore that left hand of his to his lips, and held it there.

Long afterwards, he was to confess that when he fell asleep that night under the stars, it was with the feeling that some of the vileness had been washed from him by a woman's compassionate tear.

In the Toulousain a hundred and fifty years before there had been a de Bernis who was a poet of some merit. I suspect that something of his spirit survived in this buccaneering descendant of his.

## 14

# The Nymph and the Satyr

WHEN Major Sands and Monsieur de Bernis came to break their fast in the hut next morning, Miss Priscilla met de Bernis with a complaint concerning Pierre.

This was the third morning in succession that the half-caste had been absent when breakfast was to be prepared, with the result that she had been alone in preparing it.

'He is nowhere to be seen. Each day he does not appear again until close upon noon. What can he be doing? Where does he go?'

'He is seeking yams, perhaps,' de Bernis replied casually.

'If so, he never seems to find any. Both yesterday and the day before I saw him return, and he came empty-handed from the woods.'

'Perhaps the yams are becoming scarce, and he is driven farther afield in his search for them.'

His apparent indifference to his servant's evasion of duty seemed curious to her, as he might have read in the glance with which she searched his face.

'Could he not leave those quests until after we have broken our fast?'

'Perhaps he likes to find the yams still moist with morning dew.'

At this absurdity her stare became more marked. 'I wonder why you should jest about it.'

'In our situation there are so few things that lend themselves for jesting that I may surely be forgiven if I neglect none of these few. But I will speak to Pierre. I will see what can be arranged.'

This, she thought, was an oddly offhand way to treat the matter, of slight importance though it might be. And to say no more in conclusion than to promise to see what could be arranged, when a simple word from him could remove the cause of her complaint, seemed almost discourteously casual. She pressed the matter no further; but a sense of annoyance remained with her.

Later in the course of the morning, the Major and the Frenchman went off to their daily secret sword-play beyond the bluff.

Captain Leach was strolling alone at the time on the damp firm sands at the very edge of the receding tide, a vivid figure in his scarlet suit. Impatient to be afloat again, and so safe from surprise, he came from urging the men in the completion of the work; for now that the tarring of the hull was finished, only the greasing remained to be done, and in three days, or four at the most, the Black Swan should be ready for launching again.

From where he paced he saw the two men move away from their sequestered little camp and disappear into the woods. He had already observed these morning absences of theirs, and he halted, wondering vaguely whither they went. When his attention was attracted by the green-clad figure of Priscilla Harradine coming forth from her hut. From the distance he watched that trim, graceful shape with eyes of kindling admiration. He watched her turn to the right, and set out briskly, like one who was guided by a definite purpose. She proceeded for some little way along the summit of the beach, then she, too, vanished into the wood.

From wondering whither she might be going so unfalteringly and definitely, he reached almost at once the desire to ascertain. Resentment of the barrier raised against his attentions to the lady had never ceased to smoulder in him; and it was accompanied by a growing impatience for the time when, the business of the Spanish plate fleet being concluded, this barrier would definitely be removed. It had not often happened to Tom Leach to be under the necessity of restraining his lusts, and he remained unschooled as a savage in the art of it. Also, as is the way of unruly, undisciplined men, he must ever be preferring that which lay under his hand at the moment to the greater things that might be achieved by planning and waiting. It is an indication of his rudimentary intelligence.

It is doubtful, therefore, whether in obeying now the unreasoned instinct to follow her, he was prompted only by curiosity on the score of her movements.

In long, swift strides he crossed the beach diagonally, straight to the palm tree with the arnotto roses clustering about its stem by which he had marked the spot at which she had vanished into the wood. Once himself under the shelter of the trees, he had little difficulty in picking up her trail. It was plainly marked in the undergrowth, thinner on the edges of this jungle than in the depths of it.

Cautiously, unhurried, but purposefully now as a hound upon a spoor he followed. The trail led upwards over rising ground. At the summit of this, the hard dry earth between the sparser palms was almost bare, and the trail lost its distinctness; he quested there for some moments, to be led eventually towards the open by signs which might be those of someone's recent passage that way. But having reached the edge of the bluff, he was entirely at fault. She was nowhere to be seen. Below him, like a gigantic emerald set in a vast cup of rock, he beheld a pool so clear that through its smooth, unruffled surface he could see the fish moving in the depths of it. Saving the unsuspected little platform under the black canopy of rock immediately beneath him, he could survey not merely the beach of this tiny cove, but long stretches of sand beyond the barriers of rock on either side of it, and nowhere in sight was Miss Priscilla.

He concluded that she must have continued through the wood, and went back to endeavour to pick up the trail again. Ahead, where the ground began gently to slope once more and the undergrowth increased again, he saw signs that it had been trampled, and cursing the time he had wasted, he was moving forward, when suddenly a splash below, too loud to have been made by any leaping fish, arrested him.

He turned. He saw wavelets moving outwards in widening circles, from some point which the rock screened from his gaze, rippling the mirror-like surface of the pool. A moment later, whilst he was staring frowning inquiry, he saw that which made him catch his breath, and instinctively drop upon hands and knees amongst the trees so as to avoid, himself, being seen. A nymph of an incredible whiteness was swimming out across the tiny lagoon. As beheld through the water, her limbs seemed of marble.

Leach, so pale through his tan that his countenance seemed almost green, feasted hot eyes upon that vision of incredible loveliness. At one moment he made an animal noise, something between a grunt and a groan, and held his nether lip thereafter caught in his strong white teeth.

As she turned to swim back, he dropped still lower, into a supine position. In this, wriggling upon his belly like a snake, he thrust himself forward to the very edge of the bluff, above which, had she looked up, she would have beheld no more than his head from the eyes upwards. Thus he remained until she had passed again under the screening canopy.

He scrambled to his feet then, and took off his hat to dash the perspiration from his face. That face, leering now like a satyr's, was at the same time overcast with thought. His little eyes were narrowed and calculating. There was blood on his lip where his teeth had fastened on it, and a little trickle of blood was on his black tuft of beard.

In that moment de Bernis, the Spanish plate fleet, his officers, his lawless followers and the account they might demand of him if the enterprise of the plate fleet were now wrecked, had ceased to be of any deterring account. All that he considered was whether he should leap down from that bluff or fall back and wait here among the friendly shelter of the trees. In the end he decided for the trees, and went recklessly crashing through the undergrowth to conceal himself amongst them.

Livid, panting, his heart beating in his throat, he crouched there waiting, a beast in ambush for its prey.

At last she came. He saw first her head, that golden head about which the sunlight seemed now to place an aureole, and then her bust, and gradually the whole of her, as, demurely clad once more in her gown of green,

133

she reached the summit of the bluff, from which the path ran back to the encampment.

His pulses galloped. Pausing there just beyond the screen of trees, she whipped up by that pause his intolerable impatience. But he knew that he could afford to wait a little moment longer, wait until she had come within that green shelter, when she would no longer be within range of any stray eyes from the encampment.

But, as if further to try his patience, she remained poised there, looking away to her left, down the southern slope. And when at last she stepped under, within shadow of the palms, she was still half-turning to the left, and as she advanced, to his unutterable rage and horror, she flung up an arm as if in greeting and beckoning, and he heard her voice suddenly raised to call.

'Pierre! D'où viens tu à cette heure-ci?'

A moment later his furious eyes beheld the half-caste advancing rapidly with that long, loping stride of his, and answering her as he came, though what he said, Leach in his seething, baffled rage, neither heard nor cared.

Not until Pierre was at last level with her did she turn to her right, and set out along the path by which she had come, the tall, lithe half-caste, in his cotton shirt and rawhide breeches, trotting after her.

Tom Leach made animal noises through his clenched teeth as he stepped forth from his ambush, and moved to follow them. For once he was utterly without weapons, otherwise it is possible that he might in his madness have added murder to what else he contemplated. As it was, the long athletic limbs of the half-caste made him think twice about falling upon him with his bare hands.

He paused a moment on the path, watching them as they receded and widened the distance between themselves and him. Then, without precautions, since he was no longer the stalker, he set out to follow. Instantly the head of the alert Pierre was turned to look over his shoulder. Having seen who came, and no doubt reported it, the two went on without change of pace, whilst

Leach with a leisurely step kept in their wake, carrying hell in his evil soul.

By the time the Captain came level with the hut, Miss Priscilla had already entered it. From his tent, a little farther on, Pierre was in the act of taking the fresh-water cask, to go and replenish it. He delayed but a moment over this, and was off again, almost at once, along the beach.

The Captain checked in renewed hope. Opportunity, it seemed, was to serve him, after all.

He allowed Pierre to go some little way, before deliberately advancing to come and place himself before the entrance of the hut, from which the heavy curtain was lifted.

Within stood Miss Priscilla with comb in one hand and a hand-mirror in the other, to repair the disorder in her moist hair. As the buccaneer's shadow fell across the threshold, she looked up quickly. Seeing him, his face still oddly pallid, his eyes glowing curiously, she stood at gaze, incomprehensibly perturbed.

He showed his white teeth in a wide smile, and doffed the hat from his short curly black hair.

'God save ye, mistress,' was his odd greeting.

And then before she could even answer him, the crisp voice and light, ready laugh of Monsieur de Bernis sounded close at hand, reassuringly to herald his opportune return.

In the darkening brows and harshly twisted features of Tom Leach she read the need for that reassurance.

As the Captain stepped back, Monsieur de Bernis and Major Sands came up.

'Ah, Tom,' was the Frenchman's easy greeting, 'were you seeking me?'

'Seeking thee?' the other was beginning in scornful, fierce repudiation. But he controlled himself in time. 'Aye,' he added slowly.

'What is it?'

'Why, naught. I were just passing by, so thought I'd see if thee was here. We never sees thee at th' camp nowadays. We hasn't seen thee for days.'

After that, dissembling ever, he spoke grumblingly of the progress of the work. It went slowly. It would be another four days, perhaps five, before they could get the ship afloat again. Was de Bernis quite certain that they were not behind time?

De Bernis reassured him. The appointed date for the sailing of the plate fleet was the third of July. It was certain that it would not sail before that date, probable that it would not sail until a few days later. No Spaniard was ever known to be ahead of time. Procrastination was in the blood of Spain. In twenty-four hours Leach could easily reach the point at which de Bernis proposed to intercept the Spanish ships, and he would prefer not to take the seas any earlier than was necessary.

With mutterings of reassurance, Leach took his departure. But de Bernis did not immediately turn, or immediately speak when he had gone. He remained standing there, looking after him with brooding, thoughtful eyes. He had discovered something queer, something uncomfortable, furtive, and constrained in the Captain's manner, qualities these not usually displayed by him.

At last Monsieur de Bernis turned to Priscilla. 'Of what was he speaking when we arrived?' he abruptly asked her.

'You did not give him time to speak of anything. You were here as soon as he had greeted me.' She laughed as she answered him, and scarcely knew why. All that she knew was that she wanted to laugh, in the sudden relief from the indefinable fear which the sight of Captain Leach's face had inspired in her.

'I have spoken to Pierre about his morning absences,' she went on to say. 'But he gives me no satisfaction.'

'He has returned?' said de Bernis; and added sharply, 'Where is he?'

'He has gone for water. He will he here soon.'

'Gone for water?' de Bernis echoed, and his tone had changed. The eagerness that momentarily had gleamed in his eyes died out of them again. He shrugged as he turned away, leaving her alone with the Major.

She had missed none of this, being naturally alert. Trifling though it seemed, there was something odd in it, and it left her preoccupied, returning vague answers

136

to the Major's idle chatter, as he sat there cooling himself in the shade of the hut.

Monsieur de Bernis had gone to Pierre's tent. He remained there until Pierre returned, bearing the refilled water-cask on his choulder.

Watching and listening, she heard de Bernis greet him.

'Eh bien?' And the Frenchman's dark eyes might almost have seemed anxious as they scanned the half-caste's face.

Pierre lowered his water-cask to the ground. 'Still nothing, monsieur,' Miss Priscilla heard him reply in French.

'Sh!' De Bernis dropped his voice, and muttered rapidly, almost it seemed impatiently, ill-humouredly. She wondered was his master speaking to Pierre about his early absences. But from the manner in which the conversation had opened, she could hardly suppose it. She strained her ears. Probably it never crossed her mind that she was spying; had it done so, she would have accounted that all the circumstances justified it. The Major's chatter prevented her from hearing more than the murmur of those rapid voices. But in a pause he made, she caught again the voice of de Bernis.

'We have still five days, according to Leach, and the weather is fine.'

'Too fine, perhaps,' said Pierre. 'It may be that.'

Again they became inaudible, and so continued until de Bernis turned away, and came slowly back, his fingers tugging thoughtfully at his nether lip.

If de Bernis had admonished Pierre at all about his absences, the admonition produced no change in his habits. For when on the following morning, being dressed, Miss Priscilla lifted the curtain from her door, and called Pierre, it was de Bernis who came from his tent, dressed only in shirt and breeches, and carrying a tray that was laden with the requisites for breakfast.

'Monsieur de Bernis!' she cried. 'But where is Pierre again?'

Smiling and speaking easily, Monsieur de Bernis replied: 'I have sent him on an errand, Priscilla. But I will help you to contrive without him.'

'You have sent him on an errand? But on what errand could you send him?'

'Lord! Here's curiosity!' he laughed. 'Shall I indulge it? Faith, not I. He has gone on an errand. That is all. Come, let us make ready before that ravenous wolf the Major awakens to be fed.'

And that was all she could elicit from him, to her annoyance and even uneasiness; for her environment and circumstance were not such as made it possible to bear with equanimity a mystery, however trivial it might seem.

## 15

## *Pearls*

TOM LEACH, deliberately and calculatingly watchful, observed from a distance the departure that morning of Major Sands and de Bernis. He recognized it to be in accordance with a daily habit that had become established, just as he knew that their absence commonly endured for a couple of hours. Curiosity as to whither they went so regularly had never really pricked him. After all, within the limits of Maldita it could have no significance.

If curiosity had not been aroused before, it was certainly not aroused this morning. Since yesterday the buccaneer had been wrapped in a moody absorption which seemed to render him indifferent to his surroundings. The disturbing vision of the bathing-pool abode with him so that he could see nothing else. Before his eyes swam ever the incredible beauty of that slim form, with limbs, seen through water, as white and smooth as alabaster, a loveliness such as Tom Leach had never suspected to exist in nature. To the feverish, gloating contemplation with the eyes of memory of that irresistibly alluring vision was added an unreasoning, savage, torturing rage at the chance frustration yesterday of his intentions, and an unreasoning, savage, blind resolve to take amends for that at the first opportunity.

Congreve had not yet written that line so apposite to Captain Leach's case: 'Woman is a fair image in a pool; he who leaps at her is sunk.' But if he had written it, and Captain Leach, acquainted with it, had perceived in it a warning to him now, in a double sense of which the poet had no thought, he must still have disregarded it. For if, contrary to custom where his lusts were concerned, the buccaneer may have chanced to weigh the consequences of what he contemplated, it follows that they did not daunt him.

It was within those consequences—unless he were exceptionally fortunate—that he would have to reckon with de Bernis. But when had he ever shrunk from a reckoning? What man had ever made him quail, or deviate by a hand's breadth from an evil goal? He would take a short way with that impudent, supercilious Frenchman whose days, indeed, were already numbered.

To Bartholomew Sands he did not even give a thought. The fellow was utterly negligible. And he would have accounted de Bernis just as negligible save that the consequences of quieting him would involve abandoning the enterprise of the Spanish plate fleet. This might make trouble with the buccaneers. But Leach would justify himself with the tale that de Bernis had attacked him, and that he had killed him in self-defence. Very probably, he thought, with a grin, the tale would be true.

As for the loss to himself of his share of the Spanish gold, what was all the treasure of Spain to him compared with this other treasure which lay here ready to his hand, tormenting him with its irresistible allurement?

In his madness either he did not reflect, or else he was impatient of the reflection, that, by the exercise of patience and by proceeding according to the intentions which Wogan had first inspired in him, he might reduce into possession both the treasure and the girl. Patience

139

was in the eyes of Tom Leach a weakness, almost a form of cowardice.

And so you see him purposefully crossing that beach, so soon as Monsieur de Bernis and his companion had passed into the wood, and gaining the threshold of the hut, in the shade of which Priscilla sat now alone.

Something in his attitude, above all the leer with which, bare-headed, he appeared before her, instantly shattered that sense of security in her which had seemed so solidly founded on the manifest chivalry of Monsieur de Bernis.

Looking up, she strove to conceal the sudden alarmed flutter in her breast. If her eyes dilated a little, at least she compelled her utterance to be calm, level, and unhurried.

'You seek my husband, sir. He is not here.'

The leer broadened. 'I know that. I saw him go. So, ye see, it's not him I's seeking.'

On that he paused. His close-set eyes were pondering her, so white and slim and golden. They stripped away the long-waisted gown of green taffetas with the ivory-coloured lace bordering the low-cut line of neck, and glowed as they beheld her once again as he had seen her yesterday in the pool. And yet, for all his ardour, he faltered a little, now that he was face to face with her, now that his eyes met the clear, candid gaze of eyes from which she spiritedly banished every trace of fear. He knew no way of wooing that was not rough, direct, and brutal, like all else that he did. Yet here instinct informed him that something other was demanded; that too rude a grasp might merely crush this fruit for which he thirsted.

He was glad, therefore, of an inspiration which had come to him that morning and which was responsible for the line he took. From an inner pocket of his faded scarlet coat he drew a little leather bag. He untied the neck of it as he came forward to stand by the table.

'I've brought thee a little gift,' he said. He opened the mouth of the bag, and, placing his right hand as a barrier on the table to prevent the contents from rolling too far, he poured forth a dozen shimmering, lustrous pearls of price.

140

'Beauties, isn't they?' Still leaning over the table, he grinned up at her in expectancy, for she had risen from her seat.

He had experience of the queer fascination such toys can exercise upon a woman. More than once he had seen covetousness gleam in a woman's eyes as they considered those lovely, lightly iridescent spheres, and a hunger of possession whose gratification was not to be denied, whatever the cost. He had memories of reluctances defeated in Campeche, in Tortuga, in Mariegalante and elsewhere by just a couple of these seductive baubles. Never yet had he poured out as a gift to a woman so incredible a cascade as this; but then never yet had he seen a woman so incredibly desirable.

Every man's view of life is based upon his own experiences. Like drawing like into its intimacies, the vile man meets only vileness and therefore accounts the world vile. So it was with some confidence that this crude animal displayed his dazzling offering.

The result, however, was not at all what he expected. If for a moment—breathless to him—her eyes were caught and held by those gleaming orbs, in the next they were regarding him so oddly and coldly that it was clear she had entirely escaped their fascination.

'I do not think my husband would wish me to accept a gift.'

So that was it. She went in fear of that pestilent husband.

'Damn husband! There's pearls. Aye, and beauties. Fit for thee neck they is. They mind me of you, sink me. Just as sleek and lovely as thee, my pearly lass.'

Frozen in a make-believe composure, she coldly answered him: 'I'll tell my husband that you think so.'

'Eh?' The leering smile faded from his swarthy, hawk-like face. He gaped at her, momentarily nonplussed. Then he laughed outright to cover a certain sense of discomfiture. His tone was of a grossly playful gallantry. 'Can ye not forget this plaguey husband for a while?'

She curbed a desire to answer sharply. Although fear grew in her, it did not cloud her wits. She must humour this horror of a man, fence with him as best she could,

141

so as to ward off indignities. And she must maintain an air of fearlessness. Therefore, lest her tremors should betray her real feelings, she sat down.

'Were you never married, Captain Leach?' she asked him, with significance.

But this merely opened for him a line of direct attack. 'Not I. Ye see, it isn't many of us has th' luck o' Topgallant Charley, to find such a rare lass as thee. If that had happened to me, I might well ha' done the same as him.'

'I'll tell my husband what you say. It will flatter him.'

His colour darkened. She began to exasperate him with this persistent mention of her husband, and he was not deceived as to her motive, nor did she desire that he should be. 'Thee's well-matched with him in pertness, lass,' he growled. Then he, too, began to play comedy, and covered his rising anger with a mask of playfulness. 'But that's naught against thee. Odds fish! I loves a lass o' spirit, and I hates your mealy-mouthed sickly doxies, I does.' He flung himself down on the ground at her feet. 'Now where's harm o' praising thee beauty? Dunnot thee like a man to speak his mind?'

She answered him readily out of her simulated boldness. 'That depends upon what's in it.'

'Ye should be able to guess what's in mine, if anybody could.' Leaning upon his elbow, he looked up at her, leering again. 'Shall I tell thee? Shall I?'

'I am not curious, Captain Leach.'

Nevertheless he answered his own question. 'Thee self,' said he. 'Just thee self. There's been little else in my mind since first I seen thee, that day we took Centaur.'

His ardent, watchful eyes observed a growing agitation in her bosom, which argued to him that at last he was upon the course that led to port. He was pleased with himself for having adopted now these tactics. Although this form of dalliance was entirely new to him, yet it was clear that his instincts steered him shrewdly. 'There's naught I wouldn't do for thee, lass. Naught as ye could ask me.'

'Is that really so?'

'Try me. Put me to th' test.'

'Very well. I ask you to leave me, sir, and to take your pearls with you.'

He flushed again. Under his little black moustache his lip curled in a vicious grin that laid bare a dogtooth. 'And is that so? Is that all ye can ask o' me? Odds fish! Happen you ask the one thing I canna be granting. See? As for th' pearls, I want to see them worn against thee neck. Thee whiteness'll set t'm off, or maybe shame them. For thee's wondrous white. White as a lily thee is, from head to foot, as I should know.'

She threw up her chin sharply, her brows knit, her voice stern.

'As you should know?'

He gloated over the answer it was his to return to that pert question. He laughed a little. 'If a man may believe his eyes.' He came up on his knees, suddenly to confront her, and she observed that he had lost colour, that his eyes smouldered as if a fever raged in him, whilst his full lips writhed in a smile that made her shudder. 'Dunnot be afeared. I seen thee yesterday, whiles ye swam in the pool yonder, the loveliest sight as ever I saw. D'ye marvel now, lass, that I bring pearls to deck thee loveliness?'

Slowly the colour rose in her until her face and neck were a scarlet flame. She attempted to stand up. But his arms were suddenly across her knees, pinning her to her chair, his face was close to her breast.

It was only then, under that intolerable contact, that she realized the full horror of her situation, alone there, with Monsieur de Bernis, Major Sands, and Pierre all absent and not likely to return for perhaps an hour.

Bravely she sought to struggle with her mounting fears, to preserve control of herself that thus she might still perhaps preserve control of him. By an effort she kept her voice firm and hard.

'Captain Leach, let me go. Let me go!' Then, fear beginning to conquer prudence, 'Let me go, you beast!' she added.

She attempted to elude the pressure of his arms, so as to thrust back her chair, and rise. But Leach was suddenly rendered mad by rage at this clearly expressed loathing of him. He told himself that he had been a fool to waste time and words with this cold proud piece. He was rightly served for his folly by her insult. He should have taken the short way with her from the outset instead of wasting patience in this mawkish dalliance.

'Beast, am I? Well, well, my lass, mebbe I'll give thee cause to call me that. Mebbe thee'll be less likely to call me that when I've done so. I've tamed hawks as proud as thee afore now, made them that tame they'd coo like turtle doves. Mebbe thee'll learn to coo as gently. And if thee dunnot, what odds?'

Still kneeling before her, so that she could feel the buckle of his belt pressing against her knees, he held her now firmly imprisoned in the coil of his right arm. His left hand seized and crushed lace and silk at the line of her throat. With a snarling laugh he tore the summit of the bodice.

'There's pearls!' he exulted. 'Pearls!'

She drowned his words in a scream drawn from her by his brutal violence.

'Thee'd best save thee breath, lass. Screeching won't help. Cooing may, though.'

Slobbering and snarling, he drew her irresistibly towards him, out of the chair, which he intended to knock from under her.

Her livid face was distorted now into a grin of stark terror. 'God! O God!' she cried, and never was prayer more fervent.

Nor was ever answer more prompt. Suddenly before her dilating, terrified eyes, as they looked over the shoulder of Captain Leach, surged the tall figure of Monsieur de Bernis.

Providentially that morning, as he was proceeding with the Major to their practice-ground beyond the bluff, it had occurred to him to step down to the beach for a word with the men at work upon the hull of the careened ship, and so as to see for himself precisely the stage which their work had reached.

Standing there in the open, the distant scarlet figure of Captain Leach had caught his eye. He had seen him moving swiftly across the shore in the direction of Priscilla's hut, and he had seen him vanish into it.

144

Without apprehending anything approaching the truth, it had yet seemed to him that it might be as well if he were to return and join them. Under the eyes of the buccaneers he had begun by sauntering casually back towards his own encampment, followed by the Major, who, having observed nothing, went plaguing him with questions as to this change of intention. Midway, Monsieur de Bernis had suddenly lengthened his stride, and left the Major, to whom hurry was distasteful in that heat, to follow at his leisure.

In those long, swift strides of his that made no sound upon the sand, Monsieur de Bernis reached the hut to see for himself how urgently his coming was required.

Captain Leach, too absorbed to observe the shadow cast by this newcomer, was startled by a sudden sharp tap upon the shoulder.

'You are at your prayers, I perceive, Captain. I am desolated to disturb you. But Madame de Bernis is not an object for your so immediate adoration.'

Tom Leach leapt up and round with the athletic agility of a cat, his hand going by instinct to his belt.

Monsieur de Bernis had stepped a little aside, so as to leave the entrance clear. His face was very white, and it wore a smile rendered terrible by the expression of his eyes.

'By all means continue in your worship of Madame de Bernis. I desire it so. But at a distance. At a distance in the future, if you please. Let your worship of her be such as you might bestow upon a saint in heaven. Thus it will be better for you, safer for all.'

Imperiously he waved an arm in dismissal, indicating by it the exit which he had left clear, but beyond which the sturdy figure of Major Sands was looming.

Leach, with his back turned now upon Priscilla, stood, breathing hard, crouching a little as if gathering his muscles for a spring. He spoke in a thick voice that rage was strangling. 'By God! You grinning jackanapes! D'ye know what happens to them as gets spry wi' Cap'n Leach?'

'You would do better to ask yourself what may happen to him who gets spry with Madame de Bernis.' And again it was his gesture that uttered dismissal.

145

'Hellfire! I admire thee boldness! But don't carry it too far with me. See?' He slunk a step or two towards the door and the round-eyed Major, but keeping his glance the while on de Bernis. 'Thee's a tall fine figure o' a man, so thee is. But I've made carrion o' finer fellows than thee, Charley, and don't thee be forgetting it.'

'I'll remember it,' said de Bernis grimly. 'Meanwhile, you'ld best go while my patience lasts. Ye may have heard that it's not eternal.'

'Ye threaten, do ye! Well, well! I wonder is there another man alive who can boast that?'

He stepped out of the hut, and, coming suddenly against Major Sands, thrust him roughly, vigorously out of his way, glad to find something under his hand upon which to express in violence the rage that was choking him. But before he had gone six paces, de Bernis' voice arrested him again.

'You've forgotten something.'

Monsieur de Bernis stood at the entrance of the hut, holding in his hand the pearls which he had swept up from the table. As he spoke, he flung them at the Captain.

Some of them struck him, and some did not, but all of them—a dozen pearls that he would not have sold for a thousand pieces of eight, but which in his stormy condition he had forgotten—were scattered in the sand.

After a breathless, raging moment, he went down on hands and knees spitting and snarling like a cat to grovel for them without any thought for the ridiculous, ignominious anti-climax which this supplied.

## 16

## The Apple of Discord

WHILST Tom Leach grovelled there, ignomíniously, within a dozen paces of the hut and in full view of those within it, and whilst Major Sands looked on in bewilderment, his indignation at the manner in which Leach had handled him partly soothed by the spectacle of the buccaneer's discomfiture, Monsieur de Bernis was turning to Priscilla, where she stood, her left hand instinctively repairing the disorder of her bodice.

It was a Monsieur de Bernis whom she had never seen until this moment. Hitherto she had beheld him so calm and saturnine in the face of everything that she had come to consider him utterly imperturbable, a man of a self-control that nothing could abate. She beheld him now so pale and shaken that she understood by what an effort he had commanded himself so long as Tom Leach had stood before him.

He stepped up to her in quick concern, and she felt the trembling of the hand he set upon her arm, heard the faltering quiver of his muffled voice as he uttered her name. With a deep, shuddering sigh, she sank against him, limp and helpless now that the strain was overpast. His arm went round her, to support her. And it supported her morally as well as physically. Her spirit was uplifted to feel herself thus, within the compass of an arm, as if within a protecting, sheltering wall. For a moment he held her so, tenderly, reverently. Then, commanding himself, he spoke and his voice vibrated oddly.

'I trust, I pray, that animal did not unduly frighten you.'

She shuddered against him. 'Thank God, oh, thank God that you came!' The very fervour of her thankfulness seemed to feed his wrath.

147

'Let that evil dog, too, give thanks. For had I delayed, I must certainly have killed him.'

She clutched his hand, and looked up at him in a new fear, her face close to his own. 'You will do nothing more? You will not pursue it?'

His pale lips twisted in a smile of bitter self-mockery. 'I dare not,' he confessed. 'In all my life I have never known the need for so much self-control, to prevent me from doing that which might have ruined us all. But it was hard, dear God! It was hard! To see you held so by that foul beast! Priscilla!'

It was a cry from the depth of a man's soul. Into that utterance of her name he seemed to have packed a dozen emotions: there were anger, grief, tenderness, renunciation, and something too of heart-break. All this and more she heard in it, and to the spirit in that cry she made surrender of her own spirit. She nestled closer, softly murmuring to him: 'Do not leave me alone again while we are here! Promise me.'

'Can you suppose it?' he answered passionately. 'Can you dream I should ever again leave you exposed to that?'

He bent down to the golden head that rested against his breast, and reverently touched it with his lips, scarcely aware of what he did, as he thus expressed an overmastering emotion into which his fears for her had betrayed him.

It was at this point that the Major, a spectator in whom amazement had been piled upon amazement, accounted it necessary to interfere, before Priscilla, newly wrenched from the importunate arms of one buccaneer, should melt too completely into those of another.

'Stab me!' quoth he, rolling forward, 'what's here?'

The indignation rumbling in his voice, awakened de Bernis to realities, arrested him in that easy and increasing surrender to emotion. His recovery of his ready wits was abrupt and complete. Without relaxing his hold upon the girl, or making the least change in his attitude, he spoke swiftly through his teeth.

'Will you ruin all, you fool? What are you supposing? Is she not my wife in the eyes of that man who is gaping at us at this moment? I have a part to play, sir. Begone! Leave me to play it.'

The Major gaped, relieved.

'I beg your pardon, de Bernis.' He hung there, hesitating. 'As her brother, it is natural I, too, should remain to comfort. I have done nothing to betray you.'

But Miss Priscilla evidently considered that the comedy had gone far enough. As if also recalled to realities, she disengaged herself from de Bernis' arm, moved away to a chair, and sat down, like one exhausted. She was still very white, and dark shadows had gathered under her eyes. Her left hand was still clutching to her breast the tattered portions of the bodice.

'If you would both leave me for a little while,' she begged them.

Understanding, they went. They paced the beach awhile, the Major inveighing furiously but impotently, and seeming to embrace Monsieur de Bernis together with Tom Leach in the scope of that windy invective. Monsieur de Bernis, heeding him not at all, indeed scarcely hearing him, paced beside him in moody abstraction. He awakened from that at last to hear the Major saying:

'Of late, sir, I have been giving you my trust. But I warn you that, unless you can keep these cutthroat friends of yours in order, that trust will be destroyed.'

'In such a case, sir, you would have my sympathy,' said de Bernis, and upon that abruptly quitted the Major's side.

Looking round for an explanation of a conduct that seemed to him so odd, Major Sands saw Pierre emerging from among the trees. It was towards him that de Bernis was hurrying. The Major followed, grumbling ever.

He heard the faint mutter of Pierre's rapid French as de Bernis approached him, and at what the half-caste said, his master's shoulders sagged a little, and he stood very still and very pensive, his lip between finger and thumb.

After a moment, by when Major Sands was at his elbow, he spoke, but whether to himself or to Pierre, who stood before him, waiting, was not plain. Even the Major's scant knowledge of French enabled him to understand what de Bernis said.

'Nevertheless, it is necessary to do something.'

After which he paced away slowly towards the hut, and then, like a man who takes a sudden resolve, swung on his heel, and set out briskly to walk across the beach towards the buccaneer encampment.

As he approached it, a couple of men who were boucanning turtle over a fire, looked up and greeted him with the friendly familiarity which he had encouraged in them. But for once he swung past them without noticing it.

It was already a little after noon, and in the Captain's hut, the leaders were sitting down to dinner, when Monsieur de Bernis suddenly made his appearance among them, his aspect stern and forbidding.

Tom Leach, who by now had cooled to a state of viciousness that superficially at least was normal, eyed him furtively and at first, startled by that sudden entrance, in apprehension. But the emotion was not one that ever lasted long with Leach. It passed in a flash, leaving him armed in brazen impudence to meet the attack which he had every cause to expect.

Monsieur de Bernis came to the empty foot of the table, directly facing Leach who occupied the head. On the Frenchman's right were Bundry and Halliwell, on his left Ellis and Wogan. All four of them looked up from their meat, to gape at his preternatural gravity.

His voice was cold and hard and brisk, his speech direct and peremptory.

'You may have some notion of what brings me, Captain. I have a warning for you. I need waste no unnecessary words upon it. If the plate fleet matters to you and you wish me to bring you to it, you'll be civil henceforth, and you'll avoid my quarters.'

'By God . . .' Leach was beginning, half-rising in his seat.

'Wait!' thundered de Bernis, and by tone and gesture thrust him back momentarily silenced. The Frenchman swung to Leach's officers. 'If the plate fleet matters to you, and you desire that I bring you to it, you'll see that he obeys my injunction. If I have a repetition of what happened this morning, if Tom Leach ventures within twenty yards of my encampment again, come what may, I dissociate myself from you, and I vow to you here that not a single piece of eight of all that treasure will any one of you ever touch. If I am to respect my articles, Tom Leach shall respect my wife, and you others shall see that he respects her.'

The Captain's dark eyes gleamed their hatred and malice as they met the bold, challenging glance of de Bernis across the length of the table.

From the others there were mutterings of resentment provoked by the Frenchman's arrogant tone and air. But one there was who spoke out, and this was the impassive, clay-faced Bundry. He turned his shoulder to de Bernis, so as to face the Captain.

'So you've neglected the warning we gave you, Captain?' he said, in that level voice of his that could be so threatening in its iciness.

The momentary flash of de Bernis' eyes might have betrayed the discovery made to him by those words. But at the time all were looking at the Captain, awaiting his reply. Surprised, however, by Bundry's cold, obvious challenge, Leach was momentarily at a loss; whilst de Bernis, encouraged by signs of a support he had not suspected, took advantage of the pause to turn the sword in the wound, which, exceeding all expectations, he perceived he had made.

'I have this to add, Tom, and you would do well to reflect upon it, and to take it for a compass by which to steer your course: To the success of this enterprise against the Spaniards, I am necessary. You are not. The enterprise can quite well go forward without you. It cannot go forward without me. I say no more. But if you have any prudence in your foul head, Tom, you'll use it to rake together some scraps of decency, and put them in your conduct. That is all. The quarrel may end here if you so choose; or it may go forward if you choose. I leave you to decide it.'

And without giving Leach time to assemble words in which to reply, he turned on his heel and departed as abruptly as he had come, leaving ferment behind him.

Leach was on his feet, ordures of speech on his

writing lips, and Wogan was supplying a chorus to him, when Bundry's contemptuous voice interrupted both.

'Quiet, Wogan, you fool! There's mischief enough without your adding to this hell's brew. As for you, Tom, you've heard, and I suppose ye've sense enough left in yourself to recognize sense when ye hear it.'

'Rot you in hell, Bundry! Does thee suppose I'll stomach the impudence o' yon pimpish ape? Does thee suppose . . .'

'I suppose ye know the plate fleet matters to us more than you!' thundered Bundry, getting to his feet, losing control of himself for once, and banging the table before him.

A silence followed until broken by the Captain's voice, soft, sly, unutterably wicked. 'Be that so, Bundry? Be that so?' His hand was groping slowly round his belt, his eyes never leaving Bundry's mask-like face.

It began to look as if Monsieur de Bernis had flung the apple of discord amongst them to some purpose, as if in a moment blood would be shed over that table and those buccaneer leaders would be at one another's throats. It was Halliwell who averted it. He rose and leaned forward, so that his great bulk was interposed between the Captain and Bundry.

'In the name of God, Tom, come to your senses. Will ye ruin all out o' impatience for a whey-faced doxy who'll be safely under your hand once the pieces of eight are under ours?'

There was promise here as well as admonition. Leach, with all his impatiences quenched at the moment by other matters, was steadied by it, at least far enough to look at the others. Bundry's mind, he knew. Ellis's he read in the scowl of disapproval with which the mate of the Black Swan was regarding him. Halliwell, it was plain, would join them if it came to a trial of strength on this issue. The only one upon whom Leach could count in that moment seemed to be Wogan, and how long Wogan would remain on the weaker side was not a matter in which Leach could put much faith.

With inward rage, which he strove to dissemble, the

152

Captain perceived only defeat ahead of him if he persisted. Topgallant Charley, that sly French devil, had been too clever for him, and had so shifted the quarrel that it now lay between Leach and his officers.

'Aye, aye,' he growled, 'mebbe I's acted foolish like. There's sense in what thee says, Ned. But there's poison in what yon Bundry's said.' He fetched a whine into his voice. 'To say that th' plate fleet matters more to you than I does!'

' 'Twas ill said, Bundry,' Wogan censured him. 'So, God save me, 'twas ill said.'

'So ill said that it's my right to ask satisfaction.' Leach was looking at the pallid shipmaster.

If Bundry trembled in the heart of him, aware of the vaunted deadly swordsmanship of his Captain, and of what might betide him if Leach were to succeed in making of this affair a personal quarrel with himself, his countenance remained unmoved.

'Ye've afforded it,' he said, 'when ye confessed that ye may have acted foolish. Let it rest there.'

Leach perceived fear in Bundry's desire to drop the matter. He perceived also that the others held aloof now, and took no sides in the personal issue which he had given the matter. By this he took heart again.

'That's easy said, Bundry. But will it rest? After all, here's a deal o' pother about naught, made up by that slippery devil Bernis. Am I to turn t'other cheek to him, or slink about before him like a cur wi's tail atween his legs no matter what he may do or say, just because he's got th' secret o' th' plate fleet? Sink me into hell! That's no gait for a captain, and it's not th' way o' Tom Leach. Let it be understood. So long as Charley's civil, I'll keep the peace; but not a moment longer, plate fleet or no plate fleet. And if ye expects more o' me, you, Bundry, or any other of ye—a God's name say so plainly now, and let's know where we stand.'

'Sure that's reasonable enough,' Wogan supported him.

Ellis and Halliwell, whilst saying nothing, showed by their attitude that they were not disposed to dispute a matter which Leach had found a way to render personal with any one of them who might oppose him. United they must easily have subdued him. But the mistrust of each for his neighbour dissolved the momentary bond that had existed amongst them, and no one of them would take it upon himself to bell the cat, lest he should find himself suddenly abandoned by the others.

Bundry perceived clearly the crude subtlety and cunning by which Leach had caught him; and he knew that it would be suicidal to pursue the matter as a personal quarrel with his formidable captain. So he abandoned the position which he had so boldly taken up.

'No one could expect more of ye, Captain. But ye'll remember that we expect that much.'

'That much ye shall have. Ye can be sure of it.'

Upon which, with peace restored, they sat down to resume their interrupted meal.

17

*Temptation*

THAT night, wakeful under the stars, Monsieur de Bernis waited in vain for Miss Priscilla to lift the curtain of her hut and come to sit in talk beside him. The events of the day seemed to have created the need for so much to be said between them. There was so much that he felt the need to explain. But apparently, on her side, there was no corresponding need to hear these explanations; for the night wore on, and the curtain remained closed.

At last, understanding that this must be by design and not by chance, he fell to speculating in distress as to the reason. He could conceive that he had offended her. When he had taken her so tenderly in his arms, he had perhaps overstepped the boundaries of the relations she was disposed to tolerate between them. And

yet surely she must have perceived the almost unavoidable need to create that appearance of uxorious-
ness, and by this have deflected any resentment.

Lest it should be so, indeed, the need to explain
became of an increasing urgency. He ended by softly
calling her. Three times he repeated that call before
the curtain was raised. Nevertheless, despite the urgency, prudence compelled him to keep down his voice. It
followed, therefore, since she heard him, that she, too,
was awake.

'You called?' she said between question and assertion, and added: 'Is anything amiss?'

He had risen, and stood with the long enveloping
cloak hanging loose from his shoulders.

'That is what I desired to ask you. I was led to fear
it from this breach of custom. I mean your absence.
Will you not sit?'

'You have something to say to me?'

She heard his muted, whimsical laugh. 'That seems
to have been my constant affliction. But tonight I have
something more than usual.'

She lowered herself to the cushion which served him
for a pillow, and which as usual he had set for her,
and he sank down beside her.

'Be frank,' he invited. 'You did not come, you would
not have come had I not called you, because you are
offended with me.'

'Offended? I? How could that be?' But her voice had
the frosty tone of one who fences.

'It should not be. But there is always the danger of
being misunderstood. I feared I had incurred it. You
might have conceived that I made too free today. It
was that. . . .'

'This is unnecessary,' she interrupted. 'There is no
misunderstanding. None is possible. I heard your explanation to Major Sands. It was comedy you played
for the information of Captain Leach. I perceived the
necessity.'

Yet there was nothing gracious in her tone, no
lessening of its distant frostiness. It puzzled him.

'And you condone it?' he asked.

'But, of course. You play comedy very well, Monsieur de Bernis.'

155

'Ah?'

'So well that for a moment you misled me. For a moment I actually conceived that your alarm and your concern were genuine.'

'I assure you that they were,' he protested.

'But. . . . hardly to the extent which I was so foolish as to suppose.'

He was betrayed by that complaint into a display of fervour. 'Whatever the extent to which you may have supposed me moved, your assumption will hardly have done justice to the fact.'

'And yet the fact left you under the necessity to play comedy so as to provide all that you conceived the situation to require.'

'Ah, mon Dieu!' he exclaimed, lapsing into his native tongue as he sometimes did when deeply moved. 'Can you mean. . . .' He checked himself in time. He was about to add: 'Can you mean that you are aggrieved because what I uttered of tenderness was uttered only in make-believe?'

'What were you going to say?' she asked him, as he fell silent.

'Something unutterable.'

Her tone softened a little. 'If you were to utter it, we might reach the truth between us.'

'There are truths that it is better not to reach. Truths that are like the forbidden fruit on the Tree of Knowledge.'

'This is not Paradise, Monsieur de Bernis.'

'I cannot be so sure on that. In these last days it has grown nearer to Paradise for me than any I have known in life.'

This created a silence, which endured so long that he began to fear he had now, indeed, offended. And then at last, in a small voice, looking straight before her down the pallid beach to the dusky shimmer of water beyond, and the shadowy silhouette of the Centaur where she rode at anchor in the lagoon, she answered him with a question.

'Do they play comedy in your paradise, Monsieur de Bernis?'

If he had doubted until now, he could doubt no longer on what it was that she desired his frank avowal. The invitation could scarcely have been more plain had it been plainly uttered. He passed a hand across his brow and found it moist. True, the night was warm. But not warm enough to draw the sweat from such a frame as his. It sprang, he knew, from the labours of his mind.

He answered, at last, slowly, in a voice which being of necessity muted was thereby the more easily kept level.

'Priscilla, count it my saving grace that I know where the frontiers of reality are set for me.'

'Can you think only of yourself?'

'It is perhaps my only unselfishness.'

Again there was silence; of frustration for her, of agony for him. And then, woman-like, she came back to the beginning.

'Then it was not comedy you played today? Not quite?' Her voice was coaxing.

'What else? I am I; you are you. The only bridge that Fate can fling between us is a bridge of make-believe.'

'Fate, perhaps. But you, yourself. You . . . you build no bridges?'

Almost roughly he answered her. 'There is none would bear me. I am too heavily laden.'

'Can you throw off no part of this load?'

'Can a man throw off his past? His nature? It is from these I derive my load of shame.'

She shook her head slowly. She leaned against him, as she answered.

'Your nature is not so laden. I have studied it. As for the past. . . . What is the past?'

'Our heritage in the present.'

'May not a man discard his heritage?'

'Not when he inherits from himself. It is a part of him.'

She sighed. 'How obstinate you are! Are you quite sure that your humility is not a form of pride?'

'Pride?' he echoed in repudiation, and upon the word fell silent, thoughtful, to say at last: 'Perhaps it is. An obstinate pride to serve Honour at last, that in serving it I may be worthy at least of the passing thought you have bestowed on me.'

'And if it were not passing?' she softly asked him.

'It must be.' His voice was firm. He drew away a little, as if so that the warm, sweet contact of her arm upon his own should not enfeeble his stout purpose. 'Later—soon—when you are restored to your own people and to the ways of life to which you belong, you will look back on this adventure as upon some incredible nightmare from which you have happily awakened. Take nothing from it with you into that waking future to mar its sweet serenity.'

'Charles!' She set a hand upon his, where it rested on his knee.

His hand turned in her grasp to close upon her own and press it. Still holding it he rose, and drew her up with him.

'I shall remember, Priscilla; always shall I remember; and I vow to you here that I shall be the better for remembering. So much as you have given I shall treasure till I die. But you shall give no more.'

'If it should be my will to give?' she asked him, scarcely above her breath.

His reply came instantly and firmly.

'This pride of mine will not suffer me to take such gifts. You are you, and I am I. Think well what this means: what you are, and what I am. Good-night, my dear.' He raised her hand, and bending his head pressed his lips upon it. Then he released it, and lifted the curtain for her.

'Tomorrow this will be a sweet dream that I have dreamed here under the stars and you on your couch in there from which I should not have summoned you.'

For a long moment she remained standing before him, her face a white blur in which the dark pools of her eyes were turned towards him. Then, bowing her head a little, she passed into the hut without another word.

Her demeanour next morning, when again he came to act as deputy for the mysteriously absent Pierre, accorded with his injunction that what had passed between them in the night should be regarded as a dream. If she was pale and of a heaviness about the eyes that argued lack of sleep, her manner at least was

158

normally bright, and it was of the absence of Pierre that she spoke. As usual he evaded her questions on the subject. He could not again pretend to have sent the half-caste on an errand. He met her with assumptions that Pierre had taken a fancy for early morning wandering and a curious disposition to indulge Pierre in any such fancies, however discomposing in their consequences.

After breakfast there was that day no question of the usual sword practice with the Major. Following upon the events of yesterday it was tacitly agreed that the two men should never both be absent at the same time from their encampment.

Monsieur de Bernis wandered off to the northern end of the beach to observe the progress of the work upon the careened hull. The tarring was nearing its conclusion. By tomorrow, the men told him, as he mingled with them, they would start the greasing that marked the end of their toil. They would be thankful, they asserted with many a foul oath, to have the Black Swan afloat again. He jested with them, as usual, and encouraged them again with a reminder of the golden harvest they would sail away to garner. He was still in talk with them when Leach sauntered up.

There was a deliberate, sly, and wickedly purposeful air about the Captain as he joined them. It coloured the manner in which he growled at the men, reminding them that progress with the work was slow enough without their suspending it to stand idly in talk. Did they want him to spend the remainder of his life on Maldita? Then he obscenely invited Monsieur de Bernis to find other employment, and not to stand there wasting the time of the hands.

Curbing himself before the captain's calculatedly offensive manner, Monsieur de Bernis shrugged, and began to move away without other answer. But this did not satisfy the Captain, who came briskly after him.

'D'ye shrug your shoulders at me, Bernis?' he demanded, loud enough to be heard by the men.

Over his shoulder, without checking in his stride, de Bernis answered him: 'What else would you have me do?'

'I'ld have ye attend. I'll have ye know I'm captain here, and when I speak I expect an answer.'

'I obeyed your wishes. Is not that answer enough?'

He halted now, confronting Leach. They had moved out of earshot of the men. But they were still under their eyes, and those eyes were watchful. The buccaneers had sensed the beginnings of a very pretty quarrel in the Captain's opening words, and it being in their natures to love a fight, they looked on hopefully without even a pretence of attending to their work.

Leach considered the Frenchman with an eye of cordial dislike.

'Ye shrugged at me,' he complained truculently. 'I'll have no man shrug at me when I gives orders. Least of all a French pimp.'

Monsieur de Bernis considered him in his turn. Himself armed, he observed that Leach, too, had hung a rapier at his side. Nor did a certain eagerness in Leach escape him.

'I see,' he said. 'Ye want to put a quarrel on me. But ye dare not do it openly, lest your followers should call you to account for it. So ye think to provoke me into striking you, with Wogan looking on up yonder. That, you suppose, will justify you in their eyes. Do I read you aright, Tom?'

The other's furious countenance told him that he did.

'Be sure as I reads thee aright, Charley. Thee's just a cowardly cuckold, impudent so long as thee counts theeself sheltered.'

But de Bernis laughed aloud. 'Maybe you are right,' said he shamelessly. Then he sobered. 'There's a day for everything, Tom. Ye may be athirst for my blood. But this is not the time to drink it. The draught would poison you. Haven't they warned you of it—Bundry and the others?'

In words at least Leach could vent some of the hatred into which de Bernis had come with him. 'Ye pitiful, tale-bearing craven!' he said, and spat deliberately in token of his contempt. Then turned on his heel, and moved away, in the direction whence Wogan was uneasily advancing. But he went ready to swing round at the first sound behind him, confidently expecting de Bernis to throw caution to the winds before that crowning insult.

Monsieur de Bernis, however, disappointed him. He remained looking after that leisurely departing scarlet figure, with narrowing, calculating eyes, and the faintest shadow of a smile under his little dark moustache, until the Captain was joined by Wogan. Then he, too, moved away, returning to his own side of the beach.

And meanwhile there was Wogan confronting Leach, arms akimbo and remonstrance in his lean, crafty face.

'Och, now, Captain, darling, I was afeard you'ld be letting your temper run away with you. Bad cess to it!'

Leach laughed at him, his countenance baffled and unpleasant. 'See thee, lad! Leave me to settle my own affairs in my own way.'

'Faith, but I'll be reminding you that this is the affair of all of us, so it is.'

'When I settles it, I'll not forget that.'

'But if ye were to kill Charley, there would . . .'

Scornfully Leach interrupted him.

'Kill him?' He laughed aloud, in contemptuous repudiation of the notion. 'I's no bungler. I know what's to do. I's not killing him. But, by God, I'll cut his poxy comb for him. I'll mutilate him, make him helpless so as he'll not swagger any more.'

'But that's as bad now.' Wogan's alarm was clear.

'Is it?' Leach closed an eye slowly. 'Thee's no faith in me. Once I have him powerless, crippled, does thee think I've no ways to squeeze this secret o' th' plate fleet from him? Woolding mayn't do it, nor a match between his toes. But there's things we might do to that proud cold piece of his, to Mistress de Bernis, things we might do under his eyes, the threat o' which would mebbe loosen his stubborn tongue. There's more ways nor one o' persuading the dumbest man to talk.'

Wogan's eyes grew round in wonder. 'The Saints preserve us, Tom! It's a devil ye are.' But his tone was one of admiration.

They departed arm-in-arm, to their own quarters.

Monsieur de Bernis found Miss Priscilla, who was now reduced to being her own tire-woman, occupied with needlework within the hut. The Major had been

161

seated there, too, in talk with her. But at sight of the approaching Frenchman, he rose and went forth to meet him.

'Will you walk, sir?' he invited him. 'Since we do not fence this morning, we might saunter here awhile within reach of Priscilla. I have something to say to you.'

There was an unusual geniality in his manner which took Monsieur de Bernis almost by surprise. Of late the Major had been more friendly; but never genial. There was always in his bearing a certain aloofness, suggesting that he never lost sight of the fact that he was a gentleman of family holding the King's commission and that de Bernis was just a pirate rogue towards whom necessity alone prescribed a certain degree of civility.

'At your service,' said Monsieur de Bernis, and they fell into step and paced on towards the southern rampart of rock, beyond which, unknown to them, lay Priscilla's bathing-pool into which she was not likely again to venture.

'I am distressed, stab me! I tell you frankly, de Bernis, I am distressed. You seem at odds with these buccaneer rogues, Leach and the rest of them. I ask myself, if harm should come to you, what is to become of us, or, rather, what is to become of Priscilla.'

'Can you suppose, sir, that I am not considering it?'

'You are? You relieve me a deal. Yet not altogether.' The Major was very grave. 'Bear with me a moment, de Bernis. You were impatient with me once before when I asked you what is your intention by us when you sail away on this Spanish raid. Yet now that the time is drawing near, I am driven to ask this again. To ask it again. You cannot surely intend that we should sail with you. It would be—ah—unthinkable, stab me, that you should take Miss Priscilla into the horrors and the dangers of a seafight.'

'You might remain here at Maldita until I return to take you off,' said de Bernis.

'Ah!' Some of the gloom lifted from the Major's countenance. 'Yes.' His tone was musing. 'It is what I had thought possible. Yet . . .' He paused, stood still,

162

and confronted his companion. 'What if you should not return, Monsieur de Bernis?'

'You mean?'

'You go into danger. You go into a deal of danger as it seems to me. There is danger from the Spaniards, and then there is danger from your associates. You are making bad blood with them, I fear. Bad blood. At least, after what happened yesterday with this blackguard Leach . . .'

'Would you have had me civil to him?'

'Sir! Sir! Can you suppose it? Stab me!' The Major became consequential. 'You bore yourself as I would have borne myself in your place. Do not misunderstand me, I implore you. Do not misunderstand me. What happened could not have been avoided. But it alters things between you and Leach. It occurs to me that he may curb his rancour only just so long as it suits his ends. And that once you have led him to the plate fleet, once you are parted with your secret, he may take a revenge upon you. Perhaps this had not occurred to you.'

Monsieur de Bernis smiled. 'My dear Major, do you suppose that it is from blindness to the obvious that I have contrived to survive all the perils of such a life as mine?'

The Major did not like his tone, and the reflection it contained upon his own acumen. His manner lost some of its geniality.

'You mean that it had already occurred to you?'

'And not merely as a possibility. Long before our yesterday's disagreement, I have known that it is not the intention of Leach to keep faith with me. He has confidently been counting upon slitting my throat and possessing himself of Miss Priscilla once I have led him to the plate fleet.'

'Oh, my God!' said the Major in a horror that blotted everything else from his mind. 'Then . . . Then . . .' He was utterly at a loss. He had stood still again. His heavy face was pale as he turned it upon de Bernis. 'But if this is so . . .' Still he could find no conclusion to his sentence. There was a sort of chaos in his dull mind.

Monsieur de Bernis smiled. 'It is something to be

163

forewarned. Things may not fall out quite as Tom Leach expects them. Indeed, they may fall out very differently. I, too, have my intentions and my plans.'

The Major stared, his mind in labour. 'I suppose you think you can depend upon his followers, upon the leaders?'

'What I think is of no great account. It is what I know that matters. And what I know is that I depend upon myself. Not for the first time, Major Sands.'

Considering him, so straight and calm and resolute, Major Sands came nearer to admiring him than he had yet done. This, after all, seemed to be a man upon whom it was good to lean in an awkward situation.

'You have no anxieties, then?'

'Oh, yes. I have anxieties. Few things are certain in this life, however shrewdly a man may plan. And too great a confidence is, they say, unlucky, which possibly is true because it makes a man careless. That, at least you may depend that I shall not be. Hitherto, Major, you have placed no great trust in me, I know. At least let my deep devotion to Priscilla and my deep concern for her assure you that I have no thought but to make her safe. In that safety you will share.' His eyes travelled up the beach towards the hut, as if following his thought. 'Ah, there is Pierre returning,' he said, and on that left the Major where he stood and strode rapidly across the sands.

The Major stared after him with a brow of thunder. 'His deep devotion to Priscilla!' he said, speaking aloud. 'Damnation take his impudence!'

Monsieur de Bernis, unconscious of the resentment he had loosed behind him, was overtaking the half-caste as he entered his tent. But before he could ask the question that trembled on his lip, the half-caste presented a blank countenance to him, thrust out a nether lip, shook his head, and shrugged.

'Rien du tout,' he said dismally.

Monsieur de Bernis' eyes dilated under a frowning brow.

'Ah! But this becomes serious.'

## 18

## *The Assault-at-Arms*

ON THE following morning, Monsieur de Bernis, a
little grey of face and with the deep lines in it more
marked than usual, sat brooding alone on a little knoll
at some distance from the hut, staring out over the
sunlit lagoon at the Centaur, riding there with bare
trees.

A fresh breeze had sprung up from the north at
dawn, and the fronds of the palms were rustling softly
behind him. From the northern end of the beach came
the voices of the men labouring about the hull of the
Black Swan which so soon now would be afloat again.
Three days, at the utmost, was all that remained of this
sojourn on Maldita. And it was this imminence of departure that was so deeply fretting Monsieur de Bernis,
that had stripped him of that air of assured confidence
which hitherto he had worn.

Pierre, as usual, was absent. In the last two days this
absence had not merely been confined as previously to
the morning, but had been repeated again in the late
afternoon. According to the custom he had established,
his return was not to be expected until midday. But
now, suddenly, although it could not yet be nine
o'clock, he appeared at Monsieur de Bernis' side, to
arouse his master from his preoccupations. So effectively
did the mere sight of him move Monsieur de Bernis
that he was on his feet before Pierre had even spoken.
His expression so strained as to be almost scared, he
clutched the half-caste's wrist, and stared questioningly
into his face.

Pierre grinned and nodded, showing signs of excitement. 'Enfin,' he said. 'Les voilà!'

'C'est bien vrai?' Monsieur de Bernis demanded, like
a man afraid to believe, lest his hopes should fool him.

'Venez donc voir, vous-même.' Pierre drew a telescope from inside his cotton shirt, which once had been white but now was grey, and handed it to de Bernis.

Then the two of them turned, and set off up the beach, Monsieur de Bernis observing that the Major was with Miss Priscilla, and satisfied that he would remain there on guard. They vanished into the woods, taking the path across the island by which Pierre had once conducted Miss Priscilla.

In less than half an hour they came out upon the western shore, and halted on the very edge of the sands to gaze out to sea in the direction in which the exultant Pierre was pointing.

Less than five miles away three great ships were beating up to eastward, close-hauled to the northerly breeze and listing to starboard under the weight of it until the edges of their white bellies showed below their red hulls.

Monsieur de Bernis levelled the telescope and for some moments stood carefully scanning them. They flew no flag; but their lines left him in no doubt of their identity.

As he closed the telescope, a grim smile was stamped on his dark, narrow face. 'In an hour they will have the island abeam. Come. There's no time to be lost.'

They sped back as swiftly as they had come. In all they had not been absent above an hour when they stepped out of the woods again beside their hut. There Monsieur de Bernis paused. From under his arm he took the telescope, which he had retained until now, and handed it to Pierre, who went off with it to his tent.

Monsieur de Bernis stepped into the hut, where the Major sat drowsily watching Priscilla, who was again busy with her needle. They looked up as he entered and went to take down his sword and baldrick from the hook where it was hung.

'Why that?' the girl asked him sharply.

Monsieur de Bernis shrugged. "Feeling running as it does, it is well to go prepared.' He passed the heavily encrusted baldrick over his head, and settled it on his

166

shoulder. 'It inspires respect. It acts as an inducement to civility.'

Reassured by that smiling explanation and his easy manner, they let him go.

Outside the hut he paused. Knowing what he went to do, he was moved to a last word with Priscilla, a last instruction to the Major in case the worst should befall him. Instead, however, after an instant's thought, he passed on to the half-caste's tent.

'Pierre, if the worst should happen to me, see to Miss Priscilla. You should meet few difficulties.'

Pierre's eyes, dark and soft as velvet, were filled with alarmed concern. 'Monsieur! Could you not wait? Is there no other way?'

'No way so sure as this. Besides, I owe it to myself.'

'Sure?' the half-caste echoed. 'But not sure for you.'

'Eh, pardieu! But yes. Sure enough for me.'

Pierre clutched his master's hand. He bore it to his lips.

'Dieu vous garde, monsieur!' he prayed.

De Bernis patted the bowed head. 'Sois tranquille, mon fils.' And upon that he departed resolutely.

Chance favouring his design, he came upon Tom Leach walking with Wogan within fifty yards of the buccaneer encampment. He gave them a friendly goodday; gave it deliberately with a flourish. Tom Leach looked him over without friendliness.

'What d'ye want here?'

'What I want?' Monsieur de Bernis displayed only surprise, to mask his satisfaction at finding the Captain so readily disposed to create the situation which the Frenchman desired. 'What I want?' he said again, his eyebrows up, his lip curling, his eyes looking down his nose at the buccaneer.

The very insolence of his attitude was steel to the flint of Leach's humour. 'Aye, what ye want. If thee's come to make mischief again, thee'd better ha' stayed away.'

They were making excellent progress, thought Monsieur de Bernis. He stepped close up to Leach, with arms akimbo, whilst Wogan looked on inscrutably. 'I don't think ye're civil, Tom.'

'Civil?' The Captain spat with deliberate offensiveness. 'I sees no call for civility.'

'So? In fact, Tom, I find you damned provocative.'

'Provocative! Ha! He finds me provocative, Mike! 'Slife! Are you to be provoked? Seems to me yours is the kind o' courage that likes to have a shelter, to make cat's-paws for itself.'

'That is what you know of me, is it?'

'It's what I's seen.'

Wogan accounted it time to make a pretence of intervening. 'Och, now, will ye be remembering what's ahead of us? Won't ye be making the peace, now, both of ye, and working together like good Brethren of the Coast. Come, now.'

'It is what I most desire, Wogan,' lied Monsieur de Bernis. 'I've been thinking that yesterday Tom said that to me which hurt my honour. If he'll unsay it now, I am ready to forget it.'

Thus, in his desire that the provocation should appear to come entirely from the other side, he gambled upon his knowledge of the Captain's mood and nature. The result did not disappoint him.

'Honour!' Leach crowed derisively. 'Your honour! Faith! That's good! That's very good for thee!' And he laughed, his eyes inviting Wogan to join him in his derisory mirth.

But the tall, lanky Irishman preserved a preternatural gravity. Nor was he entirely without anxiety. He was almost as solemn as Monsieur de Bernis, who was asking in solemn tones: 'Will you tell me what's to laugh at, Captain?'

'You! You and your honour, you cuckoldy jackanapes!'

In the next moment he was reeling under the sound and unexpected cuffing he received from the Frenchman. Monsieur de Bernis, accounting that things had gone far enough, and that Leach's words were more than sufficient to justify him, had acted quickly before Wogan could intervene.

Leach, recovering his balance, momentarily unsettled, fell back a pace or two, aghast and furious. His eyes blazed in his livid face. He began to unfasten his coat. 'By the living God! I'll cut your liver out for that, you French kite.'

'Steady, Captain! Holy Virgin! Steady, now!' cried Wogan.

Leach turned some of his rage upon him. 'Does thee think I'll take a blow from any man? I'll be steady when I's skewered his lousy vitals!' There was froth on his lips, madness in his eyes.

Wogan wrung his hands in distress. 'Och, now, Charley, what have ye done, ye fool?'

Monsieur de Bernis, following the example set him by Tom Leach, was already peeling off his coat of fine violet taffetas. 'What I had no choice but do. I'll ask you to bear witness to it, Wogan. Could I have my honour mocked by that dirty cut-throat, that foul son of a dog?'

In sheer amazement Leach suspended his preparations. Not in years had any man dared apply such terms to him in his hearing, and the last man in the world from whom he would have expected it was this Frenchman who only yesterday had swallowed his insults with such cowardly meekness. When he recovered from that gasping astonishment, he loosed a volley of obscenity, at the end of which came blood-curdling menaces.

'I'll flay thee bones for that, thee French pimp! I'll carve thee lousy hide into ribbons or ever I kills thee, thou dawcock!' He drew his sword with a vicious flourish, and flung scabbard and sword-belt from him. 'Guard thee self!' he snarled, and bounded in, to attack.

So treacherously swift and sudden was the action that Monsieur de Bernis was almost taken unawares. His sword was no more than half out of the sheath when that murderous lunge was aimed at him. He parried in the last fraction of a second with the half-drawn blade, still holding in his left hand the scabbard from which the baldrick trailed. Having parried, he broke ground, so as to disencumber himself. He cast scabbard and baldrick from him, and came on guard again promptly to meet the pursuing onslaught.

Fifty yards away the men at work on the hull of the Black Swan had seen these preliminary signs of an assault-at-arms. Now, as the blades clashed and ground together, the swordsmen feeling each other's strength, tools were dropped, and the buccaneers came swarming across the beach. Others who had been at rest leapt up to join them. They came laughing and shouting like children to a show. For there was no spectacle in the world they loved better than this which was now offered to them. The gold of the plate fleet which might be lost to them by the issue of that combat, if remembered at all, weighed for nothing at the moment by comparison with the combat itself.

Halliwell and Ellis, who came running up with them, perceived this, and paused to restrain Bundry, who was angrily insisting that the fight must at all costs be stopped. That pause for argument destroyed any chance that Bundry might have had of successfully interfering. By the time he and his two companions reached the scene, the buccaneers had formed a dense ring about the combatants through which the shipmaster sought in vain to break. The perception of his intention was enough to increase the resistance of the men, and after that it was idle of Bundry to attempt to assert authority with scoundrels who recognized no authority, bowed to no discipline, save only when in action.

Meanwhile, gleefully watching the fight, the buccaneers laughed and cheered and flung their comments freely at the fighters, as if this were just some game or friendly contest being played for their amusement.

The display was certainly a brave one, fully deserving the enthusiasm it aroused in the spectators.

The swordsmanship of Tom Leach was his one redoubtable accomplishment. Often in the past had it been tested; for having come to account himself invincible, it had afforded keenest delight to his crude, feral nature to observe the growing consciousness of helplessness, the agony of assured defeat and inevitable death in the opponent with whom he toyed before finally dispatching him. He had been at pains to acquire his skill and he supplemented it at need by a half-dozen tricks picked up in different parts of the world.

So it was with an exultant confidence that he engaged this detested de Bernis, whose arrogant existence alone offended his self-love, rendering him hideously conscious of his own defects, and for whose wife he was stark mad with covetousness. As Wogan knew, it was not the Captain's intention to kill the Frenchman. But, having defeated and disabled him, he would use this attack which de Bernis had made upon him as a pretext for cancelling the articles between them and for having recourse to those fiendish measures which he had yesterday disclosed to Wogan. Thus, without further preamble he would end the existing situation. He would squeeze the secret of the Spanish plate fleet from de Bernis and possess himself of de Bernis' wife. In the circumstances none would deny him, but, if any did, Leach would know how to deal with him.

For forty-eight hours now this had been the evil dream of Tom Leach, as he had shown Wogan yesterday when he opened his mind to him so as to deflect the Irishman's opposition.

And now, at last, his cunning had found a way to provoke the Frenchman into single combat, and here was de Bernis before his point, at his mercy.

In that spirit Tom Leach went into the engagement. And because of all that hung upon it, despite his confidence, he went into it cautiously and craftily. He knew that de Bernis enjoyed some repute as a swordsman. But there was nothing in this to intimidate Tom Leach. He had faced in his time other swordsmen of repute, and their repute had availed them little before his own superb mastery.

Agile as a cat in all his movements, and crouching a little as he fought, he advanced and retreated by little leaps, testing the other's guard at each disengage.

Erect and easily poised, parrying closely, and making no attempt to break ground, de Bernis mocked his antics, and sent a shiver of laughter through the spectators.

'Are we fighting, Captain, or are we dancing a fandango?'

The jest, combined wihh the easy firmness of the Frenchman's close guard, which depended upon the play of the wrist alone, momentarily angered Leach, and urged him to attack with greater fury and vigour.

171

But when at the culmination of this attack, a swift, sudden unexpected counter drove him back, he recovered his poise and grew calm again by instinctive perception of the necessity for it. He was realizing by now that he had to do with a swordsman of more than ordinary strength, and that he must go cautiously to work.

But he lost none of his confidence in the skill with which it had thrilled him in the past to send many a tall fellow to his account.

He advanced again; and again the blades sang together. He thrust high. De Bernis parried lightly, using the forte of the blade with great effect, and countered promptly. Leach beat the blade aside with his left hand, and lunged with confidence, so as to take the other in the shoulder, but only to find his own blade set aside in the same manner. This brought them close to each other, each within the other's guard. Thus a moment they stood, eye to eye; then Leach recovered, and leapt nimbly back. Even as he did so, de Bernis' point whirled after him, swift as lightning. He parried; but he parried late. The point driven straight at his breast, was swept by him up and outwards; but not swiftly enough. It ploughed a furrow in his right cheek,

Infuriated by that first hit and even more by his near escape of worse, he crouched lower than ever. He was breathing hard, and his face had become livid save for that crimson line from which the blood was running down his neck.

He heard the excited chatter of the crowd, and the thought of this humiliation suffered in the eyes of his followers served to steady him. The disgrace of that wound must be wiped out. He had been rash. He had underestimated his antagonist. He must go more carefully to work. He must wear down that infernally close guard from which de Bernis derived his plaguey speed, before attempting his gradual subjugation. Hitherto he had led the onslaught and had not spared himself. He had better now leave that to the other, let the Frenchman spend himself in vain attack. And as if yielding to his wishes, it was now de Bernis who advanced upon him, and the Frenchman's glittering point was everywhere at once to dazzle him. It seemed to break up

172

into two, four, six, several points that came at Leach at one and the same time, so that whilst Leach instinctively circled his blade so as to cover himself from this terrible ubiquity, yet, pressed as he was, he found himself falling back, again and yet again, for very life's sake.

It was only when at the end of a half-dozen such disengages, de Bernis failing to follow the Captain's last backward leap, Tom Leach could at last pause for breath, that the realization began to break upon him, in furious surprise and mortification, that at last he, in whom past victories had bred the insolent conviction of invincibility, had met his master.

Whilst he knew nothing of the assiduous practice with which de Bernis had been exercising and keeping alive his skill, yet he began to realize that he, himself, had rusted for lack of sword-play, and that, too confident of himself, he had neglected to preserve his speed in the only way in which a swordsman may preserve it.

Into his soul crept now the horrible, paralyzing anticipation of defeat and death which in the past he had with such gloating inspired in others. As he realized it, a change came over his face, which was grey and smeared with sweat and blood. In his eyes de Bernis read the despair that told of his conviction of defeat, and feared that perhaps, as a last treachery, Leach might throw down his sword in the hope thereby of forcing his men to intervene. Lest this should happen, de Bernis gave him now no time, but by a vigorous renewal of the attack compelled him desperately to guard himself. And now, as in the course of that forlorn defence, the Captain continued to fall back, de Bernis mocked and insulted him again.

'Will you stand your ground, you mangy dog? Or must I follow you round the island in this heat? Name of God! D'ye call yourself a swordsman? Stand, you cur! Stand for once and fight!'

Thus apostrophized, fury mounting above his terror, Leach not merely stood, but bounded forward like a panther, but only to waste his energy upon space; for de Bernis, side-stepping to avoid his charge, made him instantly spin upon his feet to meet the thrust with which from his disengage the Frenchman riposted.

The promptitude of his own recovery from that position of disadvantage revived Leach's fading courage. It was an evidence of his strength and skill. He had despaired too soon. There was no reason for it. He might yet prevail. All that he must abandon was that hope of reducing, as he had intended, a swordsman so formidable as this opponent. That, however, was no reason why he should not succeed in killing him. There were tricks he knew. He had never yet had reason to have recourse to any one of them. But he had reason now. He would show this Frenchman something.

In his new-found confidence, he fenced closely until he found the position he desired, following upon a parried thrust. He feinted in the high lines, aiming at de Bernis' throat, and as the Frenchman's blade moved up, Leach went swiftly under his guard, and with that feline agility he commanded stretched himself in a lunge; but it was not an ordinary lunge; it was an extension of it in the Italian manner, in which the whole body of the lunger is parallel with the ground and supported immediately above it upon his left hand. Thus, like a snake, almost upon his belly, he sent his point ripping upward under de Bernis' guard, assured that he must spit him like a lark, for there is no straight parry that will deflect such a lunge once it is well launched.

But de Bernis was no longer there when the other's point drove home. Pivoting slightly to the left, he averted his body by making in his turn a lunging movement outward upon the left knee. So hard-driven had Leach made his lunge in his confidence of sending it home, that, meeting no resistance, he was momentarily off his balance. A full second at least must be delayed in his recovery. But that recovery was never made. For in that unguarded second, de Bernis, whose queer, un-academic movement had placed him low upon his opponent's flank, passed his sword from side to side through the Captain's extended body.

There was an outcry simultaneously from the crowd of buccaneers, then utter silence, as Monsieur de Bernis, having withdrawn his sword, placing one foot for the purpose against the body of his fallen opponent, stood erect and grim, breathing a little hard and mopping the sweat from his brow with the sleeve of his fine cambric shirt.

Standing over Tom Leach, as he lay coughing out his evil life upon the sands, Monsieur de Bernis ruefully shook his head, and in the silence his voice rang clear.

'Too fine an end for such as you, my Captain.'


## 19

### The Head of Tom Leach

THE last choking cough of the buccaneer was uttered; the twitchings of his body had ceased, and he lay on his back grinning up at the blue sky that was like a dome of polished steel, before there was any movement in the surrounding crowd. After that single outcry, when their captain had gone down, an awed silence had fallen upon those wild men. Accustomed though they were to scenes of violence and to sudden and bloody deaths, there was something in this abrupt passing of their leader to inspire awe in those wild breasts.

Leach had been of such vitality, and had come scatheless through so many fierce encounters that he had seemed almost immortal to the men he led. And here, almost in the twinkling of an eye, behold him stretched stiff and stark. Wonder, too, now that the thing was done, was stirring in their minds as to what must be the consequences to themselves of their Captain's death.

The silence endured until Bundry roughly now broke his way through the ranks which yielded as readily as earlier they had resisted him. Ellis and Halliwell followed through the gap his passage made.

Monsieur de Bernis looked up at their approach. He was not entirely without alarm, although he contrived to conceal it; but in the main he conceived himself sufficiently protected by the circumstances. Standing where he did, with one shoulder to the sea and the other to the woods, he commanded a wide field of vision. Twenty yards away and above him on the beach, he beheld Miss Priscilla and the Major standing at gaze, and he conceived the fears that must be distressing her, if not on his account, at least on her own, since even now, if this affair should find issue in the avenging upon him of the Captain's death, she must suppose that she would be left at the mercy of these ruffians.

For the moment, however, the buccaneers still made no movement. Perhaps they considered that the matter was one beyond their judgment, and they were content to leave it to those four leaders who were now confronting Monsieur de Bernis within the space they ringed about. For Wogan was there, too, having been there indeed throughout the combat, and it was Wogan whom de Bernis immediately cited as a witness in his own defence when Bundry challenged him.

'How did this happen?' Bundry had asked, his tone harsh, his countenance forbidding, his eyes piercing as gimlets.

'It was forced upon me. I take Wogan here to witness.'

Bundry turned to question Wogan with his eyes, and Wogan blinked nervously and answered, as de Bernis counted that he would answer. He might have been less confident had he known of the understanding that had existed between Wogan and the Captain. But the Captain being dead, Wogan swiftly made up his mind that, since Leach's plot had failed, it only remained to ensure the preservation of one upon whom depended the capture of the Spanish plate fleet.

'Aye, it's the truth. Bad cess to it! Ye all know how the Captain was feeling towards him, and this morning his humour bubbled over, and he put this quarrel upon him. In fact, as some of ye may have seen, he attacked him before he had even got his sword out, and if Charley hadn't been quick and active, it's murder there would ha' been.'

Encouraged by this to greater self-assertion, Monsieur de Bernis supplemented that assurance.

'It would have been unlucky for all of you if things had fallen out otherwise. There would have been no Spanish gold, no broad pieces of eight for you if Leach had killed me as he intended. The dog might have thought of you if he had no thought for his own share of the treasure before yielding to his thirst for my blood. Well, well!' He touched the body with his foot. 'There he lies as he deserves, for his treachery to you and to me.'

And Bundry, grim-faced ever, and seeing no profit in going against de Bernis at present, nodded slowly. 'I warned him. But he was ever a headstrong fool. Maybe he's best quieted.'

And by the men, who had listened and who had been persuaded by what they heard, this seemed to be accounted a sufficient funeral oration, and closed the matter.

Monsieur de Bernis had been reasonably confident that ultimately he must prevail with them, by means of the prospect of that Spanish gold. But he had expected at the outset a violent explosion of passion over the death of their leader, and he had been bracing himself to meet it. It took him by surprise to discover how little any such effort would be required of him. In the circumstances in which it had befallen, Tom Leach's death was no calamity to any of those predatory rogues who followed him. What mattered was that the man who was to lead them to fortune had been preserved.

And so, with scarcely a lowering glance to follow him, Monsieur de Bernis was permitted to sheathe his sword and resume his garments.

The buccaneers broke up the circle and fell into babbling groups, busily discussing the event, its details and its consequences. Already even sounds of laughter began to punctuate their arguments, whilst the dead man lay there almost at their feet, staring up at them from glazing eyes. Wogan actually came to help Monsieur de Bernis into his coat.

They were at some little distance from the others, and Wogan, with his back to them, muttered so that only de Bernis could hear him.

177

'You'll come to the hut presently. We'll be after electing a new captain, and you'll be needed.' More softly still he added: 'Ye'll not be forgetting how I stood your friend, Charley, just now when ye called upon me, and that but for me ye might be carrion this minute. Sure, now, didn't your life hang upon my answer?'

'Did it so? I thought it hung upon the Spanish plate fleet. But if ye covet dead men's shoes, ye may have them for me. I'll follow presently.'

He turned from the Irishman, and went briskly up the beach to the three who remained there still at gaze.

Miss Priscilla watched his approach with eyes that were almost of awe. He was so calm, so entirely master of himself, so apparently unruffled, as if he came from some normal daily task. Was he made of iron that he could bear himself thus within a few moments of himself facing death and after killing a man?

At closer quarters, when at last he stood before them, she saw that he was very pale under his tan, and she was thankful, relieved—though she scarcely knew why—to discover in him at least this sign of feeling.

'I hope that you were not unduly alarmed,' she heard him saying, in his pleasant, level voice. 'It was my wish that you should be spared that spectacle.' Then he was addressing the Major, who stood there goggle-eyed and loose-mouthed with little of his usual colour in his florid face. 'Our practices were not in vain, you see. I had a presentiment that I should need them before we left Maldita.'

'Have you . . . Is he dead?' the Major asked him, stammering.

'I do not do things by halves, Major.'

There was a significance in this that prompted an awed question from Priscilla.

'You meant to kill him? You sought him for that purpose?'

He sensed the recoil in her. 'It had become necessary. For some days, indeed. But I had to wait. I had to wait until the time was ripe for it. It was not easy waiting; for he had become a danger. Above all, he had become a danger to you, Priscilla.'

'Was that . . . Was that why you killed him?' she asked in a hushed, faltering voice.

He considered her gravely an instant before replying. 'Not entirely. But if it did not supply all the reason, it supplied all the desire. Because of you, and because of what he had dared and what he hoped, I killed him without compunction.'

She set a hand upon his arm. At the impulsive gesture, the Major frowned a little and looked down his nose. But no heed was paid to him.

'I was afraid—so afraid—that I supplied the only reason. If you had fallen . . .' She seemed to choke. When she recovered, she continued on another thought. 'Afterwards, I was even more afraid. I thought his men would have torn you in pieces. I still do not understand. It seemed to me you must be in great danger.'

'I am in danger,' he answered quietly. 'But I was in no danger there. The danger is still to come.'

As he spoke, Pierre, from a pace or two in the background, leapt suddenly forward.

'Monsieur!'

De Bernis turned to face the sea. Into view round the shoulder of the bluff, a cable's length beyond the entrance of the cove came three tall red ships, sailing almost abreast, and taking in sail as they majestically advanced into fuller view. Across the water came the creak of blocks and the rattle of spars.

Monsieur de Bernis appeared to stiffen. 'It has come, this danger,' he said, in a low voice.

On the beach below them the buccaneers stood staring out across the lagoon in an utter stricken silence, as if suddenly paralyzed. Thus for a half-dozen heartbeats. Then, as the Union flag broke from each maintruck, and the ships began to swing into line to starboard, heading straight for the entrance of the lagoon, it was as if hell had vomited all its devils onto the shore. Shouting, cursing, raging all together, the groups broke up and the men ran this way and that, blindly, aimlessly scattering. Thus had de Bernis seen rats scamper and run when into the dark hold of a ship a light had suddenly been lowered.

In that first sudden panic, only a few of them were

purposeful in their flight, and ran deliberately for cover behind the careened hull of the Black Swan. For the thought in the minds of all must have been that these heavily armed vessels, obviously hostile, and probably belonging to Morgan's Jamaica squadron, which for months had been scouring the seas in quest of Tom Leach, would presently be sweeping the beach with their guns.

It was Wogan who led the way to cover, whilst Bundry stood and cursed him for a loathly coward and a fool, who by his very conduct was betraying them all to observant eyes upon the ships. For Bundry kept his head, and succeeded, when that first spasm of surprised terror had spent itself, in recalling the main body of the buccaneers to their senses and to some semblance of order.

'What's to alarm you, you rats?' he roared at them, straining a voice that was anything but powerful until it cracked upon his words. 'What's to alarm you? Whoever these may be, what can they know of us? What can they see here except a ship careened, and another riding peacefully at anchor?'

Men paused, steadied themselves, and came clustering about him to hear him.

'Keep your heads,' he bade them. 'Why should these ships be hunting us? They may be coming here for fresh water. How should they have known we are here? Don't you see this is but a chance arrival? Even if they be Morgan's ships, how should they recognize the Black Swan, careened as she is? If they see you scuttling to cover like those who've followed that fool Wogan, they'll learn the very thing we must conceal from them. Calm, then, in hell's name. Let 'em land, if so be that wants to. We'll see where we stand then, and what's to be done.'

Thus he harangued them, and thus restored, gradually, some of their spilled courage. Ellis and Halliwell, themselves encouraged by Bundry's obvious commonsense, went to his assistance in this task of restoring order. The buccaneers broke into groups again, and squatted on the sands or moved now, as if unalarmed, like men whose consciences are at ease. Thus, until the leading ship, a powerful vessel of forty guns, being within the neck of the lagoon, swung broadside on, and revealed open gun-ports with the guns run out ready for action.

At this the buccaneers fell again to muttering ominously, their adopted calm dissolving before that menacing sight. Still, Bundry held them in leash.

'A pox on you, you fools! What if she shows her teeth? What then? Not knowing who we are or what we may intend, she puts herself on guard. That's all.'

But, to give him the lie, a white cauliflower of smoke broke suddenly upon the flank of that leading ship, followed instantly by the boom of a gun, and simultaneously with this the Centaur staggered where she rode so peacefully at anchor, and, with a crash, there was a flight of splinters from her bulwarks where they had been struck high up by that shot at short range.

A cloud of gulls rose from the bluff, and circled mewing in affright at this sudden shattering of the silence. And like those white birds, the buccaneers too started up again in panic from the calm into which Bundry had laboured to bring them.

A second shot, following hard upon the first, to batter the bulwarks of the Centaur, riveted them there at gaze, awe-stricken and momentarily silent, expecting a broadside to follow that should sink the appropriated merchantman.

But none came. That second shot evoking no response from the Centaur, her gun-ports remaining closed, and her decks displaying no sign of life, the newcomer held her fire. She had taken in sail by now, as had the other two; and in the queer, uncanny silence rang the rattle of chains and the creaking of windlasses. They were coming to anchor there in the roadstead, within a half-dozen cables' length of the shore.

That the buccaneers had to deal with a foe, and with a foe who was well-informed of their identity, they could doubt no longer in view of that demonstration against the Centaur. What particular action would be taken by these ships when they had anchored, these men could not surmise. But that it would be action to their undoing they were assured, and in their rage at finding themselves thus trapped, helpless here ashore, in the very situation that Leach had always feared, they cast about them for a scapegoat, as stupid men will in their anger.

Thus it happened that presently there was a surge of them up the beach to the spot where Monsieur de Bernis was standing, with Miss Priscilla on his left, the Major on her other side, and Pierre, with a strained and anxious look on his coppery countenance, in the immediate background.

Monsieur de Bernis, who never in all his adventurous life had been more alert and watchful than in the last few moments, expecting precisely this development, and exercising his wits as to how to meet the onslaught when it came, drew closer to Miss Priscilla until his arm touched her shoulder.

'It comes now, this danger,' she heard him murmur. 'Stand firm, and do not be afraid.'

With that he stepped forward boldly to meet this human wave that was sweeping forward to engulf him. Very straight he stood, his chin high, his plumed hat slightly cocked, his left hand resting on the hilt of his long rapier, so that the weapon standing out behind him made a right angle with his body.

Wildly clamouring, that fierce wave—that mob of close upon two hundred men—came to break and recoil a little at his very feet. A sea of angry, evil faces confronted him; curses and foulnesses almost deafened him; brawny bare arms were outflung towards him; fists were shaken in his face, and one there was at fairly close quarters who brandished a machete as if to cut him down.

He stood like a rock before it all, dominating them by his height and his intrepidity. His voice rang like a trumpet, clear and sharp, audible even above their howls.

'What's here?' he demanded. 'You fools! Do you attack the only man with the wit to save you from this danger?'

Their noise fell to a mutter, a rumble as of receding waters, and presently it was still so that they might hear him before they made an end of him. Bundry, he saw, was trying to break his way through to the front rank. And presently that clay-faced, resolute shipmaster struggled up to him, and there turned to wave the assailants back. Bundry, after all, had a practical mind. He was not a man to be swept by passion into blindness. Never in any situation did he lose sight of the essential thing.

'Wait! Back there!' he croaked at them. 'Give us air! Let's hear what Charley has to say.' And he turned to de Bernis. 'What are these ships? Do you know?'

'Don't you? The leader there is the Royal Mary, Morgan's flagship. They are all three of the Jamaica squadron. We've Morgan on our hands. Sir Henry Morgan. But he comes too late for what he seeks. It's Tom Leach he's hunting.'

They roared at him that they, themselves, still remained to be brought to account, and how did he suppose that they would fare at Morgan's hands?

'I know how I shall fare,' he answered them, and he actually laughed as he spoke, though with more than a touch of bitterness. 'There's no doubt at all on that score. No need to be a prophet to foretell it. So if ye want to cut my throat, so as to thwart Morgan of the pleasure of hanging me, by my faith, ye're welcome. I dare say it will be the pleasanter end.'

This reminder that, whatever might betide any of them at Morgan's hands, he, who had been Morgan's lieutenant, and who, deserting, had taken to the sea again and gone a-roving in their company, would certainly meet with no mercy, gave them sudden pause. Here was something they had overlooked. There was no argument by which he could have made a stronger appeal to their sympathy.

And then, suddenly, Wogan came sliding through them. He had come from cover with several fellows at his heels, intent as most of the men were intent upon making a scapegoat of de Bernis; intent that, since destruction perhaps awaited most of them, de Bernis should certainly not escape, but should be the first to pay.

And there he stood, tall and lanky, threshing the air with his long arms in his excitement as he poured forth his venom.

'Let him talk as he pleases, it's Topgallant Charley we've to thank for this. It was he brought us here! It's his fault, so it is, that we're caught with never a keel

183

under us: trapped like rats in a gin, and helpless at the mercy of Morgan!' He flung out an accusing arm, so that his hand almost struck Monsieur de Bernis in the face. 'It's Charley's doing! Bad cess to him!'

With that he thought to destroy de Bernis, and might have destroyed any man less prompt and resolute. As it was, and as he was presently to learn, he merely supplied de Bernis with a weapon at once defensive and offensive.

Before the rage which Wogan fanned in those wild ruffianly souls could blaze forth, de Bernis was answering him, and by tone and manner and very words was compelling attention.

'Will you make a scapegoat of me for your own blundering incompetence, you lubberly oaf?'

He paused upon that question which struck Wogan dumb with amazement and arrested the attention of all. Then, with an increasing vehemence, with a simulation of indignation, he went on to scarify the Irishman.

'If we are helpless as you say, the fault lies between you and that dead cut-throat Tom Leach whose worthy lieutenant you are. If either of you had known anything of your trade, there would be guns emplaced on that bluff with which to have given Morgan a warm welcome.'

Again he paused, and this time no fear of interruption made him hurry to resume. He knew that what he had said must whet the men's appetite for more. It was something that leapt to the eye when uttered. One and all of them must perceive the force of it, and, perceiving this, they would wait for his amplification of the charge he brought, he, the accused, turned suddenly accuser.

'Pardieu! You come bleating here to make it seem that I am to blame, you numbskull! Ha! Why, you and Tom Leach between you were never fit to command anything, afloat or ashore! And here's the proof of it: in the disaster to which we are now betrayed. And you say it was I. I brought Leach to careen here because there is no better beach than this for careening in all the Caribbean. But I did not tell him to take no precautions against surprise. I did not tell him to pile his guns there on the shore like so much rotten dunnage.' He pointed to the spot where the guns had been stacked when first they were landed from the Black Swan. 'How do you know that I did not warn him? Do you suppose that I did not advise him to set up earthworks on the bluff there, and mount guns to command the entrance of the lagoon? We dispose of sixty guns between the two ships. With those we could have defied the whole Jamaica squadron. We could have sunk any ship that tried to force an entrance here. But how did he receive my advice?'

He was never allowed to tell them. For here, Wogan, quivering with fury, interrupted him. 'It's a lie! Don't be listening to him! He never advised it at all! It's a lie!'

'Is it?' quoth de Bernis, and now he was actually smiling, if very grimly. 'We will agree it is a lie. We will agree I never warned him; I never told him or you that guns should be emplaced there.' And now his voice suddenly swelled up. 'But, my faith, what were you doing, what were you and he doing, that you did not think of it for yourselves? He was the captain and you were his lieutenant, Wogan; and between you lay the responsibility for the safety of your men. How does it happen that neither you nor he thought of placing this cove in a state of fortification? Can you shift the blame for that on to any other shoulders? Leach is dead, and cannot answer. But you are alive, and you can answer. There are your men: the men who, through your carelessness and incompetent leadership, are now trapped here as you say. Answer to them, then! Answer them!'

And from the throats of those buccaneers whom de Bernis' indictment had lashed into sudden fury came in a raucous roar the demand: 'Answer! Answer!'

'Holy Virgin!' screamed Wogan, in sudden affright to see the storm so swiftly and craftily deflected upon his own head. 'Will ye be listening to this liar? Have ye never heard tell of Topgallant Charley's artfulness, that ye'll be deceived by it? Will ye be the dupes of his foxy, cozening tongue? I tell you he's . . .'

'Tell us why ye mounted no guns on the bluff!' a buccaneer interrupted him.

185

'Answer for your cuckoldy self!' cried another, and—
'Answer as he bids you, you son of a slut' a third
demanded, whereafter in a roar he was assailed by the
cry: 'Answer! Answer!'

Quaking and livid, he stood before them, accounting
himself lost, seeing himself in fancy already torn to
pieces. But de Bernis, having used Wogan as a lightning conductor so as to deflect their frenzy from himself, could now afford to despise and spare him. He
stepped forward once more to claim and hold attention.

'Let the fool be!' he admonished them. 'After all,
considering where the blame lies will not save us from
this danger. It's how to meet it we must consider.'

That made them all attentive. He saw the round
moon face of Halliwell turned upon him, and the fiery
Ellis at the ponderous shipmaster's elbow. Bundry, dry
and snappy, at his side made an interjection.

'Faith! It'll need a mort of considering!'

'Courage, Bundry! There's no reason yet to despond.'

'I don't want for courage,' Bundry snapped back.
'But I don't want for sense either.'

'A man may have both, and yet want for invention,'
said de Bernis.

'If ye can invent anything as'll help us, Charley,'
cried Halliwell, 'we'll follow you to hell after this!'

And from the men came a roar of confirmation to
encourage de Bernis. His brow was dark with thought.
He turned his shoulders upon Wogan, who, shaken and
still trembling from the fright he had sustained, had
fallen back a little, and waited white-faced and half-
numbed for whatever might follow now that he had
shot his bolt and found it turned into a boomerang.

Monsieur de Bernis was smiling wistfully as he replied. 'I doubt if Topgallant Charley will lead any
buccaneers after today, whatever may betide the rest
of you. And yet, voyons, it is possible that I may save
myself with you; for you, I think, I certainly can
save.'

There came from that villainous multitude an inarticulate sound such as is made by a great wave against
a rock. It was a gasp expressive of their incredulity
before such an announcement. And then, as the sound

of it was dying down, a gun boomed from the flagship, to turn them startled towards the sea once more.

The shot had been fired high to draw their attention. The ball crashed into the palm trees beyond them. And now, as they looked, they saw the reefed foretopsail being raised and lowered. Monsieur de Bernis, with his eyes upon that signalling, was quietly counting.

'It is a call to send a boat.'

They turned to him again for direction. He took command, quite naturally. 'We must obey, or we shall be swept with langrel. Some of you launch the long-boat. See to it, Halliwell.'

'D'ye want me to go?' quoth Halliwell, aghast.

'No, no. But be launching the boat, so as to let them see that we are obeying. Thus they will hold their fire. Take your time in doing it.'

Halliwell picked out six or eight men for the task, and these reluctantly departed, stifling their curiosity to hear what de Bernis might have to propose, by what means it was in his mind to work this miracle he had promised them.

The Frenchman addressed himself particularly to Bundry, but spoke so that all might hear him.

'You are to remember that there is one thing that Morgan wants, and that he wants it desperately; one thing that he is seeking, one thing for which, in the name of the English Crown, he has offered five hundred pounds. That is what he offers. But if I know him at all, to secure that thing which so long he has coveted, he would pay even more; a deal more. It might be possible even to drive such a bargain with him as would secure the lives and liberty of all of us in exchange for that one thing. Fortunately we are in a position to offer him this to him so precious object. It is the head of Tom Leach.'

Bundry sucked in his breath in surprise. He under-stood; but he was mistrustful. Not so the men; there was a stir among them, even a laugh or two. They perceived a grim humour in such a bargain as Mon-sieur de Bernis proposed to drive; an ingenious swin-dle, diverting to the rascals that were to profit by its perpetration; for Morgan was not to know that Leach was dead already.

And then Ellis, stepping forward, showed a difficulty.

'Aye, aye. That may well be. But who's to bear him that offer? Which of us would be safe in Morgan's lousy hands? I knows the mangy old wolf of old. If any of us was to go to him with this, that one'ld never return. Morgan'ld hang him from a yardarm and demand Tom's head as well. That's if he'ld consent to the bargain at all.'

'He'll never consent,' said Bundry, with sudden conviction. 'Why should he? He has us all at his mercy. The old wolf'll ask unconditional surrender, and you should know it, de Bernis. Ye're a fool to think otherwise, and we're fools to listen to you.'

There was a momentary start from de Bernis. But he recovered at once.

'Fools, maybe. But not because you listen. Are you so sure he has us at his mercy? What if we take to the woods? Will he dare to land a force and follow us? Has he no ambush to fear? And how long would he take to starve us into surrender?' He felt about him a revival of the hope which Bundry had momentarily damped. 'What I propose may be a forlorn chance. Morgan may utterly reject it, as you fear. But at least let us try him with this bargain. Remember how desperately he covets the head of Tom Leach; in what danger he stands of disgrace with his Government until he gets it.'

The men loudly insisting, Bundry was overborne. He shrugged. 'Very well. But, as Ellis says, who's to bear that message? Which of us can trust himself in Morgan's hands? Unless we send Wogan. And, faith, why not? It's Wogan is to blame next to Leach for this situation.'

'Me?' cried Wogan. 'Rot you, ye swine, Bundry! Ye're as much to blame yourself!'

'I'm but a shipmaster, not a fighting seaman,' Bundry answered him.

Monsieur de Bernis interposed. 'Wait! Wait!' He half-turned and looked at Priscilla, who, with the Major's protecting arm about her waist, stood there aloof, with all the sense of living through an ugly, terrifying dream.

'There is my wife,' he said. 'Morgan does not make war on women. He never did, not even before he came to be Governor of Jamaica. Nor can he treat a woman as a buccaneer. She will be safe in his hands. Her brother and my servant Pierre will suffice to man the longboat and pull her out across the lagoon. That resolves the difficulty. She shall bear our message, our offer to Morgan: our lives and liberty, with freedom to depart from here in our ships, in exchange for the head of Tom Leach.'

'Can ye hope he'll accept?' quoth Bundry, his beady dark eyes searching the calm face of the Frenchman.

'But why not?' He spoke confidently. 'He looks upon Leach as the soul and brain of you all. It is his conviction that, if Leach were taken, this company would disband. Moreover, as I've said—and it is upon this I stake all—he fears that unless he can shortly report to the Government that he has made an end of Tom Leach, the Government may make an end of him.'

There was some muttering and some considering among the men, some argument between Ellis and Bundry.

But whatever they considered, it certainly played no part in their deliberations whether Morgan would be as tender of Madame de Bernis as her husband hoped. If they thought he took too sanguine a view of that, they did not allow the thought to weigh. What mattered was that here was someone who would bear the message. What might afterwards befall her was purely the affair of de Bernis who had proposed it.

And so in the end it was even with a measure of gratitude, and a deal of admiration for the wit which had discovered this possible way of escape, that they urged de Bernis to put his plan into execution.

189

## 20

# Sir Henry Morgan

MISS PRISCILLA went down the beach to the boat which Halliwell's men had launched. She walked between Monsieur de Bernis and Major Sands, with Ellis and Bundry hanging on either flank, Pierre following at their heels, and a few of the buccaneers straggling after them; and she walked as she had walked in dreams, her mind clouded by a mist of unreality.

Few words had been employed. When the matter was settled between Monsieur de Bernis and the buccaneers, the Frenchman had stepped up to her.

'You have heard what is required of you, Priscilla?' he had said, and he was gently smiling encouragement.

She nodded. 'I have heard,' she said, and there checked, staring at him, her face blenched, deepest trouble in her clear eyes.

Gravely he answered that look: 'You have nothing to fear. Sir Henry Morgan will treat you with consideration.'

'I could not suppose that you would send me unless you were convinced of that,' she answered steadily. Then she asked the question that revealed the real source of her fear. 'But you?'

'I?' His smile deepened a little. He shrugged. 'I am in the hands of Fate. I do not think he will treat me unkindly. It depends now upon you.'

'Upon me?'

'Upon your bearing this message for us and upon how you deliver it.'

'If that is really so; if this is really for your good, you can depend upon me indeed.'

He inclined his head in acknowledgement.

'Come, then. We have no time to lose. The boat is ready. I will recite the message for you as we go.'

Thus they had set out, the Major silent, endeavouring to preserve a stolidity upon his broad florid countenance, least he should betray his surprise and satisfaction at beholding the opening of a door of escape from circumstances which to him had been intolerable as a nightmare.

As they went, Monsieur de Bernis gave her the terms of the message she was to deliver, and he desired Major Sands's attention to it also. They were simply to offer Morgan the head of Tom Leach, upon which he had placed the price of five hundred pounds, in exchange for the lives and freedom to depart, at their own leisure in their own ships, of all those now upon Maldita. If more were needed, and as an earnest of their good faith and their intention to quit piracy, they would disarm their ships, and cast their guns into the sea under Morgan's eyes.

If Morgan would not agree these terms, then let him know that, abundantly supplied with provisions and ammunition, they would take to the woods, and if he chose to pursue them there, he would do so at his peril. In such circumstances, they would be in a position to hold out indefinitely.

At his request, she repeated the words after him, as did also Major Sands. Ellis and Bundry nodded their gloomy approval of the message, and so they came to the wet sand at the water's edge, where half-a-dozen men, knee-deep in the sea, held the long boat in readiness.

Halliwell offered to carry the lady to the boat, the Major and Pierre could wade for themselves.

But now Priscilla, white and trembling, turned suddenly fully to face de Bernis, and caught him by the arms above the elbow.

'Charles!' was all that she could say. 'Charles!' But there was agony in her voice, a haunting fear in her eyes.

He bowed his tall uncovered head, and a smile of encouragement, sweet and rather wistful, irradiated the swarthy gloom of it.

'Child! I repeat, you have nothing to fear. Nothing. Morgan does not make war upon women.'

There was a flash that was almost of anger from her eyes. 'Have you not yet understood that it is not for myself that I am afraid? Must you always think so meanly of me?'

The smile passed from his face; pain was reflected in it; his eyes, considering her, grew sad.

'Brave little soul . . .' he began, and there checked. He turned to Ellis and Bundry who stood by. 'Sirs, give us leave apart a moment. It is possible that I may never see her again.'

Ellis made shift to move away. But the cold, calculating Bundry resolutely stood his ground. He tightened his thin lips and shook his head.

'It will not serve, Charley. We know the message that she carries now. We don't know the message she may carry if you speak to her apart.'

'You don't trust me?' He seemed genuinely taken aback.

Bundry spat thoughtfully. 'I'ld rather trust myself if it comes to trusting anybody.'

'But what could I do? What other message could I possibly send? What bargain could I drive for myself, since that must be what's in your mind?'

'I don't know. But, not knowing, we'll keep on the safe side. Come, man. Take your leaves here. What the devil! You're man and wife, ain't ye? What need to be so coy?'

Monsieur de Bernis sighed, and smiled again, a little sadly. 'So, Priscilla. There is no more to say. It is perhaps just as well.' He bent and kissed her. It was his intention to kiss her cheek; but she turned her lips fully to meet his own.

'Charles!' she said again, in that low, anguished voice.

Monsieur de Bernis stepped back, and waved to Halliwell. The corpulent shipmaster obeying the signal picked her up in his arms, and waded out to bestow her in the stern-sheets of the waiting boat. Then the Major and Pierre followed, swung each a leg over the side, took their places on the thwarts, and got out the sweeps. The buccaneers gave the boat a forward thrust, and so she was launched upon her voyage, a little white flag of truce fluttering in her bows.

Monsieur de Bernis stood with the wavelets rustling at his feet watching the boat for a little while. Priscilla did not look back. She sat in the stern-sheets, with her shoulders to the shore, a little crumpled figure in green. At last he turned, and very slowly, with his chin sinking into the ruffles at his throat, he moved up the beach, Bundry and Ellis following him with no word spoken.

In the longboat Priscilla was softly weeping, so that at last Pierre, who sat beyond the Major, was moved to comfort her. He spoke to her over the Major's shoulder.

'Mademoiselle,' he begged her in French, 'do not weep. There is no need. All will be well with Monsieur de Bernis. He knows what he is doing. Believe me, all will be well with him.'

'And, anyway,' said the Major, 'it's no great matter if it isn't.'

Thus he expressed the bitterness aroused in him by that little scene he had witnessed at the water's edge. It provided a fitting, exasperating climax to all that he had been constrained to endure in this past month. It was high time, he thought, to restore things to their proper places in their lives, high time that Priscilla should recover the perspective which she appeared, from her latest conduct, utterly to have lost. The vision of that kiss was something that haunted the Major, and set his memory shuddering with horror. Roughly, then, did he attack the business of correcting the focus of Miss Priscilla's mental sight.

His words certainly had the immediate effect of checking her tears. Momentarily, at least, her concern, anxiety, and grief were overcome by indignation. From a white, tear-stained face her eyes blazed as they encountered the Major's.

'What do you dare to say?' she asked him, with such scornful anger that he would not have had the temerity to repeat his words even if she had given him time. 'Is that how you speak of a man who has placed himself in danger, who has pledged his very life to ensure our safety, to provide us with a means of escape?'

The Major, meeting resentment with resentment, answered sullenly.

'I don't perceive that at all. Stab me if I do.'

'You don't? Then you are even more stupid than I have been supposing you.'

'Priscilla!' He stopped rowing in his unutterable stupefaction.

Pierre's oars, sweeping rhythmically forward, struck his own suspended ones, and jarred him unpleasantly, and almost knocked him off his thwart. But he paid little heed to that. Recovering his balance mechanically, he sat with fallen jaw and goggling eyes, staring incredulously at this fledgeling who had dared to say such a thing to him. It was the end of the world. Only the realization that, overwrought, she was not responsible for her words enabled him to condone it. He smiled with the patient, exasperatingly indulgent amusement of noble minds.

'How rash you are in your conclusions! You display the intolerance of youth and inexperience.'

'Better than the mean intolerance of age from which you appear to be suffering, sir.'

This was a cruel thrust under the Major's guard. But, having recovered from one stupefaction, he was now prepared for anything. In the same indulgent tone he continued.

'This pirate fellow is using us for his own ends. If you can't see that, you must be purblind, Priscilla. Consider the terms of the message . . .'

'There is nothing to consider but what he is doing. No perversity, no meanness, can change the appearance of that. He has had no thought but to deliver us. It is noble of him. It justifies all my steady faith in him.'

The Major permitted himself to laugh at this. Looking at his face, distorted by that sardonic hilarity, she considered it the most repulsive she had ever seen.

'Noble!' he mocked, and went on to explain his point of view. 'That nobility is rooted in concern for his own skin. Finding himself caught, this thieving pirate hopes to make terms; and he counts himself lucky to have us under his hand, so that he may send us with his message. That's his nobility, as you shall see, child.'

From behind him came the gentle voice and the imperfect English of Pierre.

'If Monsieur de Bernis escape himself from t'is, he shall be tol' what a good opinion you 'ave of him.'

'Why, so he shall! I shall tell him so, myself,' the Major snorted, in fresh anger at this further opposition.

Ill-humouredly he bent to the oars again, and after that an angry silence reigned in the boat, Priscilla disdaining to push the argument further.

In this mood they came bumping alongside of the Royal Mary, Morgan's flagship, until Pierre, standing at the bows, steadied the longboat at the foot of the entrance-ladder.

Miss Priscilla, disdaining the assistance of the Major's proffered hand, but accepting that which Pierre extended, was the first to climb the tall red side of the ship, with Major Sands following close behind to save her from falling, in case of need.

At the head of the ladder she was received by a middle-aged, overdressed man of an almost obese habit of body, whose yellow fleshly face, adorned by a pair of drooping moustaches, was coarse and unprepossessing. This was Sir Henry Morgan. From the bulwarks he had watched her ascent of the accommodation ladder with a scowling stare. He advanced to hand her down into the waist of the ship. Having done so he stood back a pace to survey her. Behind him, beyond the main-hatch stood a score of musketeers drawn up in file, a youthful-looking officer standing a few paces in front of them. Like Morgan they, too, stared, when they saw the lady standing at the head of the accommodation ladder.

'Save us! What's here?' he asked, when he stood level with her in the waist. 'In God's name, who may you be, madam?'

She answered him steadily. 'I am Priscilla Harradine, daughter of Sir John Harradine, who was lately Captain-General of the Leeward Islands.' And she added: 'You will be Sir Henry Morgan?'

He removed his gaudily plumed hat from his heavy periwig, and made a leg. There was something ponderously sardonic in his manner, yet with a hint of gallantry behind it, as if in that obese and sagging body still smouldered embers of the romantic fires of sprightlier days.

'To serve you, madam. But what may Miss Priscilla Harradine be doing in the blackguardly company of Tom Leach and his crew? Odd company that for a Captain-General's daughter.'

'I come as an ambassador, Sir Henry.'

'From those cut-throats? Od rot me, madam! But how do you happen amongst them?'

The Major who had meanwhile climbed the ladder, and for a moment had paused at the head of it, stepped down into the waist and thrust himself forward selfsufficiently. At last he found himself among men who could not ignore his rank and consequence.

'I am Major Sands,' he announced. 'Major Bartholomew Sands, second-in-command at Antigua to the late Sir John Harradine.'

The dark eyes of Morgan considered him, and the Major was not reassured. He found those eyes of a singular, mocking malevolence. The heavy face, darkened by a frown at the roof of the prominent predatory nose, reflected none of the deference the Major had hoped to command by the announcement of his name and rank.

'That being so, and Sir John being dead, what the devil are you doing so far from your command? Were you both kidnapped from Antigua by any chance? If so, I hadn't heard of it.'

In dignified resentment of Sir Henry's manner, the Major answered loftily. 'We were on our way to England on a ship named the Centaur. She's over there.' He pointed to her where she rode within the lagoon. 'With us travelled a French ruffian named de Bernis, who once, I believe, was your lieutenant.'

'Ah!' the dull yellow face lighted suddenly with interest. The sneering malevolence of its expression seemed to deepen. 'That ruffian de Bernis, eh? Continue, pray.'

Miss Priscilla would here have interrupted the Major. But he would not be interrupted. He swept on headlong with his tale of the boarding of the Centaur by Tom Leach, and the manner in which de Bernis had revealed himself to the pirates. He was still sketching

196

what had followed and abusively qualifying de Bernis' name at every mention of it, when Sir Henry, standing before him with wide-planted feet and arms akimbo, roughly interrupted him.

'If ye're telling me the truth,' he said, 'seems to me this de Bernis has saved your lives and perhaps more.'

'*If* I am telling you the truth?' quoth the Major, with immense dignity. '*If* I am telling you the truth, do you say, Sir Henry? That is very nearly to give me the lie circumstantial.'

'Devil take your vapours, sir,' Morgan roared at him. 'What then? Unless you're a liar, you're the meanest pimp I've met in years.'

The Major, going red and white by turns, drew himself up. 'Sir Henry, I have the honour to hold the King's commission, and . . .'

'Why, so have I, sir. So have I. And so has many another scoundrel. That proves nothing.' He made a repudiating gesture with an enormous freckled hand. 'We're wasting time. What I desire to know is how you come here aboard my ship, and why.' He swung to the lady with a smirk and a bow. 'Perhaps you will tell me, madam.'

Eagerly she complied, glad that the poison Major Sands had been pouring forth was stemmed at last. 'We bring you a message, Sir Henry, from Monsieur de Bernis.'

'Ah!' He was all attention, ignoring the Major, who had fallen back, and livid with anger was biting his lip.

'An offer of terms, Sir Henry.'

'Terms?' He blew out his enormous cheeks. 'Terms!' He turned with a hoarse, fat laugh to the officer behind him. 'There's impudence! An offer of terms when we have them at the pistol-muzzle. Well, well! A God's name! What are these terms?'

She began to explain to him, as she had been instructed, that the buccaneers were not quite at the pistol-muzzle; that they could take to the woods, where they might not be followed save at great peril. She was still eloquently at this when he interrupted her, a rude, overbearing man.

'The terms! The terms!' he demanded impatiently.

197

She stated them. Monsieur de Bernis offered to give up Tom Leach, alive or dead, to disarm the ships and fling their guns into the sea, in return for the honours of war in other respects and freedom for the buccaneers to depart in their own time. Those were the terms. But she did more than state them; her tone pleaded for their acceptance as if she were advocating the cause of Monsieur de Bernis.

The dark eyes embedded in those bulging cheeks watched her curiously the while, the keen ears and keen wits missing nothing. Then Sir Henry looked at the livid Major, leaning with affectations of wounded dignity against the bulwarks, and under cover of his drooping moustache his heavy lips writhed with sardonic mirth.

'The honours of war!' he echoed slowly, a man infinitely amused.

It provoked from her a resumption of the argument of what the buccaneers could still do if their terms were not accepted. This time he listened to her, the fleshly face creased in a sly amusement that she found almost exasperating. This fat, oily, sinister man was without mercy; a man who loved cruelty for its own sake. She saw this plainly, and yet, faint and nauseated, she gallantly held her ground before him, fighting the battle of Monsieur de Bernis.

'Ah!' he said, when she had done. 'Madam, you are well delivered out of your dangers, and so are you, Major. I congratulate you both upon that. It is no wonder, madam, that you plead the case of that rascal de Bernis so eloquently. I perceive and respect the gratitude that moves you.'

'And you will agree his terms?' In her eagerness she stepped close up to him.

He smiled down upon her, and again there was in his manner that hint of gallantry. Then his eyes travelled beyond her to the Major. 'You, sir, are not so deeply concerned, I think?'

'At the risk of being misunderstood again,' the Major answered importantly, 'I must confess that I am not. Right is right, and wrong is wrong. I have a clear perception, I hope, of one and the other. As for gratitude, I do not perceive the occasion for it. This fellow de Bernis has found us convenient tools for his work. There was no man of all that crew of cut-throats who would have ventured within your reach to deliver his message.'

The great body shook with sudden laughter. 'That I can believe, by God! They've a respect for my yard-arms. You may be right, Major. You may be right.' He turned abruptly to the young officer in command of the musketeers.

'Take a dozen men, Sharples, and go ashore with a white flag. Tell those sons of dogs that before I'll so much as discuss terms with them, I demand the sur-render, not only of Tom Leach, but of this rascal de Bernis as well. When I have those two aboard here, I'll consider what's to do. Not before. And tell them that my guns are trained on the beach, and that if I see any sign of a movement towards the woods, I'll sweep them to hell with langrel. Is that clear? Away with you.'

The fair-faced lieutenant's salute was eloquent of understanding. His fresh young voice rang out in a sharp command. Musketeers stepped briskly forward in obedience, and filed towards the entrance ladder.

The Major was smiling. For this he could forgive Morgan everything. The fellow might be a rude scoun-drelly turncoat pirate, but he knew how to handle a situation.

Miss Priscilla, white now to the lips, took a stum-bling step towards Sir Henry, and laid a timid, trem-bling hand upon his massive arm.

'Sir . . . Sir . . .' she stammered pleadingly.

Peremptorily the stout gentleman waved his officer away, and turned to hear her. 'Your servant, madam.'

'Sir, what the Major has said is scarcely true. I am sure that, in sending us, Monsieur de Bernis' main thought was to deliver us from danger. I owe so much to him . . . so very much. He has behaved so gallantly . . . so gallantly. . . .'

Sir Henry laughed a deep, throaty laugh that made her shudder. Then he frowned and the frown brought back that evil, sinister wrinkle to the base of his nose.

'Oh, ah! To be sure. To be sure. Vastly gallant fellows these Frenchmen. And who more gallant than de Bernis? Oh, I'll be sworn he behaved gallantly. He was never the man to waste opportunities.' And Sir Henry winked at the Major, who thought him a fellow of unspeakable vulgarity and accounted it an outrage that such a man should hold a knighthood and a governorship.

'Sir, you misunderstand me!' cried Priscilla, distraught.

'Not I, madam. Not I. That ruffian de Bernis was never the man to waste his opportunities, any more than I was when I was no better than is he. I understand perfectly. May I be flayed else. Oh, and sympathetically. I grow fat and old, madam; but I carry a young heart under all this blubber.'

She thought him disgusting, and she shuddered under his leering eyes. But bravely she stifled her feelings.

'Sir Henry, I desire you to hear me. I implore you to hear me.'

'Be sure, ma'am, that beauty never implored Harry Morgan in vain.' He seemed to laugh inwardly, as if at memories. 'You would say, madam?'

'It is of Monsieur de Bernis, sir. I owe life and more than life to him . . .'

'Why, so I had understood.' The dark eyes twinkled odiously. She ignored the interruption. 'My father was a loyal and valued servant of the Crown. Surely, Sir . . . Surely the service rendered by Monsieur de Bernis to my father's daughter should weigh for something in his favour. Should be accounted to him in any judgment.'

He considered her with mock-gravity. Then the horrible fellow was moved again to mirth. 'It's a romantical plea and a novel. Od's heart! I rendered in my day services to many a father's daughter; but none ever counted them to my credit. I lacked your advocacy, madam.' He was turning away.

'But, Sir Henry . . .' She began again in desperation.

But Sir Henry could not stay. 'No more now, madam.' Unceremoniously he turned on his heel, and rolled away on his elephantine legs, bawling for bos'n and gunner, and issuing orders right and left.

## 21

## *The Surrender*

IN miserable dejection Miss Priscilla watched the hands mustered for shore go over the side, followed by Lieutenant Sharples. From the bulwarks she saw them board the longboat in which Pierre waited, saw it cast off and draw away towards the beach.

An officer came to her with Sir Henry's compliments and would she and Major Sands accept the Admiral's hospitality in the great cabin.

Major Sands supported the invitation kindly, gentle concern now replacing in him an indignation which he perceived could nothing profit him.

Moreover a link between them that had almost snapped was restored by his sense that they were fellow-victims of the overbearing vulgarity of that pirate-knight Sir Henry Morgan. Then, too, the Major was disposed to be magnanimous and to forgive all offence out of regard for the fact that the offender was a woman, young and tender, who had been tried beyond all endurance. It was therefore in a tone of solicitude that he said:

'You will be better in the cabin, Priscilla.'

'I thank you,' she answered coldly. 'I am well enough here.'

The officer bowed and withdrew. She remained leaning on the bulwarks, her gaze following the boat in its swift journey towards the beach, where the buccaneers waited. She could make out quite clearly amongst them, well in the foreground, the tall, commanding figure of Monsieur de Bernis. Bundry, Halliwell, and Ellis were with him, and the four of them made a group apart from the rest.

Major Sands stood at her elbow. 'My dear Priscilla, this is the end of the adventure, and we have deep cause for thankfulness that it should end so. Deep cause.'

'We have,' she miserably agreed with him. 'For thankfulness to Charles de Bernis.'

This was not at all the answer he desired. But he realized the futility of argument with a mind obsessed and obstinate. It could lead only to acrimony, and acrimony was the last thing the Major desired between them. He could afford, after all, he reflected, to be generous. The nightmare composed of all the happenings since they had first seen de Bernis climbing the accommodation ladder of the Centaur in Fort Royal Bay, a month ago, was now at an end. Soon, now, this swaggering, posturing pirate would pay the price of his misdeeds; they would be on their way to England at last, with all this happily behind them, an ugly, fantastic interlude in their well-ordered lives which time would rapidly erase from the tablets of their memories. Priscilla would be restored to the sanity disturbed in her by the passage across her tender life of that ruffling filibuster. Magnanimously Major Sands would forget the incident, and all would be again as it had been before this disastrous adventure.

Thus Major Sands reassured himself and took confident comfort, whilst Miss Priscilla watched the boat's progress towards land.

Its keel grated on the fine shingle, and Lieutenant Sharples stepped ashore alone, leaving his musketeers in the boat with their firelocks at the ready. Miss Priscilla could distinctly make out the officer in his long red coat, standing stiffly before Monsieur de Bernis and his three companions. In the background the main body of the buccaneers was assembled. They were drawn up with some semblance of order in their ranks, and it was obvious that they were attentive to what was passing between their leaders and the representative of Sir Henry Morgan.

In this group it was clear that the Lieutenant's message was creating some excitement. Bundry, Ellis, and Halliwell appeared to be talking all at once and with some violence of gesture. Monsieur de Bernis remained a little aloof looking on whilst his own fate was being decided. One only attempt he had made to sway the decision, and that was when first Lieutenant Sharples had delivered Morgan's message, demanding de Bernis' own surrender. With some heat he had taken it upon himself to reply, as well he might since he was concerned so closely.

'Go you back to Morgan,' he had said before any of the others had time to speak, 'and tell him that if that's his last word, we can take to the woods and . . .'

There, however, he had been interrupted by Halliwell. Thrusting him aside almost roughly with his elbow, the corpulent shipmaster had stepped forward.

'Hell!' he had growled. 'There's no sense in that. Morgan can sink the Centaur and riddle the Black Swan until she's just a wreck of timber, leaving us here to rot and maybe starve.'

'Steady! Steady!' Bundry had interposed. 'We're not so easily snuffed. We've timber in plenty and the means and the ability to build.'

'You would be wise to remember that Sir Henry is a determined man,' the Lieutenant had stiffly answered. 'You will not defeat him so easily, as you should know. If you defy him, be sure that he will leave a ship here to harass you, and to see that not one of you departs the island. Your only hope lies in compliance now. Deliver up Leach and de Bernis, and you may find Sir Henry merciful to the rest of you. But those two he will have; and he'll certainly have the rest of you as well, if you attempt to resist him.'

Argument followed. Wogan whiningly supported Sir Henry's envoy. 'Och now, what else can we do but comply? Sure, it's a hateful thing, so it is, to surrender Charley. But when it's either that or surrendering every mother's son of us, what choice have we?'

'And that's the plaguey fact,' Halliwell cordially agreed.

But Bundry, of tougher fibre and further vision, was for resistance. If he could keep de Bernis with them and with their ships unimpaired, even if they lost their guns, they might still try conclusions with the Spanish plate ships. Buccaneers had overcome far heavier odds in their time. So cursing his companions for a pair of spiritless rats, he pleaded that Morgan should remain content with Leach only. Leach they would surrender at once. Ellis, swayed by him, supplemented his arguments. But the Lieutenant remained unmoved. He answered shortly that he had no authority to haggle or parley, that he had delivered his message, and that the rest was their affair. It was in vain that Bundry and Ellis begged him at least to carry their answer to Morgan. Lieutenant Sharples declared it idle. The very lack of unanimity amongst them strengthened his determination. Finally he summoned them to make up their minds without further delay; and threatening to depart and leave them to their fate, he finally broke down their resistance.

Bundry turned his clay-coloured face to de Bernis, thrusting out a lip and shrugging his disgust.

'I've done what I could, Charley. You've heard.'

Monsieur de Bernis was very solemn. 'I've heard. I understand. It is finished, then.' He, too, shrugged. 'The fortune of war.' Himself he lifted over his head the silver-encrusted baldrick that carried his sword, and proffered it to Sharples in token of surrender.

The Lieutenant took it, inclining his head a little in acknowledgement, and handed it to one of his men who stood by the bow of the stranded longboat.

'And now Tom Leach, if you please,' he said, looking round as he spoke, wondering, perhaps, that he had not yet seen that redoubtable pirate, and that he should not have been present at this parley.

'Ah, yes,' said Bundry grimly. 'Tom Leach, to be sure.' He hesitated a moment, his piercing eyes upon the fair young face of the lieutenant. 'Dead or alive was the condition,' he said, between question and assertion.

Lieutenant Sharples stared. 'What? Is he dead already?'

Bundry nodded, turned, and started off up the beach towards the massed buccaneers and what lay behind them, screened by them.

Monsieur de Bernis went after him, caught and held him a moment by the shoulder whilst he murmured something to him. It was something that made that pallid mask momentarily change its set expression. Then, with a grin and a nod, Bundry went on, and de Bernis came slowly back, and at a word from Sharples entered the waiting boat.

Watching ever from the red bulwarks of the Royal Mary, Priscilla saw and understood. A little moan escaped her.

'The cowards! The treacherous cowards!' she cried. 'They have surrendered him. Surrendered him to save their vile skins.'

The Major, careful to betray no satisfaction, answered colourlessly.

'Naturally. Could anything else have been expected of them?' He set an arm about her to steady and comfort her as she faltered there, suddenly overcome, her senses swimming.

Tenderly he supported her as far as the main-hatch, and gently lowered her to sit upon the coaming. There, with her elbows on her knees, she took her head in her hands, abandoning herself to silent misery. The Major sat down beside her, and his arm was soothingly placed again about her shoulders. He could go so far as to stifle jealous resentment of this overwhelming grief. But he had no consoling words to offer her.

An officer, pacing by the rail of the quarter-deck, looked down upon them, as did, too, from the other side, some of the hands lounging on the forecastle. But Miss Priscilla heeded nobody and nothing. Grief and horror dazed her senses. It was as if some part of her had been violently wrenched away.

She was aroused at last by the gusty passage of the large gaudy figure of the Admiral, who crossed the waist with elephantine tread, a couple of men following him. As in a dream she remembered having just heard someone say that Sharples was returning. She looked up to see Sir Henry reach the bulwarks and then she heard his brazen voice raised in passion.

'Where the hell's Leach, then? Sharples hasn't got him, after all. Damn him for a fool! Below there, Aldersly. Bid Benjamin stand by with his gun-crew. He'll be needed in a moment. I'll sweep them all to hell! I'll teach the dogs! Do they think they can get gay with Henry Morgan?'

He leaned far over the bulwarks to speak to someone immediately below.

'What the devil's this, Sharples? Where's Tom Leach?'

'A moment, Sir Henry!' sang the lieutenant's voice from below.

The boat scraped and bumped against the sides of the Royal Mary as it brought up at the foot of the ladder. A pause followed, and then the staring, fearful eyes of Priscilla beheld the figure of Monsieur de Bernis gradually rising above the bulwarks, until he stood there, steadying himself by a ratline, at the head of the entrance-ladder. Calm and smiling, as she had ever known him in the face of every peril, did he now appear. It was incredible that a man should meet his fate so gallantly.

Sir Henry, standing below him and a little aside, looked up to meet the Frenchman's debonair smile with a scowl, whilst the head and shoulders of de Bernis' servant Pierre began to come into view as he climbed close in his master's wake.

'Where the hell is Leach, then?' Sir Henry trumpeted. 'What does this mean?'

Steadying himself ever by the ratline, Monsieur de Bernis half-turned to Pierre, and held out his left hand. The half-caste proffered him a bundle in coarse sail-cloth, the natural grey of which was smeared and stained with blood. Monsieur de Bernis took it, balanced it a moment, and then tossed it forward. It fell at Sir Henry's feet, with a soft thud. The Admiral looked down at it, and then up at Monsieur de Bernis, frowning.

'That's all of him you need,' said Monsieur de Bernis. 'All of him you asked for. The head, on which you set the price of five hundred pounds.'

Sir Henry breathed gustily. 'Good God!' His face empurpled. He looked down again at the gruesome bundle from which a stain was slowly spreading on the yellow deck. Then he touched it with a foot that was shod in a gaudily rosetted shoe. He touched it gingerly at first, then kicked it vigorously aside.

'Take that away!' he roared to one of the men who attended him, and upon that gave his attention once more to de Bernis.

'Ye're damned literal, Charles,' he snorted.

De Bernis leapt lightly down to the deck.

'Which is only another way of saying that I am as good as my word. Or as good as my boast, if you prefer it. It needs a thief to catch a thief, as Major Sands there thinks they knew who made you Governor of Jamaica.'

Sir Henry looked across at Major Sands where he had come to his feet in his bewilderment. He stood beside Miss Priscilla, who remained seated staring, scarcely daring to believe what was suddenly being made plain at least in part.

'Oh? Him!' said Sir Henry. 'He thinks that, does he? Bah!' And he shrugged the pompous Major out of his further consideration. 'We've other things to think of. There's a deal here that needs to be explained.'

'You shall have all the explanation you could wish when you've paid me the five hundred for that head, and the other five hundred you wagered me that I could not get it for you.'

Morgan made a wry face. 'Aye. You never doubt yourself, do you, Charles?'

'I've never had occasion to. But I have been doubting you for three mortal days. Three days late you are at the rendez-vous here, and for three days I've been in hell from anxiety, and forced to endure that dead dog's intolerable insults. But I paid him in full when you hove in sight this morning. It was necessary, too, so that I might be literal, as you say.'

'We are quits on that, anyway,' grumbled Morgan. 'For ye'ld be in mortal anxiety now but for my stratagem to bring you safely out of their hands. Where would ye be if I hadn't demanded that they should give you up?'

'Where I should deserve to be for trusting to a fool. For only a fool would have overlooked anything so obvious.'

207

Morgan blew out his cheeks. 'Oddsfish! I've never known the like of your assurance.'

'Don't I justify it? Have I done less than I undertook?'

'Oh, I'll confess to that. Be damned to you. I take it luck favoured you.'

'A little. It saved me the trouble of going after Leach as I intended. He just came blundering across my path whilst I was on my way to Guadeloupe. But it would have made no difference if he hadn't, except that I've saved the Government the expense of fitting a ship in which to go looking for him.'

'Come below,' said Morgan. 'I want to hear about it.'

## 22

## *The Madness of Priscilla*

IN THE great cabin of the Royal Mary sat Miss Priscilla with Major Sands, Sir Henry Morgan, and Monsieur de Bernis. It was by the Frenchman's request that those other two had been brought below, so that they might learn at the same time what yet remained to be learnt in explanation of events which they had so closely shared.

They were seated about the table, and with them sat Captain Aldridge, a spare, lantern-jawed, middle-aged man of a sallow complexion, who, under the Admiral, Sir Henry Morgan, commanded the Royal Mary.

Monsieur de Bernis was quietly talking, giving them closer details of the adventure and of the manner in which he had gone about carrying out his undertaking to secure the coveted head of Tom Leach.

Priscilla, so abruptly lifted out of her terrible apprehensions, sat with senses still swimming from the shocks they had sustained that morning, scarcely daring to credit what she heard and what she had seen. Major Sands was wrapped in gloom. His feelings were mixed and fraught with apprehensions. He could not even pretend that he rejoiced in this solution, although he could scarcely yet analyze his true feelings.

Morgan alone was in high glee, despite the fact that he had lost a wager of five hundred pounds. Relieved of the shadow that had been hanging over him, the dread of drastic action against him at Whitehall if Tom Leach were to continue his ravages upon the seas, he was boisterously hilarious. Once or twice he interrupted the narrative with ribald comments delivered in explosions of laughter, and in the sing-song tones that proclaimed his Welsh origin.

He was loudest in his hilarity when de Bernis gave him the facts of the boarding of the Centaur by Leach and the manner in which he had met the pirate.

'Oddsfish! If ever there was a rogue who knew how to pluck victory from defeat, how to win advantage from disaster, you are that rogue, indeed, Charles. It's not the first time ye've pushed back the springs of a gin that held ye. Ye may thank the ready fertility of your lying. Faith! Ye've a great gift of it, whatever.'

'If ye mean the fable of the Spanish plate fleet,' said de Bernis, 'you are not to suppose that was an invention of the moment. It had been long premeditated. It was the lure with which from the outset I had meant to draw Leach to Maldita. The fact that he was in need of careening was no more than I expected of him. He always was; for he was always a bad seaman.'

When the tale was done, and whilst Sir Henry was ladling out a punch of rum and limes and sugar which the steward had prepared for them, Captain Aldridge stirred in his chair to ask a question.

'You have made all clear but one thing. What I don't understand is why you should have fought Leach this morning when we were already off Maldita. Since you knew that we had but to close our grip so as to hold him, why the devil should you have risked your life against him?'

'Risk?' Monsieur de Bernis was contemptuous. 'That was no risk. Leach may have been a swordsman to pirates; to a swordsman he was just a pirate.'

'Ye'll need a better answer, Charles,' Morgan admonished him.

For once de Bernis appeared self-conscious. He hesitated; then shrugged.

'Oh, there were reasons, of course. For one thing I owed it to him.' Almost unconsciously his dark eyes travelled to Priscilla, who was steadily regarding him, then back again to Morgan's great yellow countenance. 'He had used expressions to be answered in no other way, and he had done things payment for which I choose to regard as my personal concern. Besides, Morgan, if Leach had been alive when you hove in sight, be sure there would have been no such tame surrender. His was a very desperate spirit.'

'Ah, bah! What could he have done, trapped here?'

'He could have taken to the woods with his men, just as I told you in the message Miss Priscilla bore you; and there you could not have pursued him. He might have lived to recommence. Even if he did not, before he came by his end he might have wrought such evil as I must have accounted beyond repair.'

'Why, what could he have done? What evil?' Morgan pressed him.

Again Monsieur de Bernis hesitated a little. Then, with an abrupt gesture, he indicated Major Sands and Miss Priscilla Harradine.

'This gentleman and this lady would have remained in his hands if he had chosen defiance. And that from the nature of him he certainly would have chosen.'

Morgan's brows went up, as he looked at the Major. It was as if he marvelled that de Bernis should have been moved to risks for that popinjay. But they came down again when his glance travelled on to Miss Priscilla. He guffawed his sudden understanding, and slapped the table with his great hand.

'So! So! Damme, it becomes plain. There was a rivalry between ye. Madam said you had been mighty gallant.'

His elephantine body shook with laughter. The roar of it reverberated through the cabin. The Major coughed and scowled. Miss Priscilla's face flamed scarlet, and her troubled, indignant eyes reproved the

210

indecent mirth. The lean, leathern face of Aldridge was distended in a sour grin.

Only Monsieur de Bernis remained entirely impassive. He waited patiently until the Admiral's laughter had diminished. Then he spoke icily.

'The King may have made you a knight and he may have made you Governor of Jamaica; but in spite of it, Morgan, you remain just what God made you, and why He should have made you at all remains inscrutable. Pray pay no heed to him, Priscilla. Though he sits in the cabin, by his manners his proper place is the forecastle.'

'Damn your sour tongue, whatever!' Morgan answered him, without malice, laughter still bubbling in him. He raised his glass to the lady. 'No offence, ma'am. My homage to you. I toast your happy deliverance, oh, and yours, Major Shore.'

'Major Sands, sir,' snapped the soldier, looking his disgust of the old buccaneer.

'Same thing,' laughed Morgan, to increase that disgust.

Captain Aldridge cleared his throat, and sat squarely to the table.

'Shall we come to business, Sir Henry? What's to be done with these rascals ashore?'

'Ah, yes, indeed. To be sure.' He looked at de Bernis. 'What should you say, Charles?'

Monsieur de Bernis answered promptly. 'First send a crew to take possession of the Centaur and repair the damage you've done to her. Then order the guns of the Black Swan to be hauled to the head of the bluff and cast into the sea. When that's done, open fire on the hull where she lies careened ashore, and demolish her. After that we can go home.'

'And leave those cut-throats free?' cried Aldridge, scandalized.

Nor was he the only one to experience that emotion. The Major, emboldened by a gust of indignation, ventured to interpose.

'That is the advice of a pirate! Stab me, it is! The advice of a pirate! Monsieur de Bernis has the fellow-feeling of one buccaneer for another. That's plain.'

An utter silence of amazement followed that explosion. Very slowly Sir Henry Morgan turned his eyes upon the speaker. He slewed his bulk round on his chair, so that he might the more squarely confront the soldier.

'And who the devil desired your views?' he asked.

The Major got up in a heat, outraged that anyone of these ruffians should take such a tone with him. 'You seem to overlook, sir, that I hold the King's commission, and that . . .'

'Hold what the hell you please, sir,' Morgan trumpeted to interrupt him. 'I ask you how the devil this concerns you?'

'I am telling you, sir, that I hold the King's commission.'

'The King has my sympathy, by God! Sit down, man. You're interrupting business. Sit down!'

But the Major was not disposed to be browbeaten, particularly in the presence of Miss Priscilla. Circumstances of late had compelled him to submit to play a part in which there was no glory and little dignity. But from those circumstances he was now happily delivered. He was no longer on an island, at the mercy of a gang of cut-throats; but on board a vessel of the Crown, where his rank must be recognized and respected, so that he insisted upon his due.

'You shall hear me, sir,' he answered, and was not deterred by the deepening scowl on Sir Henry's brow. 'It is my right to be heard. My right. As an officer of the Crown it is my duty to protest—to protest with all the vehemence at my command—against a proposal which is nothing short of dishonouring to the King's Majesty.'

Sir Henry, glooming up at him, with a heavy sneer that not even his heavy moustaches could conceal, spoke with ominous quiet in the pause the Major made. 'Have ye done, sir?'

'I have not yet begun,' he was answered.

'That was but the exordium,' said de Bernis.

But Morgan crashed his fist down on the table. 'Must I remind you, Major, that by the rank ye're flaunting you owe me obedience? You'll speak when you're bidden.'

'You forget, sir . . .'

'I forget nothing,' Sir Henry bawled. 'Sit down, sir, as I bid you. Show me defiance and—Od's my life!—I'll have you in irons. Sit down!'

The Major's prominent eyes still looked defiance for a second. Then they faltered under the overbearing gaze of Sir Henry. With a contemptuous shrug he flung himself into his chair again, at some little distance from the table and crossed his legs.

Sir Henry turned to de Bernis.

'Now, Charles?'

'Captain Aldridge thinks we should not leave the crew of the Black Swan at liberty. But I perceive no danger of inconvenience in that. Marooned here, without ship or guns, their leader dead, they are rendered harmless enough. If eventually they get away, they are hardly likely to recommence. The lesson will have been too severe.'

'Faith, I am disposed to agree with you,' said Morgan, and as he spoke he cast a malevolent glance at the Major. What next he added leads us to suspect that the Major's presumptuous opposition may have helped to dispose Sir Henry to agree. 'And that in spite of the opinions of Major Beach.'

The Major irritably uncrossed his legs, and sat forward. 'I have told you, sir, that my name is Sands.'

'Well?' Morgan leered at him. 'Beach is Sands, isn't it?' He got up. 'Come on, Aldridge. Let's to work. We'll take Charles's advice. It's the easiest way to end the matter.'

Aldridge rose to accompany him. As he was turning to go, the Admiral paused to speak to Miss Priscilla. 'I'll send my steward to prepare quarters for you, and for you, Charles, and you, Major.'

The Major and de Bernis had both risen. The Major bowed with cold and distant formality. But Monsieur de Bernis had a word to say.

'If you will give me leave, Morgan, I will travel back to Jamaica on one of the other ships. Perhaps I might take charge of the Centaur for you.'

Morgan stared at him, and then from him to the others. Almost despite himself, a little gasp of relief had escaped the Major, whilst Miss Priscilla had suddenly looked up and on her countenance there had

213

been a momentary expression of bewildered dismay. Sir Henry thrust out a heavy lip, stroked his long moustache reflectively for an instant. 'What the devil...' he was beginning. Then he shrugged.

'Oh, but just as you please, Charles. Just as you please. Come, Aldridge.'

He rolled out of the cabin with the lean captain following at his heels, leaving Monsieur de Bernis alone with his two fellow adventurers. Before he could utter the expressions for which he was seeking words, Miss Priscilla had risen. She was very quiet, very pale.

'Bart,' she said, 'would you oblige me by going on deck for a while?'

The Major started forward briskly, proffering his arm. 'My dear!' he exclaimed.

She shook her head. 'No, no. I mean you to go alone. I have a word to say to Monsieur de Bernis.'

His jaw fell. 'You have a word to say to him? What word? To what purpose?'

'To my purposes, Bart. Does it not seem to you that there is something to be said between us after all that has happened? I think you, yourself, might find something to say to him. We are a little in his debt, I think. Don't you?'

The Major was in confusion. Emotions conflicted in him.

'To be sure, my obligation to Monsieur de Bernis is ... very real. Stab me, very real! I confess that I have been mistook in him. At least to some extent. And ...'

'Please say no more,' Monsieur de Bernis checked him. 'You will only make matters worse.'

'You may say it afterwards,' Miss Priscilla added. 'Pray leave us now.'

'But ...' Major Sands hung there, racked by misgivings. 'But do you think ... Surely you can have nothing to say to Monsieur de Bernis to which I cannot be a witness, in which I cannot join. It is no more than natural, my dear Priscilla, that I should wish to unite with you in expressing ...'

'I have something to say in which you cannot join me, Bart. In which you are not concerned at all.'

Alarm painted a foolish look upon his face. 'But surely, Priscilla . . .'

'Oh, please go! Please go!' Her tone grew impatient.

He spread his hands. 'Very well. If it is your wish. Monsieur de Bernis, I am sure, will not abuse the situation. He will remember . . .'

And now it was Monsieur de Bernis who interrupted him.

'The only abuse that is threatened, sir, is your own abuse of the lady's patience.'

Reassured a little by this, but still extremely disgruntled and uneasy, the Major moved to the door of the cabin. 'I shall be within call, if you want me, Priscilla.'

'I do not think that I shall want you,' he was answered.

When at last Major Sands had gone, she moved from the table to the long carved locker under the stern-ports. She was pale, and perceptibly troubled. She did not look at Monsieur de Bernis, who pivoted where he stood so that he might continue to face her, and waited for her to speak.

She sat down before doing so, her back to the light and the sunlit waters of the lagoon. Calmly then she looked up at him, at last.

'Charles,' she said quietly, 'will you tell me frankly why you desire to travel back to Jamaica on one of the other ships?'

'Frankly,' he said, 'so that you may be relieved at last of a presence of which in the past month you may have had a surfeit.'

'Is this your frankness? Will you still play comedy with me, or is it that you are not at all concerned with my own wishes in the matter?'

The question disturbed him. He sank his chin to his ruffles, and paced across the cabin and back.

'Major Sands has sufficiently indicated what your wishes should be where I am concerned.'

'Major Sands?' There was a faint warmth of indignation in her tone. 'What have I to do with Major Sands?'

'He is your only mirror of the world to which you belong.'

'I see,' she said. A silence followed, which he made no attempt to break. At last, 'Needs that weigh with you?' she asked him.

'It must, since it should weigh with you.'

'It does not weigh with me.'

'I said it should.' He smiled upon her a little wistfully. 'You are to remember, Priscilla, that Major Sands is right when he calls me a pirate.'

'A pirate? You?'

'It is what I have been. The brand of it remains upon me.'

'I do not perceive it. And if I did, I should not care. You are the bravest, noblest man I have ever known.'

'You will not have known many,' said Monsieur de Bernis.

She looked straight into his countenance, and again there was a long pause. At last she slewed round on the locker, turning her shoulder to him and her face seawards, so that he might not see the tears that were gathering in her eyes. Still she was silent a little while, so as to regain control of her voice.

'Perhaps . . . perhaps, after all, I was mistook as to your motives for going on one of the other ships. Perhaps I was wrong to wish to ask you to remain.'

But the break in her voice, faint though it was, reached his ears and cut him like a sword, betrayed him into saying what he had vowed to himself that he would never say.

'Ah, mon Dieu! You were not mistook.' He crossed to her, and set a knee upon the locker on which she sat. 'Attend to me, Priscilla,' he said gravely. 'I go because, as I told you that night when we talked ashore there, under the stars, I am what I am and you are what you are. I run away from you, which is what you supposed. I run away from you for your own sake. I would not have you betrayed into a weakness because you may perceive that I have the presumption to love you. I tell you this, just as I might place a wreath upon a grave. Do you understand?'

'I am not dead yet, Monsieur de Bernis. And whilst

216

I live you have a certain claim to me. Only today you risked your life for me. I understood. Don't suppose that I did not. What that odious Sir Henry said was true. You killed Leach, you faced death from him, so as to make sure of delivering me whatever happened.'

'That was a duty.'

'To me?' She swung to face him fully, looking up at him.

'To myself. To honour. To chivalry.'

'Honour? Chivalry? Ha! And you a pirate!' She laughed from moist eyes. 'You speak of your love as a presumption. But if I account it no presumption? What then?'

'Then? Why, then—mon Dieu!—you are mad.'

'And if I am content to be mad? Consciously, wilfully mad? Shall you gainsay me?'

His dark face was grave to the point of sadness. He shook his head solemnly. 'You torture me with temptation,' he complained.

She rose and stood against him, her breast touching his.

'You may end the torture by yielding to the temptation.'

'And afterwards?' he asked her. 'If you and I should marry, your world . . .'

She stopped his mouth with her hand. 'If you and I should marry, my world will be your world, and there we may both find happiness.'

'I do a dreadful, lovely thing,' he said, and took her in his arms.